THE TWILIGHT OF THE GODS

Élémir Bourges (1852-1925) was a French novelist closely linked with the Decadent and Symbolist movements in literature. His novel *Le Crépuscule des dieux* (1884) was highly influential, being much admired by such writers as Jean Lorrain, Édouard Dujardin, and Henri de Régnier. His other works include *Les oiseaux s'envolent et les fleurs tombent* (1893), and *L'Enfant qui revient* (1905).

I0597120

SNUGGLY BOOKS

ÉLÉMIR BOURGES

THE
TWILIGHT
OF THE
GODS

THIS IS A SNUGGLY BOOK

Copyright © 2018 by Snuggly Books.
All rights reserved.

ISBN: 978-1-64525-008-1

A Note on the Text

THIS edition of *Le Crépuscule des dieux* is a reprint of the anonymously translated version published in 1928 under the title of *Chains of Destiny*. The translation has, however, been significantly modified, with numerous errors corrected, and passages restored.

The anti-Semitic segment in the last chapter of the book is, unfortunately, part of the original. It is meant to represent the opinions of Charles d'Este, but whether it represents the opinions of the author as well is not entirely clear. It does not by any means, however, represent the opinions of the publisher and even caused us some hesitation in offering this re-issue. In the end, though, *The Twilight of the Gods* is a great work of Decadent fiction, despite this flaw, and believe it should be available to a wider public.

THE
TWILIGHT
OF THE
GODS

I

JUNE 25, 1866, being the anniversary of his birth, Charles
d'Este, reigning Duke of Blankenburg, gave a fête de nuit
at his Wendessen palace. Although the political situation had
become extremely dangerous owing to the outbreak of war between Prussia and the Confederated States and to the Duke's
adhesion to the anti-Prussian side, neither this grave event
nor the recent departure of the army under Prince Wilhelm's
command with the consequent mourning, anguish and general
distress throughout the Duchy, had prevented the Duke from
indulging his fondness for luxury and magnificence. Moreover,
he considered that so haughty and outspoken a contempt for the
enemy was in the Roman spirit and a splendid way of rousing
the courage of his subjects.

The gates were thrown open at eight o'clock, and an amazing
collection of people entered the Park. The avenues were illuminated with garlands of airy lights suspended from tree to tree
and dwindling away into the distance. Rows of Chinese lanterns
framed the beds of the flower gardens, which were adorned at
intervals with triumphal arches of glowing lights. An admiring
crowd gathered before each of them, but the throng was still
greater about the Sea-Fight Fountain, the Great Waterpiece and
the Colonnade. A vast number of burning pots and pans cast
a sort of day-like brilliance over the various water-shows, bubbling fountains, cascades, sheets of water, spouts of water, and
hundreds of water-jets darting higher than the tree-tops.

But the densest crowd of all, consisting mostly of country-men in red coats and three-cornered hats, stood in a compact mass near the palace. Its broad façade ran along the top of the eminence it occupied, dominating the park with its high dome, which was surmounted by the Horse Passant of the Blankenburg arms. The immense form of the palace was aglow with lights, while a great display of coloured lanterns marked the chief entrance. Long lines of carriages, the most resplendent of which drew shouts of admiration from the rabble, kept arriving every moment at the foot of the flight of steps leading to the entrance, which was guarded by a pair of stone griffins. The guests, on alighting, passed through an ante-chamber lined with mirrors and came out on to the stairway of the Play Hall, which was adorned with vases and rare plants and gorgeously illuminated.

At the foot of this horse-shoe stairway and leaning against a green bronze statue of Tisiphone, stood a man dressed in an ox-blood-coloured coat, breeches and silk stockings, that were slung on limbs of Mephistophelian thinness. His flayed-looking face, enormous aquiline nose and fiery, vulture eyes gave him a haughty, contemptuous and sarcastic appearance. Such indeed was Count d'Oels, first gentleman-in-waiting to His Highness.

"Hallo! what are you doing here, my dear Count?" asked with outstretched hang a personage who had just entered and was wearing a braided coat and had a dress sword at his side.

"But what about yourself, Mr. Smithson?" replied d'Oels. "I thought you were still at Southampton." Whereupon the Treasurer gave an account of his journey. He had just returned from escorting thirty wagon-loads of valuable furniture, which the Duke had had sent over to England as a measure of precaution.

"Oh, I think all this precaution quite superfluous," he declared by way of a finish to the anecdotes he had been telling. "There's only one thing to be said about the matter. The Prussians won't be able to hold out."

"Phew!" said d'Oels in a tone of ironical doubt. He said no more, but started whistling to himself as he watched the procession of vehicles. Carriage after carriage kept coming up, and the footmen never ceased opening the mirror-doors, while from top to bottom of the stairway, between a double row of guards, was a moving mass of glittering gold-braid, men in gold lace and women with long trains. Some of them came and greeted Count d'Oels and Mr. Smithson, and they all began to talk about the same things: there was still no news . . . Benedek . . . the Austrians . . . and Prince Wilhelm, the Duke's brother, whom they all looked upon as the god Mars himself on account of his presumed junction with the troops of Hanover; after which came the praises due to so magnificent a gala. Richard Wagner, lent by the King of Bavaria, was going to direct the performance of several hitherto unpublished fragments of a great drama he was preparing, called the *The Ring of the Nibelung*; and the opera was to be followed by a ball, games, lotteries, masques, torch-light dances and other gallant inventions. Meanwhile, a clamour arose outside. Soldiers were driving back the invading hordes all along the avenue. An officer entered without even noticing the two courtiers and went hurriedly up the steps.

"His Highness must be arriving," said Mr. Smithson.

"Oh, we've plenty of time," replied the chamberlain.

Going outside, they had only just taken up their positions, when a light carriage came dashing up, followed by a squad of carabineers in disorder. Very low, gilt, with painted doors and looking as light as a wisp of straw to the four little ponies that drew it, the quaint little carriage was driven at full speed by Otto, the Duke's youngest son.

The boy was bordering on twelve years of age, but looked quite sixteen; tall and strong with an impudent look and dark-reddish hair. His sister beside him was very pale and extremely fair, even to her eyebrows and eye-lashes. Dressed in flowered damask of a dull silver shade, she looked like a frail, haughty Infanta in a picture. Sitting at the back like a couple of servants were Baron Cramm, tutor to Count Otto and a young Italian woman in fairly modest attire, who was placed there that evening in the place of the governess Claribel, recently deceased. She had been chosen on account of her fine eyes, and being very well made and having far more of the manners of the world than belonged to her humble job of maid of the wardrobe, Emilia was quite capable of figuring in the turn-out without ridicule.

They all got out of the carriage and stood in a group at the top of the steps, where Count d'Oels and Mr. Smithson showered their gallant attentions on the two children. They were the only two of His Highness's five bastards that had been legitimised and treated on the same footing and with the same honours as legitimate princes, even so far as to be baptised with the famous onyx ewer that had served in the coronation of the Kings of Jerusalem. The Duke was only waiting for the whim to take him, when he would give serious thought to the future and have bestowed upon his beloved Otto the title of heir presumptive to the Duchy, so great had been his love for the children's mother, a rather ugly woman, to speak truth, but one he would no doubt have married, had she not died before the Duchess.

There appeared in the avenue a squadron of green chasseurs with drawn swords, blaring trumpets and beating kettle-drums. They rode before a gorgeous landau drawn by six high-stepping, foaming horses with a couple of old and velvet-clad out-riders and a third postillion holding a torch before them. Four persons were seated in the carriage. On the front seat was one of the Duke's sons, Count Hans Ulrich, dressed in the black uniform of a colonel of the Guards. Next to him was his sister Christiane, while in the body of the carriage sat Count Franz, the eldest of the five bastard children of Charles d'Este, smothered in ribbons and orders, and his mother Augusta Linden of Vienna, the only one of so many favourites who still managed to keep a little credit with the Duke.

"Christiane!" Claribel called out, clapping her hands and running down to throw her arms around her sister's neck, while Otto, out of boyish devilry, pretended to carry her train.

But Hans Ulrich put a stop to his tricks with an angry gesture. He was a rather small young man, very dark and not too well set up, and had all the aspect of dreamy suffering, which showed itself in his bunched-up, rather snub-nosed face. The Duke had had him in Russia by a serf of the Orlovs, when as heir to the throne he was travelling about Europe. He took the child home, bestowing on the serf a gift of money, with which she got married. And so Hans Ulrich had grown up by the side of Christiane, the daughter of an Irish mother. Hence their surprising friendship. They were so much devoted to each other that they scarcely ever parted company whether at work, games or on walks. She was very gracefully turned out, tall and slim, goddess-like in walk, very fair, with a child's large blue eyes and a pink and white skin, all of which were in keeping, that night, with her dress and jewels which were aqua-marines and the finest opals. She wore them in her hair mingled with feathers and marabouts. An emerald necklace was clasped round her throat. And her crepe de Chine robe, of a green silvered almost white, was embroidered with silver foliage and buttoned with fine pearls.

Meanwhile, acclamations burst out anew and a long procession of Body Guards appeared. The lights were reflected in their plumed helmets, as, boot to boot, they gravely marched forward with little steps. Then followed the Duke's liveried servants, halberdiers in dark green, officers of the household, footmen, butlers, major-domos carrying truncheons encased in silver gilt and tipped with the Horse Passant; finally at a distance of some twenty paces, alone in the middle of the avenue, the ducal coach appeared.

It was drawn by eight white horses decked with palls and led by hand. Glittering with windows and a gilded roof that bore a golden crown upheld by heralds blowing trumpets, the coach rolled majestically along on its four gilt wheels with silver-gilt flamboyant felloes. And from cornice to axles, box, doors, scrolls, main braces and the rest, the heavy and gorgeous machine shone with gold like a sun. A powdered coachman led it, holding the lantern under his arm. Two footmen in cocked hats stood up behind as stiff as statues; and in the body of the coach, alone, with his greyhound before him, the Duke Charles was perceived lolling on cushions of crimson silk.

The coach drew up at the foot of the steps, where the bright light of the lanterns made it glitter amazingly. Suddenly the trumpets sounded, a voice gave the word of command, thousands of throats cried "Long live the Duke!" and shouted long hurrahs, while the drums beat on all sides without interruption. Rockets hissed, filling the sky with marvellous, constant, criss-crossing fire, shedding stars and showers of golden rain. Two pyrotechnic dragons on either side of the entrance writhed and wriggled, vomiting roses. Then, of a sudden, everything grew pale in an immense greenish light, that came from the Bengal fire.

It was lighted around a rock about fifty feet high, especially constructed for the occasion. It was loaded with statues and columns and all the various knick-knacks that His Highness's theatrical fondness could imagine. From top to bottom it was covered with vines, the grapes of which were made of green, white, rose or topaz coloured glass and had each its flame of gas. They were lighted all of a sudden by an electric spark, and at the same time a stream of wine sprang forth and flowed down the heights in a foamy trickle.

It was an ancient custom which the Duke had revived after more than forty years' disuse in order to arouse the enthusiasm of the people and regain some show of popularity. Indeed, the crowd began to shout excitedly. An onrush broke the line of the soldiers and all the common people and rabble that filled the avenues rushed towards the Wine-flowing Rock. An incredible disorder ensued. There were shouts, blows, scuffles, arms lifted in the air, countless struggles and imprecations and the harsh wailings of women, many of whom carried babies at their breasts. Being in the whim to enjoy the scenes of the populace, the Duke had ordered all the windows to be lowered, and holding his gold-stemmed quizzing glass before his nose, contemplated the curious spectacle, while fumbling for sweetmeats in a satchel by his side.

Suddenly he fell back in a fit of hilarity. One of the rascals in the crowd had taken it into his head to fasten a sponge on the end of a stick and by this means was able to pump up the wine over the heads of the crowd. This caused the Duke to laugh so heartily that he dropped his quizzing glass and his shoulders shook convulsively. In the midst of his spasms he ordered d'Oels to bring the fellow to him. The man was just about to leave the crowd. A footman went up to him, whispered a few words in his ear and the funny fellow, who at first was rather surprised, hastened towards the door of the coach, where he started bowing profusely and kept repeating, without raising his eyes off the ground:

"Ah! Great Prince! Magnanimous Duke!"

His painful Italian accent only served to double the Duke's mirth. Tears were in his eyes as he looked the creature up and down. Tall, alert and loose-limbed in body, he seemed to be so in mind as well. With his white teeth, high nose, saucy look, brass jewellery and dirty hands, he looked just like a country comedian.

"Oh, you gallows bird!" exclaimed His Highness in French. "Have you sworn to make me die of laughter?"

"Me! Sublime, great monarch!" and he threw his hands up to the heavens, "this poor unfortunate Arcangeli who would consecrate his life to the service of your illustrious majesty!"

"Really!" exclaimed the Duke, laughing. "And what if I took you at your word?"

"*Viva Monseigneur le Douc!*" cried out the Italian wildly. "*Viva le Douc!*" And flinging himself on to his knees he seized His Highness's foot resting on the rim of the open doorway and kissed his diamond-buckled shoe.

"Enough!" said the Duke, who broke into another spasm of laughter. "You shall follow Hildemar or Joseph, who will give you my livery, and I will bear you in mind when the occasion occurs."

Then, standing upright, he commanded:

"D'Oels, your arm!"

✳

Slowly he ascended the stairs with his greyhound Caesar at his heels, while the rest of the company followed a few paces off. They passed through a row of silent, brilliantly-lighted rooms, gorgeous with marble, painted ceilings, mirrors and gilt. Otto and Claribel walked together hand in hand. Christiane exchanged a smile with Hans Ulrich occasionally, while Count Franz ogled Emilia Catana, the Italian waiting-maid, who was beginning to make an impression on him. At last they reached a very small room, furnished in the Turkish style. A door led from it into the ducal box, and the Count was about to open it when his master said to him before passing through:

"D'Oels, while I think of it! Go and order my horses to be covered up; the poor creatures were all in a sweat."

Whereupon he proceeded into the grand box, which was draped with orange-coloured velvet. As the orchestra struck up the national hymn of 1813, Charles d'Este uncovered his head and bowed to the greetings of the assembly. He was forty-five years of age that day and rather stout, with bushy eyebrows, a pimply, brown and red complexion, a scornful, fierce look and small, dark, deep-set eyes, and an enormous, hooked nose that overhung a thick beard. He wore the full uniform of a Blankenburg general, with the medals of his orders on his breast, epaulettes of yellow diamonds and seven or eight millionsworth of precious stones on his sword. The Golden Fleece hung on a red ribbon round his neck.

He sat down, placing Count Otto on his right and Christiane and the little Claribel on his left. A wealth of lights illuminated the gilded hall. Jewels, satin and sumptuous adornments sparkled and shimmered on all sides. Diamonds flashed their fires; painted fans were fluttered to and fro; many an orange-coloured or pale blue ribbon stood out against the black uniforms, while the strings of half-bare, finely dressed women in the front row of the boxes made a circle of superb necks, shoulders and bare flesh on show. It was then the fashion to wear trailing things, silver-spotted gauze, scarves with violets and forget-me-nots; chains of foliage attached a small Renaissance looking-glass to the waist; many women held nosegays of camellias; and the four tiers of boxes, glowing with soft colours and symmetrically alike, were piled one above the other in this way as high as the pink and white ceiling, which displayed an Apollo in the midst of a great company of goddesses. It was commonly held at the Court that the naked god was painted from life, after the Duke Charles.

The hymn came to an end. Rummel, the elderly musical director to His Highness, discreetly left the conductor's rack and slipped into a corner of the orchestra. He had hardly got there, when a low door on the left of the stage opened and Wagner appeared.

He bowed rather stiffly to the Duke. Whereupon His Highness replied with an inclination of the body. Everybody craned forward to get a better view of him, though not without a slight reserve, since the Duke was likely to be jealous of any attention that was not directed to him. At last silence was restored. Wagner mounted the rostrum. He sat down, gathered the musicians under his wand with an imperious gesture, cast a penetrating look round at them—they were going to play the opening symphony of *Tannhäuser* at the Duke's request—and suddenly gave the signal.

The brass instruments struck up the famous Pilgrims' Chorus. It grew less, trailing away into the distance, and mournful puffs of sound expressive of the hymn's wistful sighs spread around like the melancholy of twilight. Then night came, a night of magic and enchantment, the night of Venusberg, the mountain on which the goddess holds the Knight captive. A love song was heard and then the Bacchanale crashed forth. All the voices of the orchestra thundered together and their tumult rushed past like the very breath of the grotto of beauty, like a whirlwind of harmony bearing away the restless knight, Tannhäuser, in an eternal tempest of love. And however deeply surfeited the Duke may have been and thoroughly opposed to the idea of allowing himself to be moved by another man's thoughts, his heart was stirred by a little vanity. He gazed with pride on the multitude surrounding him, on his young and handsome children cluster-ing at his side, on the faithful nobles whose ancestors had served his own. Guarded by his soldiers, acclaimed by his people, he was indeed the offspring of a family of gods, the head of the last of the Guelphs, once as mighty as the Hapsburgs and as noble as the Bourbons. The long line of his ancestors suddenly crossed his mind. He recalled his grandfather, famous for his manifesto against France, Otto, who was defeated at Bouvines, the Emperor Henry the Lion, who was dispossessed and put under the ban of the Empire, and Witikind, the legendary ancestor, the greatest of the Saxons. He forgot the noise, the fête, the surrounding magnificence, and became engrossed in his thoughts. The last accords sounded, and applause crashed out on all sides, as soon as the Duke gave the signal.

"D'Oels!" he said, passing into the little Turkish room, where all sorts of fruits, pastries and liqueurs awaited him, "bring Wagner to me after the show. I want him to receive from my own hand the Grand Cross of the Order of the White Horse."

Fans were fluttering vigorously and laughter suddenly sprang up as though something more lively had spread over the assem-bly, which had been quite gloomy under the eye of the Duke and stifled with silence and constraint. Count Franz paid his gallant attentions to the young Italian. Hans Ulrich spoke with agitated accents to Christiane, while Count d'Oels at the back of the box chaffed Baron Cramm, who was very wide of girth and perspired most pitifully. But soon a clanging bell called everybody to attention. The Duke regained his armchair, where he no sooner sat down than he turned to Otto:

"How now, mignon; what if a fire broke out?" he said, laughing merrily.

The piece that was about to be performed was an act from *The Valkyrie,* one of the dramas composing the Cycle. Wagner had chosen this fragment from his great work because only three voices were needed and the legend could be easily detached from the general plan. The noise gradually died down, the orchestra played a short prelude and the curtain went up.

It disclosed a primitive dwelling, a hunter's lodge. Monstrous boars' heads, wolf and bear skins, a veritable slaughter of elks adorned the walls. The trunk of an enormous beech-tree filled the centre of the hut. Outside the storm raged, while a woman on the stage offered drink to a tired and hungry warrior. The scene went back to those legendary times when the Gods wrestled with Dwarfs and Giants and the hero sons of the gods went through fire to win maidens. Finally, a rugged theme burst out, a hurried step was heard, and Hunding, the husband of Sieglind and the master of the dwelling entered.

But the attention of the audience was not towards the scene. It was directed with sundry furtive glances and hurried whisperings towards the ducal box. At the sound of Sieglind's song the Duke had suddenly lifted his head in surprise. He looked at his programme printed in letters of gold. Sieglind's name was Giulia Belcredi. She had been brought from Munich by Wagner himself, to whom she had offered her services as soon as the gala had been announced. The Duke had scarcely noticed her the day of the presentation and had since forgotten her so utterly that he failed to recognise her. He examined her through his quizzing-glass and she appeared to him very touching in her ample white robe as she bent her love-filled gaze upon Siegmund, her unknown brother. Displeased at being observed and anxious to thwart the inquisitive, Charles d'Este began tranquilly to sip a Sherbet that stood on a table at his side, and from time to time he looked through his quizzing-glass at the assembly, trying to guess the women's faces by their shoulders—there were in fact very few women of his court that he might not have had at his orders—and trying to see if anyone was absent from the fête. But of course not; all Blankenburg was there, and the Duke suddenly remarked, as though reminding himself:

"Have you at least intimated my orders to Bergmuller, M. d'Oels?"

This was the name of the only accoucheur in the whole Duchy. The fact was that Baron von Lauingen had suddenly gone away without giving the Duke warning, and the latter, infuriated by the Baron's treachery, had vented his wrath on the Baroness, who was about to be delivered of a child.

"I have forbidden him in Your Most Serene Highness's name to attend Madame von Lauingen," replied d'Oels, bowing.

Immediately appeased, the Duke turned his gaze once more upon the stage. To the accompaniment of blaring trumpets and a war-like tumult, Hunding was challenging his host; chance had brought Siegmund to the home of his most violent enemy. But let him sleep without fear; the house was friendly to him till dawn. Then the fight would begin and the conquered one would be given no quarter. Pale Sieglind went out to prepare the evening beverage. Weighed down with wrath and fatigue, Hunding followed her to the nuptial bed. At last Siegmund is alone. A silence charged with passion wraps him round, as he dreams in the ingle-nook. Little by little the fire dies down. A deeper night descends. The door opens. Sieglind appears.

The Duke took up his quizzing-glass, and all eyes were fixed on the scene. For a whole week previously people had been talking of the marvellous beauty of the love duet that followed. All who had assisted at the rehearsals were agreed that it was far superior to all the rest. The women leant forward more eagerly. A dead silence took possession of the hall. Wagner stood upright before the music rack, his grey hair falling dishevelled about his temples. Lean of body, hook-nosed and sharp-eyed, he beat time with slow gestures. The Sword theme blazed out from the orchestra. Sieglind was showing Siegmund the gold hilt of a sword in the side of the beech tree. A passing stranger had thrust the sword into the heart of the tree. . . . Something began to trouble her, a sort of love-languishing. Panting silences broke up the dialogue. Sighs heaved her breast. The supreme avowal slipped from them.

✻

At that moment somebody tapped tentatively on the door of the box and then repeated the knocking with insistence. Mr. Smithson opened the door and found a scared-looking captain.

"What is there so very urgent, sir?" asked d'Oels very dryly. Whereupon the other stuttered something and thrust a letter into the old chamberlain's hand. It had been brought post-haste by a soldier from the commandant of Mannersberg and the matter was of the utmost importance, as was evident from the words on the envelope: *I beg Your Most Serene Highness to open this letter at once.* Disturbed, apparently, by the buzz of the conversation behind his back, the Duke turned round in a fury. D'Oels handed him the letter, which was secured with a large red wax seal.

Charles d'Este took it with no small surprise, read the strange inscription and broke the seal immediately. He read the message at a glance. A cry escaped his lips and he rose to his feet in the midst of indescribable confusion.

The orchestra broke off, and the emotion was increased two-fold when the Duke was seen to leave the box in a violent hurry, followed by his children and household. Very soon after, the curtain was lowered and conversations flared up. Looking pale and standing upright, Richard Wagner faced the hall, and after a moment of indecision, withdrew. And all of a sudden a strange rumour spread throughout the assembly. A corps of the

Prussian Army had invaded the Duchy. The Commandant of Mannersberg had realised what was afoot and had only just had time to send warning to His Highness of this incredible coup d'état. The news was whispered round throughout the hall. At first the result was astonishment, followed by alarm. But nobody ventured to stir, the whole court looking round for somebody to give the signal. At last one or two ventured to go out, and they were followed by many others. And, His Highness not returning, the assembly broke up, in a sort of panic. Women cried out, footmen shouted. Horror and confusion reigned on all sides. The greater part began to flee in all haste, so that in a very short while the solitude in the theatre was as great as the crowd had been, and the main road of Blankenburg was covered with a torrent of vehicles.

Meanwhile, the Duke gave vent to his frenzy in one of the salons. He was choked with fury and speechless. The Prussians! the Prussians in the Duchy! . . . And almost foaming with rage he inveighed against his brother, that traitor, that coward, that rogue, and other things fit to make a strong man blench. Then followed oaths, invectives, raving and stamping, as though he imagined he was trampling on his enemy's dead body. Everything in peril so suddenly! . . . Wilhelm had declared the danger likely to be in the direction of Luneburg, and here were the Prussians pouring in through Wolfenbuttel! . . . And that traitor Lauingen! Donnerwetter! . . . And finding within reach of his hand a timepiece of old Saxon porcelain that he greatly prized, he smashed it on the floor, and collapsed speechless on to a sofa.

Nevertheless, his first rage was spent, and a moment later his children ventured to enter the room, shedding tears and embracing him, for in spite of his severity, they were moved to tenderness by the desperate situation. Seeing himself surrounded in this way, the Duke was deeply affected. Tears gleamed in his eyes. But he was ashamed of his weakness and got up in order to hide it, saying with a show of briskness:

"Well! we'll leave at daybreak. We are not the stronger. One must let the storm pass."

They discussed the ways and means, and d'Oels developed the points more or less, according to the displeasure they aroused in the Duke, who held his peace. For the time being he affected a theatrical resignation and even a certain cheerfulness that pointed to grandeur of mind.

Meanwhile a feverish activity reigned throughout the palace. Being obliged to abandon the place, His Highness counted at least on leaving as little as possible. Under Mr. Smithson's orders, a host of menservants and petty officials were packing enormous cases, which the Duke had had constructed in readiness for all events. One hundred and fifty chosen soldiers of the Guards helped the men in livery. Pictures, clocks, mirrors were taken down; carpets, damasks, brocades, velvets, tapestries were gathered up and packed. Chairs and armchairs with spiral legs, antique four-poster beds, ivory and lazulite cabinets, shepherdess screens, tables, consoles, even the negro's arms that served as candle-brackets, and a host of trifles were gathered together and packed away. D'Oels had everything taken away according to the orders of His Highness, who would have taken even the gilt off the walls, the paintings from the ceilings and the glass of the windows. A stream of men passed up and down the stairs. Fifty or sixty lorries stood before the palace and were hastily packed with articles. The drivers, who had been chosen by d'Oels from among the most reliable menservants, were to make a pretence of setting out along the Helmstadt road and then turn off in secret to a country house belonging to the Count. And as nothing, neither joy nor sorrow, ever takes place in Germany without drinking, two big barrels of beer were placed in the ante-chamber. Everybody was free to turn on the tap and drain the jug.

A very delicate task was that of taking down the great door of the Gallery of Beauties. It was a rare piece of old Italian ebony work inlaid with ivory, and came down from the Elector Anthony Ulrich, the friend and protector of Leibnitz. As d'Oels was going to see to its removal, the Duke took it into his head to accompany him, and they arrived just as eighteen soldiers were carrying the two panels down the stairs under the direction of a tall sharp-looking fellow dressed in the ducal chestnut-coloured livery. He flitted about the head of the procession, barking out encouragements, stamping and puffing, and crying out at the slightest sign of a bump:

"*Ah-ee! porco! porco! gently!*"

But when he caught sight of the Duke, Arcangeli, for it was he, seemed to melt before His Highness with enthusiasm, and falling at his feet, gave vent to his transports, gesticulated wildly, and beating his breast. . . .

"Eh! animal! I'm going to take you with me. That's settled, don't worry."

And stopping at the top of the staircase, the Duke accompanied the Italian with his laughter to the very last step. Then puffing and panting with recollection, when the rascal had disappeared, His Highness exclaimed:

"What an amusing rogue! Where the devil have I seen something like his phiz before?"

Then after a moment's reflection, he added:

"But, d'Oels, don't you think he's rather like an ugly double of the maid that took the place of Miss Phoebe with Claribel this evening?"

"I believe they're something like brother and sister," replied the chamberlain. "At least they were seen to arrive in Blankenburg together. In fact, it ought not to be concealed from Your Most Serene Highness that the police had their eye on the couple for some time."

"Well!" the Duke snapped abruptly. The spectacle before him was not likely to make him patient. On all sides lay broken porcelain, trampled fruit from the buffet, and scattered cakes and meats, soddened in pools of wine. The Duke felt his temper rise once again and belched out a torrent of abuse. Then, finding perhaps a slight consolation in the thought of his rescued riches, he spoke about his stables, the greater part of which had been sent to Frankfurt. In fact, the event had not altogether taken him by surprise, whatever he might have to say on that score, and the numerous cipher despatches that he had received and kept secret, contained the minutest details of the Prussians' advance and their evident tactic of occupying the rich territories of the enemy to begin with. But he had relied on chance and Providence, exaggerating carelessness to such an extent that he had not even taken the few simple measures that would have immediately warned him of the Prussian army's invasion.

The great clock struck two, and the Duke went back to the hall of mirrors, but nobody was there except a half-tipsy footman, who told him that his children had gone into the winter garden. A soft warm odour mingled with the hot exhalations from the ponds. In the light of the fairy lamps rose the thickets of palms, so dense, innumerable and gorgeous, that were the glory of Wendessen, while thousands of lianas, speckled with many-coloured flowers, hung in bunches on all sides.

"Oh, there's my parrot!" exclaimed the Duke of a sudden in the midst of his reflexions.

A messenger had to be sent post-haste to Blankenburg. After that, the Duke got bored, reminded himself of his night-commode, and thought he felt rather hungry. A table was put at the end of the hothouse, in the Labyrinth, a sort of trellised adjunct with pergolas and archways and teeming springs, which was all that remained of the old Dutch garden. The company foregathered there, while Christiane and Claribel hastily put on their travelling dresses. The Duke prepared to consume a full course supper: four soups, entrées, roast partridge and pheasant. He had recovered all his former cheerfulness, devouring his food, laughing whole-heartedly and so frolicsome that when he saw Arcangeli enter, he sent him to have a look at the "beasts" of the Labyrinth. These were certain water contrivances that played pranks on visitors. Water started from under their feet, a treacherous shower of rain fell upon them from imitation birds placed among the trees, while other sprays soaked the unwary to the skin, so that the Italian came back dripping wet, but looking as serious as a high priest in the midst of His Highness's roars of laughter.

"Perfect! perfect!" Exclaimed the Duke at last. "I've never seen such a splendid fellow as you!"

Then, cutting the man's demonstrations short with a gesture, he added:

"Well then, speak! What do you want?"

Whereupon the rascal explained that there were certain grave-looking persons without, who begged to be admitted into the presence of His Most Serene Highness. They said they were a deputation of nobles with the Burgomaster of Blankenburg.

Oaths and invectives were let loose before the fellow had finished, and there stood the Duke storming and pacing up and down the hot-house, with plates flying in all directions and the table knocked over. Nobody stirred save the Italian, who was twisting the folds of his coat. The Duke saw him, seized him by the shoulders, and turning him round pushed him away. But Arcangeli, without a flicker of emotion, picked up a vermilion plate, put a visiting card on it and proceeded to present it with such a brazen seriousness that the Duke could not resist a fit of laughter.

"Astonishing! . . . I attach you to the service of Otto. You will look after his wardrobe. . . . Well, what's the matter? . . . What is it now?"

"My second commission, Illustrious Majesty . . . the card of a lady, a singer, who begs to see Your Most Serene Highness."

Giulia Belcredi! She it was, whom the Duke had forgotten till that moment in the midst of the disaster and was now pleased to have shown in at once, the urgency of the situation dispensing with etiquette. Nevertheless, he was somewhat taken aback when she failed to make the three customary curtseys; and his temper affecting his sight, he thought she looked less tall than when she had appeared on the stage. As Sieglind she had displayed for admiration the most beautiful and bushy auburn hair; yet here she was, fair-haired, lily-complexioned, deep-eyed, a strange, enigmatic face.

The Duke had recourse to compliments with regard to the pleasure he had had. She showed all the ease of the social world, smiling, polished and balanced, worthy in her expression of thanks, when the Duke, following the custom of all the princes of Germany, gave her a small bracelet of jewels. Then she added, not without a certain hesitation:

"But so much kindness towards me gives me courage to make my request. . . ."

Whereupon she explained her great desire to be able to leave Blankenburg before the arrival of the Prussians. She feared and hated them. The train for Düsseldorf would not leave till the morrow and there was no earthly chance of getting a vehicle, as everybody was in terror of the enemy. Hence she had emboldened herself to come and beg His Highness (here she peeped up towards him from her lowered gaze) to be so kind as to give her and her trifle of baggage a place in one of the carriages of his suite till they were out of Blankenburg.

"Of course," the Duke replied dryly, already frowning at the mention of the Prussians and never so much taken aback as by a too direct approach. Moreover, she pleased him less than when she was acting the part of Sieglind. Turning his back on her, he beckoned to Arcangeli. And in order to nettle the venturesome cantatrice all the more by displaying a sharp difference of treatment, for he was capable of strange, petty meannesses, he asked in a tone of familiarity:

"Thou hast already a relation in my household?"

"She is my sister by birth," replied the Italian laconically, pointing to Emilia.

"Very well," His Highness continued in order not to be cut short. "From now on, I attach thee to my own personal service. Thou'lt be one of the footmen of my coach."

It was not far off three o'clock. A livid light filtered through panes of the hot-house and the Duke was beginning to show signs of impatience, when Mr. Smithson reappeared. He had been to see that the final preparations were all in order and brought with him His Highness's post chaise. Then, after pacing up and down in silence for a while, the Duke opened a door and with sombre bearing and downcast eyes descended the steps slowly, followed by all the rest.

A long row of vehicles were waiting in front of the terrace, where the last fairy lamps were flickering out. Everywhere was calm, no noise. The pillaged Wine-flowing Rock, that had ceased to flow, was strewn with litter. On the façade of the palace a row of gas-jets flashed up here and there by fits and starts, darting out bluish, sinister tongues. Dawn hovered on the rim of the sky. The great silent avenues of the park stretched away into the livid distance. Smoke was going up very straight, here and there, from half burnt-out bon-fires.

The Duke's post chaise headed the procession, drawn by six sturdy horses. Mr. Smithson handed him the key, and opening one of the doors, His Highness cast a critical eye over the interior. It was lighted by a hanging bronze lamp and upholstered throughout in buttercup satin spicked with black flowers. It contained a bed, a dressing table, a sliding table, a divan and a safe. It was more than eight years since His Highness had set foot in a railway carriage, preferring endless inconveniences for fear of an accident.

"Are the diamonds in the safe?"

"Your Most Serene Highness may rest assured," said Mr. Smithson.

"Then everything's all right. Let's start!"

But just as he turned his head the Duke noticed the Burgomaster of Blankenburg and the principal noblemen coming towards him. They had insisted on waiting in spite of the refusal of an audience and came to point out to the Duke that his flight would most certainly entail complete discouragement and abandonment to the enemy. The Duke's voice failed him. So fearful was his fury that he shook from head to foot. At last he burst out with a tone and gesture that were terrifying:

"Ah! threefold traitors!" He roared. "Hildemar! the Cuban dogs! Let them loose on this rabble!"

At the sound of this thundering voice, the unfortunate men beat a retreat in so scared and grotesque a manner that the Duke passed once more from tragedy to farce, and he got into the post chaise, shaking with laughter. Before sitting down, he called d'Oels, and ordered that Richard Wagner should be sought after, wherever he might be.

"Probably he's in the apartment Your Most Serene Highness assigned to him in Wendessen."

"Well, see that they make him get up and bring him here."

Dawn was growing in the east. A yellowish, watery light was stealing over the silent grey sky. Birds began to flit about and no sound was heard save the occasional neigh of a horse or the noise of a hoof striking the earth. The two squadrons of Hussars appointed to escort the Duke, were drawn up under the trees, their unsheathed swords glistening between the trunks. The carriages did not stir. On the box of the coach, next to Hans the coachman, sat Arcangeli, keeping an eye on Emilia, to whom Franz was talking. The others, looking wan and chilly, walked up and down, while Giulia Belcredi, alone and at a distance, stood wrapped in her great mantle, gazing at them all with her deep and wistful eyes.

Presently Wagner came down the steps, accompanied by Count d'Oels.

"Ah! Here you are, sir!" said the Duke, who immediately excused himself for having broken off the performance of *The Valkyrie* in such a manner and also for summoning him at such an hour and in such a place. "But we are fugitives!" he kept repeating bitterly. He finished by giving Wagner, as a token of his special esteem, a portrait of himself framed with diamonds, as well as the Grand Cross of the Order of the White Horse. Then he asked the musician:

"I've been told that the third part of your poem is called *Siegfried*; but what is the fourth part, Mr. Wagner?"

"*The Twilight of the Gods*, Sire."

The title seemed to surprise the Duke, and he muttered it repeatedly through his teeth, till, recovering himself, he dismissed the composer with the words:

"It is with you, Mr. Wagner, that I shall have had my last interview."

The whole suite immediately got into the carriages, while the two squadrons came and took up their places at the rear. An immense wave of golden colour now spread over the sky. The stretches of water sparkled, quivering under the breath of a livelier breeze. Scores of bird-cries were heard. There was a brief pause, then Hans, the old coachman, whipped up and the coach started off.

But the Duke put his head out of the window, raging:

"Brute! dolt! Who told you to start! D'you think I'm no longer your master?"

Then, beckoning to Arcangeli, he cried out:

"Take that idiot's place! I appoint you head coachman. Hans! Be off and drive the luggage van."

He let down all the windows and took a long look at his surroundings. The flower-beds filled the peaceful air with a delicious odour. There was a pleasant freshness in the morning haze. From time to time a deer sprang into view in the depth of the copses. A sigh heaved his breast and he called out: "Set off!" in a strong voice. The six horses scampered away, urged on by the postillions, while Arcangeli cracked his whip. And the Duke, after a last farewell to Wendessen already disappearing in the distance, stretched himself out on the Turkish divan, murmuring to himself as though in a dream: "*The Twilight of the Gods . . . The Twilight of the Gods.*"

II

IT was with slow-turning wheels and many stops that the Duke continued his flight beyond Frankfurt. In that town he suddenly dismissed his domestics and children, who were to go and wait for him at the mansion he possessed in Paris. The only suite he retained consisted of the various officers of his table, chef, iceman, butler, and Arcangeli, who had passed from coachman to bosom companion in the coach by virtue of His Highness's ever-increasing infatuation. He was always in a bad humour. The July heat was stifling in the closed-in carriage, and the Duke sought refreshment by consuming a good deal of fruit all day long, melons, grapes, cherries, which he washed down with torrents of beer. Puffs of sultry air came in through the lowered blinds, while the varnished coach blazed with sunlight in the midst of the chalky plains of the Champagne country. Then the weather changed to constant showers, and there was always the same livid grey sky, the mud-soddened road and rain pouring down the window-panes. The Duke now increased the relays and by dint of tips, oaths and whip-thongs the party reached Paris and the Champs Elysées one morning about seven o'clock.

The Duke alighted, kissed Otto and Claribel, greeted Franz, Hans Ulrich and Christiane and presented Arcangeli to them as first groom of the chamber; which certainly looked like the rise of a new sun and the reign of a favourite. Then he went to his apartment and, having had himself put to bed, stayed there ten days on end.

He woke up late, sighed, groaned, and ordered the Italian not to admit whomsoever and to keep the curtains drawn. The twilight, which he did not dislike, increased the atmosphere of calm in the magnificent room with its old-gold fringes, sombre Flemish hangings and four-poster bed surrounded by a balustrade. A complete meal was always on a table within reach: oysters, caviare, prawns, a truffle pie, baked pears, sliced oranges, all kinds of fruit, beer, chocolate, champagne iced in a silver bucket and large mother-of-pearl and silver-work salvers full of all sorts of sweetmeats. The Duke nibbled a little from time to time, but could find no appetite. He stroked Caesar languidly, stuffed his parrot with biscuits, and then sank back upon his bed exhausted and muttering that he had never known a summer so hot and wearisome.

Arcangeli tried to amuse him with other things: mechanical gewgaws, butterflies stifled in oil of rose, chariots drawn by frogs, by sowing cress on damp flannel and growing hyacinths in water. An incomparable mummer, he imitated the personality of all the members of the ducal household, the stilt gestures of Count d'Oels, the American twang of Mr. Smithson, the soft lisping of Augusta, the Viennese. He was indeed a weird favourite, who seemed to have been cut out for a buffoon. An apish restlessness seemed to carry him hither and thither, now sitting on the back of an armchair, now running on all fours. Then he would leap up and twirl about with great gestures and a loud voice. Meanwhile, wrapped in his white satin dressing-gown with its bars of red ribbon, and a nightcap on his head, the Duke killed time by twining gold thread or cutting out figures which he afterwards drew out at random. Thus the helmet-covered head of Bismarck came out by chance on the shoulders of a low-class actress, and His Highness found great delight in these ridiculous mixings.

Yet all the while he never doubted that he would soon return to Blankenburg. In this assurance he was maintained by Arcangeli, who unscrupulously pandered to him with false reports of the triumphs of the Austrian army. Though he had not been to Paris for a considerable while, he did not wish to see anything this time, saying that he was determined not to set foot out of doors except to enter the coach that was to take him back home. Letters, newspapers, packets, even the despatches of Count d'Oels, were allowed to accumulate, till one day he suddenly took it into his head to attack the pile at last.

Then the truth was quite plain to him. The entry of the Prussians into Blankenburg the day after his flight had been the signal for a universal outcry. Everything was brought in accusation against him: his caprices, his tyranny, his refusal to sign the laws voted by the Landtag, the badly paid troops, the decaying trade, the finances drained by exactions, the mourning and suffering throughout the entire Duchy. Some he had banished; others he had imprisoned or despoiled. So out of his mind and frantic had he been at times that the Landtag had even thought once of appointing a secret commission *de lunatico inquirendo*.

Bad news followed bad news. The Prussians discovered the hiding-place of the furniture taken from Wendessen, and the pillage spared only what was of no value. And when Count d'Oels protested in the name of the reigning Duke, the Prussian officer had replied:

"Your master reigns no longer!"

In fact, Prince Wilhelm had been taken prisoner together with the Hanoverian army and had now been summoned to headquarters in order to come to an arrangement with the victors regarding the re-organisation of the Duchy.

The Duke's rage beggared description. Foaming at the mouth, stamping his feet, banging the furniture, roaring he would send Wilhelm a challenge that would rouse all Europe, he scared the whole house with his follies. He ordered at Larribeau's, the famous Army supply stores, 25,000 White Horse cockades, had printed 1,000,000 copies of proclamations and decrees and held himself ready to quit Paris. The extreme anxiety that surrounded him kept everybody gazing out of the windows in the expectation and apprehension of decisive news. There was no noise. Only a gloomy silence reigned everywhere. Glances were exchanged, nobody daring to speak except a few words slipped hastily into the ear. Sick with impatience, the Duke was on the verge of doing something rash when the news of Sadowa came with a rumble, grew louder and finally burst—with all its details.

It was a terrible blow for the Duke Charles. He shut himself up in his room, passed the night with lighted candles about his bed and Arcangeli watching over him without uttering a word. On the following day, however, he recovered some hope and he thought he was going to work wonders by sending Baron von Cramm as his plenipotentiary to the Berlin Government. The emptiness of the commission was quite in keeping with the ludicrous personage. His instructions were to submit, kiss the boots of the conqueror and protest unfailing devotion for the future. And the Duke relied above all on a letter in his own handwriting which he addressed to Count Bismarck, a letter by him, Charles 1st d'Este-Blankenburg, head of the House of the Guelphs.

At first he had thought of sending one of his elder sons instead of the old fogey. But he feared lest they might become emancipated if he brought them out of their obscurity. They might even make an effort to save their own little barque in the shipwreck that was threatening. Moreover, he was not at all fond of Hans Ulrich, while Franz had grown up among the petticoats and hated trouble and business matters. His mother, weak like himself, had always kept him near her and consequently had brought him up in the Roman faith. He was the only one of Charles d'Este's children who did not follow the Lutheran religion. Augusta's religion, chiefly confined to Agnus Deis and blessings of the Pope, did not interfere with her amorous pleasures. Magnificent and disorderly, as could be seen by her crooked coiffure and sagging dresses, she lived in a welter of debts and had been ruined by her passion for gambling. Nevertheless, advancing age filled her with a dread of death and she had gradually become one of the most fussy and precautionary of women. And now this mania kept her in bed for weeks at a time, though she did not love it as did Charles d'Este, but merely submitted to it for the sake of her health. She never got up for more than a couple of hours each day and then only to adorn herself or play at battledore with her maid. She was never seen outside of the little apartment that had been allotted to her, consisting of three quiet remote rooms overlooking the garden.

When the Duke's bellicose fury subsided, he set about putting his house in order. There was Claribel to be thought of. Emilia still continued to take the place of the English governess, Miss Phoebe, who had died. But whereas the latter had tyrannised the poor child with her stern formalism, the Italian made haste during the journey and the freedom of the first days after their arrival to win her attachment by dint of care and affection. Her lively ways, effusions and that caressing manner peculiar to women who are destined to become mothers, together with a little flattery, promptly captured the heart of the poor little solitary and inspired her with a tyrannical, childish passion for her friend. Thus it came about that when she was told by her crafty companion of all that was threatening them both, she ran broken-hearted and in tears to the Duke's apartment.

"Oh, my daddy! my daddy! let Emilia stay with me, if you love me!"

"Always address me as My Lord my Father," said the Duke, somewhat aghast, for surprise always put him out of temper.

Nevertheless he showed a good heart and descended from the lofty rainbow from whose summit he generally looked at all things, and tried to find a way to satisfy Claribel. But he did not think it would be possible to give the title of governess to Emilia Catana. How incongruous it would be to have such a name in the Court Year-book and how could it keep its place in the midst of so many titled people! The Duke took Arcangeli into his advice and the latter proved to be a very generous brother—oh!

one ought not to judge Emilia by himself. She was the daughter of a priest, a Monsignore, and brought up in one of the convents frequented by the Roman nobility. The death of her protector had reduced her to poverty and she had been obliged to seek employment, first at Wiesbaden, as reader to Princess Kolovrath, and then as wardrobe maid in the Duke's household.

"A good sister, my lord! It was she who got me to come to Wendessen, hoping to get me later on into Your Highness's service. . . ."

So many cunning praises succeeded in warding off the choice of a new governess for some time and made the Duke wish to judge Emilia himself. Proud, dull-complexioned, with flashing eyes and the large regular features of Sultanas and Junos, whose imposing gait was also hers, she was not at all unpleasing to His Highness, who easily took a liking to a face. So, while nothing definite was settled, she remained with Claribel. It was desirable not to subject the little countess to too many changes of hand. Moreover, there was no need at all to place her in the charge of a blue-stocking, for Claribel was far beyond her age in intelligence, sharpness of wit and repartee.

She was particularly wonderful to Count Franz, who seemed to evince a sudden devotion to his sister and was constantly in her company. But his attentions seemed to be addressed more to Emilia than to Claribel. He had always been fond of the company of women, revelling like them in tittle-tattle, gossip and petty squabbles. Smothered with perfumes and jewels, handsomely fair and bright-featured, sporting cameo cravats and side-whiskers, the young Count was the Beau Brummel of Blankenburg. He had had his amorous adventures there, not without a fair amount of noise. Being well up in the subject, he laid his plans like a strategist; sighs to begin with, glances, exclamations half aloud, long pauses before the idol. Following these preparations, a few gifts of flowers. Then, finding that the Italian refused to listen to him, he bombarded her with bouquets. Emilia said nothing and treated him with a proud and challenging coldness, waiting for him to go as far as the case of jewellery, which she promptly returned to him. He tried to make her yield; but she requested him so dryly to discontinue his visits that he was taken aback and kept away for a while.

But the least seen of all were Hans Ulrich and Christiane. They had been relegated to the far end of the mansion a couple of days after the Duke's arrival, because he could not stand their music.

"Besides, they will probably thank me for it," he said to himself afterwards by way of justification.

They seemed indeed to be quite sufficient to each other and to have no need of anybody else. Their mutual attachment took in all their feelings, thoughts and emotions and made of brother and sister a single heart and mind. One might have seen them blush and grow pale together. Hans Ulrich heard Christiane's footsteps at an incredible distance. And if one of them was absent, the other wandered vaguely about as though looking for his or herself. Nobody disturbed their long *tête-à-têtes*, for Augusta, who was nominally lady-in-waiting to the young Countess, had managed to take cold during the journey. And in this way their life went on in a calm and delightful intimacy. Gifted with very fine voices that would have made their fortune on the stage, they never tired of singing, except to read of Desdemona, Cordelia, Ophelia and Gretchen in the dramas of Shakespeare and Goethe. And Christiane would shed tears, for she loved these heroines as a sister.

She was indeed their sister in appearance. Fair, noble, modest, natural, with charming, naïve features, she possessed an angelic goodness, which had caused her to grow attached to Ulrich, because he was ugly, unlucky and crushed. He had been born with a superior mind, but was cheerless and chary of speech, succeeding neither in the fencing school nor the riding-school and standing in awe of his father to such an extent that his thoughts dried up in his presence. From an early age, he had fed his melancholy humour with art, literature and poetry. He loved music above all and could even compose. He was equally at home with pictures, and being extremely well-read and gifted with an unusual memory, he was keenly sensitive to the beauties of books. But the Duke spoke of him with contempt, saying:

"He's nothing but a pedant."

Nevertheless, they were the first His Highness called for. The poor man was bored to death, lying forever between his buffoon and his beasts, and three days running he demanded that his son and daughter should come and sing to him some Hartz songs, such as "The Heart is a pretty bird" and "Let's drink and smoke," etc. But he only shook his head, hummed a tune, sniffed his smelling-bottle, had himself bathed with scented water, ate dishes of ice-cream, spoke in a whole morning four phrases one after another in a trailing voice and thought there was nobody on earth so unfortunate as himself.

Boredom drove him at last to keep himself less shut up, and it was not long before he had Otto and Claribel brought to his room each day. It gave him pleasure to see her with her long curly flaxen hair. The child's chatter amused him, as did her crossness with Arcangeli who gravely begged to be allowed to kiss her hand.

"I will not have you kiss it even in thought," Claribel had replied.

And gentle little thing as she was, she kept the Italian very much at a distance and snubbed him for his impudences. Once when he was gravely giving his opinion on a political matter, she went and sat down at her father's feet, saying:

"Now, papa, let's talk about State affairs, since I'm already ten years old. . . ."

Whereupon the Duke shook with laughter for the rest of the day. But his preference was always for Otto, whose roughness and dare-devil ways made an impression on his ailing mind. The young count had an overbearing, fiery temper that any trifle might upset. He foamed with rage against Heaven, if the rain or sunshine crossed his purpose, and he wanted to smash all the clocks that called him back to his lessons. Sturdy and supple, with green eyes and reddish kinky hair, he revealed gross, passionate instincts in his low, arched brow, dilated nostrils and large jaws, the upper of which almost encased the lower. He occupied himself with nothing but wrestling, kicking and punching about. He was a sort of domestic demon, finding delight in maltreating the dogs, scullions and stable boys, and even the chambermaids of the household, for he prided himself on his contempt for women on account of their pusillanimity and weakness.

One of them, however, had overcome the young monster with her cold blue eyes. Giulia Belcredi had inspired him with a deep, unknown sentiment. At Frankfurt, when they were about to leave, Otto had slipped up to her and fallen on his knees, rolled his head in her skirts and then fled. He dreamt of her, and still often. That burning sensation remained in his heart and one day he spoke to his father about the lady that they had brought with them, the one who sang, dressed in white.

"Ah! Belcredi!" said the Duke.

And his astonishment at having forgotten her so utterly left him speechless. Nevertheless, she had pleased him, though women in general did not, and he recalled all the details of the audience he had given her at Wendessen, his bad humour, haughtiness and affected brutality. He vaguely remembered that Giulia had travelled in the company of Franz and Augusta Linden. Why had she left his suite? Ought she not at least have come and taken leave of him? But such a well-known woman of the theatre could not be allowed to disappear in this way. And his caprice being stirred, the Duke ended by setting the Italian the task of finding out where Giulia was hiding. Alas! Arcangeli knew it only too well, and an ironical smile crossed his features. For over a month he had seen her every day pass and re-pass up and down the Champs Elysées. Scenting a possible rival in her . . . what was she doing in Paris indeed? . . . and fearing a secret intrigue to gain access to the Duke, the favourite could hardly breathe for fright. It was no good keeping guard. A stupid chance might at any moment reveal everything to His Highness. As indeed occurred, for one morning most of the newspapers announced that Giulia Belcredi, the celebrated diva of Budapest, was to make her début at the Théatre Lyrique in Mozart's *Magic Flute*.

The Duke read the announcement with a start and immediately sent to the theatre for Giulia's address. The Italian, who knew it quite well, would have been just as pleased to throw himself down a well. It was Hildemar who came back with the information that the singer was staying at the Grand Hotel. The Duke ordered his carriage and set out immediately. . . . A staircase, a door, and there he was face to face with Giulia.

"Ah! Mon Dieu! Monseigneur. . . . Your Highness. . . ."

Her surprise was all the greater because he had sent in a visiting card under the name of Count Doellingen, which was one of those he used when travelling incognito. He stood for a moment or two without replying. He looked at her with astonishment in the midst of all the vulgar sumptuousness of the room, where spangled stage dresses were lying about on the chairs. Giulia seemed to him altogether different, more beautiful than he had ever seen her. Her hair was gathered into a bunch at the back of her neck. Her gloves and sunshade lay on the table and she was in the act of fastening a serpent of diamonds as a bracelet.

"Were you about to go out?" the Duke asked.

"Yes," she replied, "I was going to a rehearsal." And she made a gesture signifying at nothing could be so unimportant.

"Then it's true you are billed?" he said, rising. And suddenly breaking the ice, he added, looking into her eyes and leaning with his hands on the table:

"Well! I've come to beg you not to sing in the future except for me alone."

She stood speechless, a slight flush alone betraying her emotion during the long pause that followed. Was it the joy of triumph? Had she laid her plans to capture Charles d'Este? Tall, elegant, proud and noble-looking, with a touch of the majestic in her bearing, she looked at the Duke with a Sphingine smile and deep, awe-inspiring blue eyes. She answered simply:

"Your Highness is not unaware that it is my whole future that you ask of me?"

She stood before him as though anxious to pierce him with her gaze. And seizing her hand, the Duke kissed it.

"I know," he replied, "and that is how I understand it. You will come and live in my house until we can go back to Blankenburg." And rising up, as after the settlement of an affair, he paced round the room a few times, saying nice things to Giulia and stopping occasionally to open the jewel cases or to look up at the crowns that were hanging on the walls. One of them, received at Naples, was adorned with red coral and the Duke made a joke about it. Then after a short silence, he sat down again, asked for a pen and scratched a few lines. Then raising his head, he said:

"How much is your forfeit?"

"Fifty thousand francs, monseigneur."

He wrote his signature and put the address at the bottom: *Monsieur le Baron James de Rothschild*, and handed the draft to the singer. As he picked up his hat and walking stick, he remarked:

"But don't use extract of pinks any more. I can't bear the smell of them. Well, adieu, my dear. Within three days your apartment will be ready."

On the way home he did nothing but laugh up his sleeve and flatter himself on the trick he was playing on those silly Parisians. What a sensation would occur and how people would wonder and conjecture when La Belcredi's disappearance became known! Nothing less than this idea and Heaven knows what in the shape of a despot's grudge against the public had been necessary to shake the Duke out of his apathy. On his arrival home, he was struck by the confusion and disorder and the scattering of the menservants at his approach.

"What is it? What has happened?"

And as Karl stuttered a few incoherent words, the Duke rushed towards his apartment in dread of some horrible disaster: Caesar dead or the parrot ill. All his children were there, sitting or standing, and even Augusta, whose eyes were full of tears.

Count Franz held a letter, which he tried instinctively to hide when his father entered.

"Give it here!" said the Duke. He took and read it.

The long despatch from Count d'Oels contained the text of the treaty concluded between Prussia and Blankenburg. Prince Wilhelm was appointed Duke, or in diplomatic language, invited to take charge of the government of the Duchy.

"The robbers!" stammered Charles d'Este, turning ghastly pale.

A gnawing anger and sorrow took hold of him. For three days, he did not utter a word. He was vanquished, dying, annihilated. The Italian read to him the newspapers and Count d'Oels' despatches, and his poor Highness found consolation in the misfortunes of the others. Hanover, the Duchy of Nassau and the great Electorate of Hesse were incorporated in Prussia. Bremen and Hamburg lost their privilege as free cities. Bavaria and Wurtemberg signed disastrous treaties and Austria, besides losing her Venetian provinces, had to pay a very large war indemnity. The entire political system of Germany was overthrown to the profit of Prussia.

On the morning of the fourth day, the Duke put on his full-dress uniform as Blankenburg commander-in-chief, decorated himself with all his orders, the Golden Fleece, the White Horse, Guelfs, Henry the Lion, St. Stephen of Austria, St. Hubert of Bavaria, the Lion and Sun of Persia, and ordered the horses to be harnessed to the ceremonial coach, a masterpiece by Binder. He took with him Mr. Smithson, who put on Court dress. Together they went to the Tuileries, where the Duke begged for an audience with His Majesty the Emperor of the French. He had a very little while to wait, and was admitted.

It was not the first time that the Head of the House of the Guelphs had been in the presence of the Emperor. At the time of his visit to Paris in 1862, he had been wonderfully well received at the Tuileries, and since then the two sovereigns had always kept up the most friendly relations. The Duke went up a stairway, escorted by the chamberlain in waiting, crossed a small ante-chamber and saw Napoleon standing at the door of the room. The Emperor advanced a few steps to meet

"Ah, Sire!" exclaimed the Duke, "under what terrible circumstances. . . ."

But taking him by the arm and putting a finger to his lips, the Emperor led him into his study. The door closed on them and their interview was strictly private. When the Duke returned to the mansion, he seemed much calmer and more resigned, and no doubt would have overcome his grief had not a new disaster overtaken him. The poor prince became aware that his hair was falling out abundantly, and Arcangeli could no longer hide the terrible truth from him. The days that followed were very mournful. The shutters remained closed. A couple of candles furnished the only light in the vast room, which was wrapped in a profound silence. And white as a ghost, the Duke spent the time, clad only in his great lace-bordered dressing gown sitting on his close-stool and foreseeing a gloomy future or gazing for hours on end at a bunch of his fallen hair.

The only effort he made was to write a short note to Giulia Belcredi, who came with her maid and took up her abode in the mansion. Her installation, however, took place almost without its being noticed, for Charles d'Este's children had long been accustomed to living among their father's mistresses. The same day saw the arrival of Baron von Cramm, chop-fallen, sweating with fear and already beforehand feeling on his back the furious violence of his master. The fear of being cross-examined in every possible way and of having a searching light turned on his actions, increased the little baron's anguish. So it was with a sigh of relief that he learnt that His Highness did not wish to see him.

So great was the Duke's grief that he even refused to receive Count d'Oels, who arrived a few days later with a convoy of lorries which he had picked up at Frankfurt, and the Duke's thirty-three horses. Six of them were presents from the Shah of Persia, while the rest were of the Blankenburg breed, horses with silvery coats and pink eyes, nostrils and hoofs. According to legend they were descended from the battle steed given by Charlemagne to Witikind and adopted by the Guelph princes in their coat of arms. D'Oels looked after the stabling arrangements, and his ardent, evil eyes and sinister personality were once more to be seen about the corridors of the house. He came with a stock of scathing comments on the hasty defections of His Highness's courtiers, on the Austrians, Prince Wilhelm, and even the Duke himself.

And in very truth there never was a man so full of fancies and caprices as the latter. One morning the Duke suddenly decided, without breathing a word to anyone on the matter, to return to his ordinary life. He rose, shook off his grief and thought no more of it. He inspected the mansion from roof to cellar and ordered the eighty cases that had recently arrived from Southampton to be unpacked, while he watched over their disposal. The same day he completed the reform of his household, which had been quite Bohemian while he was still living in uncertainty, and he settled the titles of his attendants. Count d'Oels remained His Highness's chamberlain and aide-de-camp; Mr. Smithson was appointed treasurer and administrator in chief of the Duke's fortune, while Baron von Cramm took the title of gentleman of the bed-chamber and tutor to Count Otto.

"As for La Belcredi," thought Arcangeli, who saw His Highness lean over and speak in a low voice to the singer, "we know what she will be."

Two days later, the Duke sent fifty thousand francs on behalf of the poor to the Committee for Public Assistance, as though to stress the fact that he was henceforth a citizen of Paris. It was a sort of housewarming present which the newspapers did not fail to celebrate in appropriate terms.

III

AFTER these events Arcangeli went about with a pensive look. Behind all his masks and grimaces the buffoon remained as serious as a Jew with regard to his interests and fortune and thought only of succeeding. At first he was filled with hope when the Duke decided to remain a recluse. He thought he was going to keep him shut up and put the key of his prison into his pocket. But when he came to know the Duke better and realised his capricious, mistrusting nature and that being in his favour was like skating on thin ice, the Italian thought it safer to look in another direction and procure a friendly backing in case of sudden disgrace. He could not remain forever dependent on such a capricious temper, that kept one in a state of constant anxiety as though a mine was about to blow up. So the wily favourite cast his eyes about him and tried to make up to the persons and penetrate the intrigues of the little court. The natural son of a police spy of King Bomba, Arcangeli knew what he was about in the job he was undertaking. He excelled in eavesdropping at doors, moving about the corridors as though on padded feet, startling people with plausible irruptions, and was just as clever in ferreting among private papers and using skeleton keys in order to see the inside of a desk. Now it happened that Count Franz had the German habit of keeping a diary of his life and filled it with opera verses, dried forget-me-nots, and his heart's outpourings in perfect confidence.

One morning at the beginning of October, Emilia was in the garden with Claribel and Count Otto, when Arcangeli approached her, and having passed the compliments of the day continued to walk by her side. The sky was calm and pale. The half-bare trees opened up vistas beyond the still flower-beds to a gold grating in the distance. And nothing disturbed the silence except the rustle of footsteps on the dry leaves and the gentle voices of the children. They were playing at the foot of a pine tree near a marble pond where some swans were swimming about.

Arcangeli, who seemed intent on enjoying the fresh air and peacefulness, said in the most inoffensive tone:

"Oh, I thought I might meet Count Franz in the garden."

She was startled, and standing up from gathering a bunch of geraniums, flashed a look from her dark pupils at him. Her face flushed and her temper was on the point of boiling over, when Arcangeli said in his most wheedling voice:

"Look here, Emilia, why do you keep me in the dark about it? You know the Count loves you."

"*Hé!*" she retorted in a muffled voice. "What does that matter to you, ruffian?"

They went on with their walk and said no more. From the end of the avenue came the loud laughter of Otto mingled with the supplications of Claribel. Brandishing an open razor, the young Count was pretending to pass it across his throat and at the same time trying to force his companion to take her hands from over her eyes.

"*Hé! sorella!*" said Arcangeli, "my little *ragazza* of the good Lord, I'm not an enemy."

He caressed her as much as he could and played the buffoon according to his habit so well that she began to laugh, saying:

"Will you never alter, Giovan?"

Recovering from her first surprise, she lent a more willing ear to his suggestion. Lively, headstrong in her desires and always bubbling over with the romantic spirit that had caused her to run away from Rome with a singer, it was only by dint of will-power that she managed to display so much circumspection in her task of seduction. Yet was she certain of holding out to the end of that long road? Knowing her weakness, in the face of infatuations, she was afraid of herself and regretted the lack of somebody to whom she could turn for advice and comfort. So, when Arcangeli spoke to her, all her hopes turned towards that dear brother. In him she saw all the patience and spirit of cunning which she lacked, and stretching out her hand to him of a sudden, she exclaimed in a fit of confidence: "Well, yes! I admit it. I was wrong not to be quite open with you."

She told him of Count Franz's attentions and gifts, how she had treated him in order to inflame him all the more and how after a short period of discouragement he had returned to the attack and ventured once more on sending bouquets. From time to time Arcangeli deigned to shake his head and approve. When her story ended, he advised her to let him manage the intrigue. No doubt the hook was well baited, but would the fish bite? . . . With slow steps they returned towards the lawn where the children were playing. Otto was now amusing himself by saying unspeakable things and frightful oaths. When Claribel grew angry and shed tears, he began to laugh and said:

"Listen, Clary. Repeat after me what I've just said to you, or else I'll throw myself into the pond."

"Oh, Otto! my brother, my little brother!" she appealed to him, half-choked with sobs and fear.

"Hurry up, or I'll throw myself in!"

And perched on the rim of the pond with his head turned towards Claribel, he appeared to be ready to take the plunge. Suddenly his foot slipped; his hands were thrust out in a vain attempt to clutch something, and he fell into the water, which was fortunately not very deep at that spot.

The young Count was fished out dripping wet and laughing heartily. After that, it was necessary to see to Claribel, who had fainted on the spot. She was brought to after a good deal of trouble. But the shock was a very strong one, and the same evening a nervous illness that had long been secretly undermining the frail child's health, made its appearance.

※

She baffled the doctors, and no remedy was of any avail. She felt a distaste for life, a strong depression with an intermittent fever, convulsive crises and such extreme suffering that the machine failed and sank into a deathly torpor. Nothing was so appalling as the length and violence of the attacks. Furious spasms shook the poor child as though her spirit was shaking off the bonds that united it with the body. She grew pale and dreadfully haggard. Her face was like wax streaked with the blue of veins, and her hair was discoloured. Reclining in the midst of an immense bed of lace she spent two months surrounded by coloured saints, rosaries and holy pictures, which the devout Emilia pinned all over the bed curtains. These amulets, medals, scapulars with a green and pink St. Clara just opposite her pillow became extraordinarily important in the eyes of Claribel, though as a devout Lutheran she had a secret contempt for the superstitions of popery.

She had, indeed, in many things the seriousness and maturity of a woman. Ever since she had been taught to read, she had been anxious to learn the history of her family; and she could proudly talk of how she belonged to one of the greatest families of Christendom. She always took pleasure in discussing the Guelphs, of whom she knew all the lineage, the tangle of the various branches, the virtuous and memorable actions. She was a strange little girl, a sort of charming freak such as belongs to a declining race, sharp-witted, frail of body, proud, though tender towards those she took a liking to. She stretched out her dying arms from the depth of the bed towards the Italian woman, wishing to keep her always at her side, embracing her and calling her *mamaccia*, my little mama, though she could not bear to be addressed as *thou* by the old doctor Ferney. And later on when she got a little better and the members of the ducal household came one after the other to congratulate her, Claribel never forgave Count d'Oels for Putting off his visit to the following day. When he afterwards presented himself, she turned her face to the wall and received his compliments without uttering a word. When Emilia reproached her an hour later for behaving in such a way, the little countess replied:

"Why did he not visit when he should have? Am I not his master's daughter?"

As her attacks now grew less, the doctors allowed her to get up. But this only meant that she changed her bed for a sort of immense niche of mattresses upholstered in green and gold satin. She passed the whole day there, smothered in a pile of lace and stitch-work, looking ghastly white with her strange pale-gold hair done up on top of her little head.

She did not feel bored. Visitors were numerous. The Duke came as soon as he was out of his bath, well-kempt, powdered and scented and spruced up. He indulged in frolics, played at pitch-and-toss and allowed his money to be won, and generally made Claribel a few presents of jewels, dainties or wonderful toys. Often he would take her by the hand and walk round the room with her. She looked such a darling and so different from her tall, robust father that she seemed to have come out of his pocket. These visits cheered Claribel up and she showed her best manners while he was there, though she greatly disliked the violet perfume with which the Duke was always scented. There were times when she turned sickly white and felt ready to choke, but she would rather have died than appear to be embarrassed or permit herself to make the slightest complaint.

Count Hans Ulrich and Christiane would come in the afternoon, and the latter would enliven everything with her nymph-like gracefulness, inventing all sorts of amusements and making Claribel join in them. The gorgeous playthings of the little girl would be taken out of the cupboards. There were dolls, marionettes, Punch and Judies, Noah's arks, perfect masterpieces of sculpture by the mountaineers of Wolfenbuttel, wonderful mechanical toys, pirouetting dancers, gilt coaches with moving horses, elephants that raised their trumpets. But the little Countess watched them with a gloomy eye and invariably asked for Micky. It was her favourite plaything, an ugly doll that had been given to her by a peasant woman one day when she was out walking. She clasped it in her arms and closed her eyelids, talking to it all the while and answering Christiane's cheering remarks with a sad smile.

Of all the household none was so constant a visitor as Count Franz. By dint of simulating the passion of love he had become its victim, and Emilia's astute tactics had soon brought it to a climax. The young man no longer went out riding on horseback; he forgot to play Strauss's waltzes after dinner, and his healthy-looking face even took on an expression of pitiful languor during his visits to Claribel. He was consumed with sighs, oglings and long silences, standing motionless and running his fine hands through his side-whiskers and becoming so utterly absent-minded in the midst of his ecstasies, that Claribel would talk to her doll, scolding and consoling it maternally, as though she was quite alone with the furniture. On one of these occasions the little old fogey von Cramm arrived and took it into his head to ask her how long it was since her doll had been weaned.

"And how long have you been?" Claribel replied, offended. "For you are hardly any bigger."

She had these ways of making sudden retorts and a peculiar fashion of saying the commonest things. Once the Duke brought her a new mechanical toy, a fox in the midst of some hens with a cock flapping its wings. As soon as she saw the fox she grasped him by the neck, as though afraid of being robbed. When they asked her why she did so, she replied with a sweet little look:

"They are so cunning in the fables!"

But when Arcangeli, who had been brought in by the Duke that day, asked her a question, she merely replied:

"Oh, I think he is even more cunning than the fox!"

The Italian bowed without a protest, and his sullen, impudent eyes glanced towards Count Franz, who was an uninterested witness of the scene. Arcangeli had got his man; he was sure at last of getting his foot in the intrigue and directing it according to his wish. Somewhat tired of perfect love and hoping that so long a respect had softened Emilia's heart, the Count had that very morning attached a most pathetic letter to his daily bouquet. It was a step in the dark. Two minutes after its reception the letter passed into the hands of the brother, and towards the end of the afternoon Giovan paid a visit to the young Count.

His subject was well prepared. He began by expressing his thanks at a great length for the favour which Franz had showed him in deigning to receive him. It was not altogether a waste of time, as he had something important to lay before him that might otherwise go astray and cause trouble. Whereupon he drew the letter out of his pocket and placed it on the edge of the table in such a way as to show that the seal had not been broken.

"Ah!" exclaimed the lover, who remained dumbfounded, while Arcangeli sat with his hands spread out over his knees and pretended to look attentive. There were green plants on a flower-stand, a panoply of Mongolian arrows on the wall; a pink candle was burning on an inlaid bureau near a jade writing desk and other knick-knacks of curiosity.

At last the Count rose from his chair and paced the room, looking very much embarrassed and muttering a string of prot-estations. Far from him was the slightest intention of wounding the person to whom the letter was addressed! How could she have supposed such a thing? . . . Thus he went on up hill and down dale regarding his respect and his feelings, speaking in vague terms all the time. As Giovan did not utter a word, the Count continued:

"Besides, my passion is sincere."

A faint smile passed over the Italian's features and he replied in a wheedling voice: "No doubt, Monseigneur, but your inten-tions . . ."

"My intentions . . ." stuttered the Count, "my intentions . . . have nothing, believe me, that could give offence to Emilia."

With a theatrical gesture, Arcangeli sprang towards him and clasped his knees frantically.

"That Your Excellency should deign to think of marriage! What an honour! *Gesù-Maria!*"

He seemed to be mad with joy, and Franz held his tongue tight for fear of laughing out. Marry the ex-chambermaid! The idea seemed so absurd that he could not believe it was sincere. And the words he heard were certainly not of a kind to dissipate his suspicions. . . .

"Ah! from that moment His Excellency could rely on the most absolute devotedness! Arcangeli, his humble servant, was his forever, body and soul! Emilia would soon be coaxed, *corpo di Bacco!* She was already only too well inclined towards the signor count!"

"Do you think so?" the young man asked with eagerness.

"Let Your Highness rest assured!" exclaimed the Italian, his face enflamed with ardour. "God damn me if the stupid creature doesn't appreciate the honour you do her! To begin with, she's going to receive from my own hand the letter she has despised!"

And, ruddy and gesticulating, he slipped the letter into his pocket, though both he and his sister knew every word it contained, for among other talents he included that of being able to remove a seal with consummate skill. At last he made for the door, as though unwilling to embarrass the young Count any longer.

"Ah! no matter what you say, Arcangeli, I fear I am not loved!" sighed the young man.

The Italian put his mouth close to the Count's ear and replied in a jovial manner:

"Believe me, signor count, if you want to catch women you must catch them as you do turtles."

The Italian set to work with so much zeal that three days later Emilia gave the Count a rendezvous in the greenhouse of the mansion, though under the stipulation that Giovan was to be present. The cunning Italian helped the enraptured lover to dress for the occasion, held the mirror up to him and chided him in a paternal manner:

"I don't like to see Your Highness so madly in love. What are women after all, signor count?" Whereupon he snapped his fingers—"I myself was in love with a grand lady once upon a time," he asserted. "But there! three or four men who had been her lovers were only too glad to get rid of her."

✳

The rendezvous was followed by a good many more. Arcangeli promptly ceased to assist at them, saying that he had to attend to the Duke. It is true that he was hardly ever away from him and had become the indispensable person of the household. Nobody would have known how to bathe, massage, perfume His Highness and brush his feet and ankles so delicately as he did; Neither could anybody go into such raptures as he did over the person of the Duke Charles, press his boot against his breast, and marvel so much at his arms, legs, thighs, and the elegance of his waist. Nor was anybody equal to him in managing a clyster, cutting corns or preparing goose-quills for his master. The latter talent served him in good stead on a remarkable occasion, which showed that the Duke knew how to dispense his favours in a striking way. In trying some goose-quills one day, Giovan happened to scribble the words so often used by His Highness:

Mr. Smithson, my treasurer. . . .

Passing through the ante-chamber, the Duke noticed the scrap of paper and read it. Sitting down, he immediately wrote after the Italian's handwriting:

Pay to Arcangeli, my housekeeping secretary, the sum of 3,000 livres by way of gift.

Having signed it, he sealed it with his ring, put it into an envelope and had it sent. In this remarkable way did Giovan learn of his new fortune and appointment to a post that had been vacant several months without anybody knowing to whom His Highness would give such a desirable plum.

Giovan's credit seemed to be definitely established. He had shackled the Duke's capricious will and gained over him an ascendancy that nobody could attempt to rival. However great the Duke's confidence in Mr. Smithson, the latter was fortunately not much to be feared, as he was continually flitting about from one country to another and only made a break of journey, as it were, in Paris. The Duke used to speak of him jokingly as "My watchdog." And he did, in fact, watch over and protect him and brought back his imprudent, hazarded millions. The American would go at one time to Spain for the salt marshes; at another, to Moravia, where His Highness was exploiting several blast furnaces. Mr. Smithson travelled about in all seasons, at all times. Quite recently he had been obliged in the depth of winter to rush to Nijhny-Taguilsk, an immense Russian region half in Europe, half in Asia, containing veins of gold, iron and platinum and the richest copper mine in the world. Moreover, he was thoroughly master of the mechanism of business, spoke little, committed himself still less and corresponded chiefly by telegrams, which saved him the trouble of sitting down to write.

It was Count d'Oels' privilege to open the telegrams and take the most interesting ones to His Highness. The chamberlain would seize such occasions to denounce everybody in the house, particularly Arcangeli, whose elevation filled his breast with gall and envy. The Duke would only laugh at it all, for in his dread of cabals, he had made it his policy secretly to maintain the enmities of his entourage, and he was not at all displeased when Otto sometimes threatened to cut off that rascal Arcangeli's ears like a dog's.

Otto hated the Italian. The latter kept out of his way for fear, knowing only too well the young Count's violent temper. He was like a perpetual whirlwind, full of cries, blows and fury that made everybody hide. Poor little von Cramm, chained to his terrible pupil, was in perpetual terror of him, neither daring to breathe a word nor to raise his eyes, but glad to be forgotten. Twice already the young Count's ferocious farces had almost cost the tutor his life, once when Otto poured some vitriol into his full glass, and again when he fired a loaded pistol at him from the top of the doorsteps.

But the more wildness and madness the boy displayed, the more the Duke showed himself indulgent, attributing these violent excesses to the boiling blood of youth. In a few months Otto had grown quite a foot. His face was no longer white and pink. It had grown bigger and freckled, smudged with brown and covered with a precocious reddish down, besides having a furious look. He was often to be seen going towards the stables, switch in hand, followed by his dogs. He would not stir from there except to bring into the rooms of the house the strong smell of manure, urine, and dogs' sweat. His fondness for low life was thoroughly satisfied there in the midst of the stable-yard grooms. He would wrestle with them, use the pitch-fork and curry-comb, assist at the covering of the mares and do all sorts of filthy things. So great was his passion for horse-riding that when he returned from his rides he would spend an hour or so doing stunts before Claribel's windows, trampling on the flowers and hoofing up the beds and lawns. And one day he nearly knocked the Duke down during one of his mad gallops; but the Duke was not at all angry with him.

It was at the time when the Duke had felt a great need of fresh air after his long imprisonment during the winter, and was accompanying Claribel, who was brought in a great gilt bath-chair into the garden, where they would go about for hours together. He even acquired the habit of driving out in his coach every morning to the park of St. Cloud or Sevres. After the grey gloomy days of winter the spring seemed even more lovely. It was in its first glory and there was something young and gay, a sort of sparkle, in the fresh, sun-lit air. Somewhat cheered up, the Duke would walk slowly about the thickets, stopping at the fountains and statues and contemplating the lonely stretches of water. Once or twice he even paid La Belcredi the unexpected attention of taking her with him. But these marks of growing favour—as also later on the small presents of jewels, fans, gloves and gewgaws—in no way altered the young woman's attitude.

His Highness had never had an official mistress so modest, retiring, and apparently so anxious to live on good terms with everybody. When one happened to meet her, one saw only her dark dress and flashing blue eyes. Nevertheless, she always wore wonderful underclothes and beautiful jewellery. This great simplicity was thoroughly in keeping with her gentle and respectful air. The Duke thought her extremely fine and soothing. He admired her charming voice and talk, her inexhaustible conversation about all she had seen in the way of people and countries. She was to him noble, polished, refined, a sort of enchanting siren, and he ended by getting as much accustomed to her, the songs of Schumann that she sang to him, and the hours he spent in her company, as perhaps to his parrot or the antics of his buffoon.

It was just what she wanted. All her smiles, charms and floweriness were but the cover of horrible vices: the lust of domination, the thirst for riches, a frightful treacherousness, infernal machinations. Beneath her reserved, indifferent exterior, the singer blazed with the most ardent ambition and pondered deep and darkly. Splendid pride and overbearing haughtiness did not prevent her, when necessary, from having recourse to a meek and humble tone, patient bearing and flattery. No matter how dark or execrable the means were, she considered them good provided they helped her to achieve her ends.

Like the Lauras of Dante and the Vittoria Accorambonas of the sixteenth century she was masculine-minded and no lovemaker. She seemed to have been cut out on purpose for those bloody times, to dominate some Italian court and dabble in politics, wars, intrigues, poisons and sonnets, with a da Vinci who would have painted her portrait. Born to be the mistress of kings and princes, Giulia had never laid her ambition aside. People in Moscow were still talking about her romance with the Grand Duke Vladimir Mikhaelovich, the Emperor's nephew, who would have agreed to marry her, had she not been suddenly driven out of Russia by an order from St. Petersburg—and forbidden ever to set foot in that country again.

But this time La Belcredi had her prey well in hand. She had every possible leisure in which to combine and arrange her threads. The undertaking was dark and risky, and seemed to require the patience of several lifetimes, for what this blonde Medea aimed at was nothing less than the title of Duchess and the fortune of the Blankenburgs; and as long as the Duke's children were still around him, there was little hope of getting more than the crumbs that fell from his table. Fortune, however, is always likely to change. So, trusting in her own powers and dark resources of inventiveness, she waited patiently, taking great care to dissemble and thickening the ice that covered all that was boiling within her. She had no other occupation but that of amusing the Duke, pleasing him, and little by little getting him into her power.

An unexpected event, however, proved to her once more how amazingly fickle Charles d'Este could be. To build on such a man was like leaning on a reed. The Duke had always seemed fond of his mansion in the Champs Elysées. At Blankenburg he had often talked about it and sometimes expressed a desire to be able to live there. Everything about it seemed to him admirable: structure, situation, the apartments all on one floor, the convenience of the various flights of stairs, even the iron-bound walls, which he was fond of saying protected his millions against fire and thieves. The latter, however, are cunning people. One evening the Duke returned from a gala at the Tuileries and found his safe wide open. He had shut it before leaving, but forgotten to adjust the secret lock. The carpet was sprinkled with diamonds and several bags of gems had disappeared. The police were immediately up in arms; telegrams flew round; and in the early morning they arrested Mr. Jackson, the thieving coachman, and Joe, the groom, just as they were about to embark at Boulogne.

So the diamonds were restored to their proper place; but the Duke took the affair to heart and began to distrust the household as after an act of treachery. In the disaster that had befallen him, he had saved his purse at least. Was he now to lose that as well? . . . And his anxiety was crowned by a second disaster that was far more annoying than the first. Owing to a rearrangement by the City Council, the number of the Duke's house was changed from 59 to 77. That was quite enough for the Duke to make up his mind to leave it at once. For many years he had had a superstitious abhorrence of the number 7 and held it to be mixed up in some sinister fashion with all the calamities of his life.

Mr. Smithson, who had just arrived, was ordered, therefore, to buy a new house for His Highness. He set about the job at once, visiting several quarters of the town. He inspected the region of Monceaux and found, not far from the Parc des Princes, a sort of miniature castle with an enchanting view. But the Duke would have none of it. Mr. Smithson then persuaded him to visit the house formerly occupied by Lola Montez, the famous Countess de Lansfeld.

It had long been uninhabited and was surrounded with a high fence. Situated at the end of the Champs Elysées, it had been much neglected. His Highness thought the garden looked wild and overgrown. Once the keys were brought and the Duke could see inside the house, he found a worse spectacle awaiting him. A musty odour came from the faded wallpaper; dilapidated furniture stood about the rooms; the sashes of the broken windows were rotten and falling to pieces. From time to time the Duke stopped to test a panel with his finger or examine the upper part of a door. He shrugged his shoulders and said nothing. He felt he was wasting his time in such a palace of dust and cobwebs, that seemed to have been asleep since the days of fairyland and crumbling with age. He went about muttering, stamping his foot, threading his fingers through his moustaches—a sign of suppressed anger—and getting very red in the face.

"I see, Your Highness, that it doesn't please you," said Mr. Smithson very dryly, turning halfway towards him.

"Doesn't please me! doesn't please me!" cried the Duke, relieved at being able to burst out at last and to find something to contradict. "Might you by chance wish it shouldn't please me? . . . In that case you are mistaken, sir. . . . I'm going to buy it."

The work was begun immediately with an amazing number of workmen; scores of pulleys were fixed to the sides of the mansion; there were lots of boilers, rails and machines and workshops were erected in the garden itself. All this activity was quite necessary, for the Duke had scarcely left anything untouched except the staircase, the four walls and the roof. He kept an eye on everything: plans, contracts, estimates. His boredom was swallowed up in this new occupation and he even went so far as to spring sudden unexpected visits on the workmen.

He also assisted in fixing the gilt bronze figures and other pseudo-Greek iron-work which he insisted should adorn the top line of his roof, for he had been born in the glorious days of bastard Parthenons. Everything was mixed up in his mind. Every kind of bad taste lived there in a muddled confusion, so that he had no scruple in ordering the pink marble front of the mansion to be adorned with mosaic medallions representing his forbears, Henry the Lion and the Emperor Otto.

His strange livery, fine turnouts, coachmen, huntsmen and postilions began to single the Duke out even in the midst of the crowd of princes assembled by the World's Exhibition. It was at its most brilliant and the whole town was en fête for the reception of the King of Prussia. The poor Duke was wounded to the heart on that account and gave way to fits of rage and sullenness when he heard that his enemy had stopped, while on a visit to the Champs de Mars, right in front of the epaulettes of yellow diamonds, which had been lent for show by Charles d'Este. He refused to go and see them until the King of Prussia had left, and the sight of the monster canon exhibited by Prussia only served to rekindle his anger, which was so great that he never went again to what he called "that bazaar!"

He became morose and eaten up with bile and boredom. Often during the night he would wake up, ring for the Italian and send him to fetch Mr. Smithson. He would then deign to inform them of some new fancy that had come to him in his sleep. Thus there appeared one after the other immense hot-houses for the hotel Beaujon, as the Duke called his house, a Turkish bathroom, the busts of the twelve Caesars, a Roman portico in the park, which soon became a copse of cedars, changed into a stretch of water, and then turned back into a forest once more. He had scores of fancies, the one more fantastic and costly than the other, in buildings, orangeries, marble and porphyry pavilions, fountains, vases and statues that only a magic wand could have brought into being.

But a still greater anxiety now began to worry the Duke. It became more and more apparent that Claribel's bright ray of improvement was fading away with the sun that had given it birth. The child was already confined to being pushed about in her bath-chair inside the house, and the time soon came when she had to take to her room.

Sad-eyed, she watched the rain rattling down the window-panes, and the clouds scudding across the sky. The shortening days, unending downpour, the dull light of that pale, lugubrious autumn and the universal silence all combined to fill the dying child's heart with an unspeakable melancholy. She was brave, however, hiding and swallowing her tears. Beauty still lingered about her face, that was worn out by the disease. She wished to be dressed and cared for even more than before, and her whims as to what she was to wear often obliged Emilia to rummage among the heirlooms of the Countesses of Blankenburg. There were satins, brocades, lace, jewels, collarets of precious stones, muslins and damasks, robes of Lyons silk embroidered with flowers of gold and silver, Brussels and Alençon stitchwork, a most wonderful trousseau, the like of which is now possessed in Europe only by one or two images of the Virgin Mary.

Her dressing finished, Claribel would remain daydreaming, ensconced in her silken niche, shivering and gloomy, her thin arms looking lost in their great puffed sleeves. But at twilight, when the embers glowed between the dog-irons in the open hearth and night gradually cast a wan tone over everything, from the bluish roses of the grey carpet to the light blue satin of the hangings and ceiling, she would suddenly burst into tears, her poor heart drowned in sadness. She would call Emilia and nestle against her bosom, sometimes asking her:

"Ah! what do the dead do, *mamaccia*? Do they suffer? Are they ever hungry and cold? Are they as unhappy as the living?"

"No, little sister, they sleep," replied Hans Ulrich one day.

"Then why am I not dead?" she answered.

And from that moment Claribel seemed to take a bitter pleasure in talking about her coming end. Nevertheless she faintly smiled when Christiane brought to her for her amusement a little ten-year-old girl, whose father was employed in the Duke's kitchen. Frida was shown a great array of toys that she might take her choice, but she was so overcome at the sight of such magnificent things that she gazed at them with gaping eyes and burst into tears.

It took several days to overcome her shyness, get her to take her arms away from her eyes and give up the quaking curtseys with which she replied to the simplest words, or looks, or even the wonderful stories that Claribel found amusement in telling her—"Hush, one must answer very softly, whisper into the ear, whenever there are any big flies in the room. They hear all that is said and never fail to repeat it. . . ."

She invented scores of other fanciful things of this kind regarding dogs, clouds, birds, trees. Frida listened to her agape. The poor naïve little girl who gazed at her with such wistful eyes was the last doll that could give any amusement to the little Countess. Claribel would kiss and pamper her, stuffing her with sweetmeats or making her do penance, dressing her up or undressing her, rigging her out in old-fashioned furbelows, high head-dresses and immense crinolines. Or she would keep her dinner in her room and stuff her playmate with it. Pale, diaphanous and so thin that she might almost have passed through a curtainring, she made a pitiful contrast with ruddy, fat-cheeked Frida, who greedily devoured the partridge, pheasant, and sturgeon in Tokay, while Claribel was bed-ridden and could scarcely suck half-a-quarter of a tangerine.

She was dying, too nervous, too fine, consumed with ardour and intelligence and already tired of life. Overwhelmed with all the favours and honey of Fortune, she had tasted their bitterness and realised, even at her age, the emptiness and transitoriness of things. Her father! Any gewgaw would be enough to console him, a neck-tie, a new ragoût, or the case of sweet lemons he was expecting from Palermo and which came from a tree he had planted with his own hands, as he was fond of relating. Franz, after so much attentiveness, scarcely appeared at all now. And as for Emilia, the child felt only too well that the Italian retained scarcely more than the outward show of affection, and had her thoughts elsewhere. Her caresses were indifferent. Oh no! nobody loved her. . . . If only she had a brother as Christiane had Hans Ulrich! In her innocence, Claribel sometimes wondered if it was possible to love one another more than they did. How Hans trembled and grew pale whenever Tina roguishly put her arms round his neck and how tenderly they smiled at each other! But why did La Belcredi look at him in such a strange way? Why did she want to fathom them with her gaze? . . . With her modest look, her real talent and the pile of music-scores that she kept in her room, especially a Handel's chorus that required three voices, she had succeeded in penetrating into Christiane's apartments. Of these frequent visits and this growing intimacy the little Countess was jealous. Her sister and brother could surely not like her, since they were on such good terms with one whom she detested. No! Nobody loved her! What would she have done in life? She could die without regret!

Nevertheless, she still wished to live a while and see at least one Christmas for the last time. The festive day was drawing near. She had formerly looked forward to it so eagerly. And her proud, commanding spirit seemed to make death obey. In spite of feverish nights, a perpetual drowsiness, and short, irregular waking periods, she reached the longed-for day. Dusk had fallen early in the foggy December afternoon. Without waiting for the evening, the Duke had his usual Christmas present taken to the sick child. It was an immense tree illuminated by thirty brackets of wax candles and loaded with toys, caskets, boxes, rings, jewels and all sorts of gifts. The glowing lights seemed to revive the child. A joyful smile lit up her deathly features and with an extraordinary effort of the will almost in the midst of the throes of death, she gave the order to have herself dressed for the feast. Her necklaces were placed round her neck; her fingers were adorned with turquoise, opal, sapphire and emerald rings; and Emilia slipped jewelled ribbons and bows into her fair tresses, while Frida held up the mirror by the bedside.

She saw herself in it for the last time, the little Countess with the hooked nose, the vague and watery eyes, the place of the peeling eyebrows. She seemed so haggard in the midst of all her fineries that she was startled by her livid aspect and asked to have her cheeks rouged. Emilia smeared her cheek-bones with some rouge and having finished her toilet, the child contemplated her Christmas tree with all its blaze of lights. Several dolls were hanging from the branches. She had them brought to her bed and turning towards Frida she said with a last smile:

"Let's put this one to bed, will you? Then we'll pretend it's dying. . . ."

And as the other girl only gazed at her with large, astonished eyes, she added:

"No, really! dolls die just as well as we do." Frida laughed incredulously and shook her big head. Whereupon Claribel said very softly:

"I assure you they die. Believe me, Frida, there is nothing more true."

And sinking back exhausted on the pillow, she closed her eyes and died after a short agony without regaining consciousness.

The Duke was immediately summoned. In the confusion of the first moments, the room remained quite empty, lighted by the candles on the Christmas tree and with nobody by the body except Count Otto.

IV

THE funeral pomp was gorgeous. There were wreaths, lights, a catafalque, and the apartment was draped with white velvet hangings with silver fringes; the hearse was covered with plumes, flowers, fringes and escutcheons. More than a thousand pounds' worth of candles were kept continually burning. It was in the midst of all this staging, the slightest details of which had been settled by His Highness, and through a vast concourse of people that Claribel was borne to her last resting place at the Père Lachaise on the seventh day after her death.

The Duke wore mourning for six months. He was very low-spirited and perturbed, less perhaps on account of his daughter's loss than by the scents, torches and the whole gloomy get-up with which the house had been surrounded. The grey skies and snow-covered roofs were in keeping with his low spirits and he suddenly sank into a stultifying sorrow. Every voice around him was hushed and even smiles were kept back. Speaking aloud, walking, laughing, whistling, became a capital crime. He passed his days in deepest gloom in the company of the lead casket containing Claribel's heart and on which he had had engraved the words:

ET FILIOLÆ ET MEUM
(*Here lies my heart, with that of my daughter*)

He would never raise his head except from time to time in order to say in the midst of a dreadful sigh:

"You see, my poor Arcangeli, nothing of all this would have happened but for that cursed re-numbering."

He often dwelt on that bogey. His sadness dried up and disappeared. The artificial movements of his sorrow came to pieces as quickly as they had been made. But he did not recover from his mourning except to live from that day on in a continual and growing dread of the number 7, as though it were a mill-stone suspended over his head and ready to crush him at any moment. He was constantly depressed and spoke in a low, whining tone, always muttering "If I'm alive" whenever he spoke of the morrow. Nothing was lacking in the comedy, not even the daily quarrels on the subject with Arcangeli.

"A number!" the Italian would say. "A lifeless thing that can't move!"

And he would laugh compassionately. He would fiddle with the enormous bunch of red coral hands dangling at his waist and declare that the little Countess had died because she had been given the evil eye by a "gettatore," Count von Plessen, whom he knew quite well. This made the Duke laugh and shrug his shoulders, so that in the end the disputes, contradictions and anger arising out of this superstition caused it to become the Duke's most cherished and blindest failing.

He worried his architects and quarrelled with them over the length of the work at the Beaujon house, though he was always adding to it with his caprices. The stables had already been settled and the woodwork got ready, when he had them changed a dozen times, and even reduced by one half when he suddenly took it into his head that he would only retain four pairs of horses for himself and his children at the Beaujon house. He intended keeping the rest at Saint Germain in immense model stables, and was only dissuaded from this proposal when he realised that some groom might for the sake of a bribe make use of the stallions and thus shatter the Duke's pride in having unique animals.

66

He became more and more distrustful and even distributed certain locksmith's work among seven or eight workmen, each of whom was unaware of the whole to which his part referred. This naturally caused further delays and His Highness grew more impatient. He grew thin with fear in the Champs Elysées house and three claps of thunder one afternoon towards the end of March nearly drove him off his head. He could stand it no longer and abandoned the accursed house, taking up his abode with Arcangeli in the Hotel Windsor in the Rue de la Paix, where he put up with the apartment usually reserved for the Prince of Wales.

He was saved. He could breathe once more. He opened his eyes and shook himself. For several days he busied himself with things in a most fussy manner; so there could be no doubt of his coming to his senses and resuming his customary mode of life. He had long conferences with Pomadère, his French tailor, bought four hundred louis' worth of perfumes and neckties, had himself bled twice in order to keep his paleness, which he deemed interesting and uncommon, and being invited to a fête at the Palais Royal, kept his feet in cold water all the afternoon in order to wear smaller boots. A great throng gathered round him, admiring the scores of jewels with which he was loaded. The women were so eager and embarrassing that he was quite overwhelmed and exclaimed in the most engaging tone:

"Mon Dieu, mesdames, if you are so fond of diamonds, I have some finer ones underneath."

And he made as though to unbutton his coat. Whereupon the inquisitive ones fled. From this time onwards the newspapers began to retail every little detail concerning him, and a paragraph sent all Paris to the Champs Elysées to watch the procession of His Highness's menservants in breeches and gilt hats. This queer procession escorted an enormous light blue ark like a sedan chair which held under a couple of padlocks the food and table service of the Duke, who continued to be served from his own kitchens. Arcangeli served up the dishes and the head major-domo himself, who had once served the Tsar Nicholas at table, tendered the serviette and carved the meat. During this process, the Duke amused himself by chiding him with feathering his nest a little too avidly.

"Look here, Michel," he would say to him. "I'll pay you by the year, fifty pounds extra, if you'll promise to be reasonable."

"Ah, Monseigneur! I should lose too much by it!" replied the other gravely, without interrupting his service. He was a Parisian and had published a large book on his art with a rather profane epigraph:

Man does not live by bread alone.

Something occurred a few days before the Duke's departure that seemed to justify his horror of the house in the Champs Elysées. One of the Cuban dogs suddenly became rabid during the night. It broke away, bit two grooms and rushed, foaming and bleeding, into the house, where it took refuge at the bottom of a passage and snarled at everybody who dared to approach it. Great was the dread and confusion of the menservants, who did nothing but talk without attempting to do battle, when Emilia came fearlessly out of her room and going straight up to Syphax, shot it dead with a revolver.

Though this hardly feminine exploit caused a stir of tongues, it did not arouse too much astonishment in the house. Maids and menservants had already begun to smile whenever the Italian's name was mentioned. She had been left to look after herself since Giovan's departure and her temper and fancies had kicked over the traces. No more circumspection, no more constraint; the real Emilia appeared, full of impulses and extravagances. After keeping Franz at arm's length for so long, she suddenly yielded at a time when he least expected it.

"Good Saint!" she had said to her plaster Santa Lucia, "I am going to commit a great sin, but you are so powerful in Heaven . . . and the poor fellow is so unhappy!"

He had, in fact, grovelled at the feet of his mistress and vowed by all that was sacred that he would marry her, though quite determined never to put his head into such a yoke.

So much romanticism softened the heart of the Italian, who lived in a world of comedies and operas, of which she often quoted snatches. She adored shows, races, galas, horses, and was always going out, hardly finding time for a single meal. Towards midday on her return from the Bois de Boulogne, having changed her dress and ready to go out again, she would send for some salt meat or a slice of ham and a few small patties, which she would eat standing and talking all the while. Her large felt hat with a grey plume, a sort of Louis VIII hunting habit with silver braid stripes on the front, her copper-heeled shoes, her buff and blue striped skirt, all suggested the queen of the stage. And this impression was certainly not contradicted by her lively, mobile, audacious and rather mad physiognomy with its flashing eyes. Franz wondered how she managed so long to make them appear so expressionless. But now her oglings, and even her silence spoke only too clearly! The whole house was aware of their secret understanding, and the poor lover, who stood in perpetual awe of the Duke, was terribly afraid lest his intrigue should come at last to his father's ears.

But the Duke was far from dreaming of such a thing. He was now busy with the details for the construction and fortification of the cellar at the Beaujon house, in which his treasure was stored. This led to amusing scenes. His mind was so muddled that he found it hard to get people to understand what he was driving at. He would fume and shout and knock the furniture about in order to inculcate his plans on the architects and Mr.

Smithson. One afternoon he could stand it no longer and in great dudgeon went off with them to the Beaujon house, where for some unknown reason he had been unwilling to appear for more than three months.

He was surprised and delighted. In place of the rough and tumble and scaffolding which he had left, he found the house looking very neat with its pink marble walls, dark blue stone steps, and immense gilt balustrade that concealed the roof. A jasper railing, breast-high, covered the kitchen area, and the Duke gazed with pleasure at the bronze statues standing on top with upraised lanterns.

The gardens pleased him more than anything. Everything had been erected one after the other according to His Highness's whims, and the muddle which the architects had vainly sought to reduce to order, formed an amazing collection of buildings, pavilions, arcades, balustrades, crescents, galleries, without any symmetry or level; a conical roof supporting a green Russian cupola; terraces loaded with orange trees and attached to nothing; everywhere a profusion of columns, metal vases, myrtles shaped like pyramids, goddesses, coloured-glass windows, black and blue marble, fountains and water-sprays. The Duke spent an hour looking at them all. Then he visited the servants' quarters, the stables, the orangery and the sheds with always the same delight. He was not even repelled by the great puddles in the garden where the holes for the trees and lakes were being dug out. And before leaving he found delight in the gilt work of one of the three doors, iron-clamped and painted in ox-blood red, which guarded the entrance to his immense palace.

Charles d'Este was encouraged by his first visit to go again. His mind found occupation in the scores of activities which he found in progress there, so that little by little he came to regard the Beaujon house as his doll once more.

He arrived every day at two o'clock even in the worst weather. He listened to the reports of the architects and inspected the works. Then he would stand on a chair and watch the ceiling-plasterers and the parquet-layers, submitting to showers of dust for a couple of hours or so, after which he asked for his porte-manteau, changed his linen and suit and went away. Mr. Smithson, who was wanted in one of the mines belonging to His Highness at Villaharton, was at last allowed to set out after a delay of six weeks.

"I will take your place at the works," the Duke had deigned to assure him, and became even more assiduous in his visits, if that were possible, especially when the time came to finish the stables, where the work went on all night.

They were built on a royal scale with oak boxes for twenty-eight horses, a marble pavement, an oak ceiling with sculptured beam ends, and an arcade of windows round the top. There was a profusion of sparkling gold and luxury, old Cordova leather adorned with valuable porcelain and an oak cornice, blazoned with an endless number of the Blankenburg Horse Passant.

"The poor beasts!" exclaimed the Duke from time to time, as he thought of his horses living in the midst of so much grandeur.

He made a great feast the day his thirteen stallions were transferred from the Champs Elysées to the Beaujon with half the coachmen. For a long time after he delighted in walking round his stables, while Otto groomed one of his favourite colts. The young Count used the most savage and intractable for his promenades each day. Five grooms were hardly enough to hold Selam or Firdonsi and keep them in the yard. And once the Count was in the saddle, it was necessary to see whether the street was empty before opening the gates, as the first spring of the horse carried him right into the middle of the roadway. And Otto's wild daring, roughness and violence made the Duke feel young once more even at the mere sight of them.

"He is my very image," he often used to say, recalling his old prowess as a boxer and rider, and all the fiery vigours of his youth. They sometimes returned to him in fits and starts, as was seen when he set about moving in. He kept his beasts, servants and even Arcangeli on hot bricks; the twenty-four hours of the day were like twelve to the Duke. In his rage of activity, he ordered a general inventory to be made of his furniture at the Champs Elysées house. Count d'Oels came every morning and read out the exact details from the book which was written by his own hand, this left him scarcely time for food or sleep. He complained and even put His Highness out of temper. As a last resource he fell back on the gout, from which he sometimes suffered, and stayed in bed. Impatient of all delay and not caring who was harnessed to the wheel as long as it moved, the Duke decided to appoint a helper and created in his household the title of Second Chamberlain.

This decision coincided very appropriately with the recommendations that had recently been made to him on behalf of M. Cordeboeuf d'Andonville, a gentleman of Normandy, who had squandered his fortune during the last ten years and was on the point of living in a hovel on his cabbages and his gun when he was taken under the wing of Madame d'Esparbes, his cousin, one of the beauties of the Court. She made up her mind that he was to have a post with Charles d'Este.

"D'Andonville, d'Andonville," the Duke laughingly repeated to the diplomats of the affair. "Do you want to deafen me in my own house with that clanking name?"

Nevertheless, he willingly allowed Mme d'Esparbès to introduce the fellow to him. He was a sort of giant in height and thickness with a jovial, enflamed look, that had something of the yokel about it and gave him the appearance of one of those loutish horse dealers with whom he had so often clinked glasses. But he also looked kind, honest and for the time being exceedingly bashful. In sitting down on the chair indicated to him by the Duke, he smashed it right away, lost his wits and could do nothing but twist his hat round and round his fingers as long as the interview lasted. His awkwardness and awe-stricken state gave extreme pleasure to the Duke, who was always highly gratified when anyone appeared overwhelmed by his majesty and its radiance. Hence he beamed on d'Andonville, and as a regiment with a band happened to be passing down the street, complained to him of the noise of trumpets, that was murdering him day after day. Whereupon d'Andonville stuttered something and then suddenly making up his mind, said:

"Your Most Serene Highness should order straw to be laid down in front of the house."

The Duke shook with laughter. He was completely conquered by such a sublime absurdity and that same evening, M. d'Andonville took up his residence in the Champs Elysées house.

It was quite time, too. Everything had got out of order. The poor major-domo had a hard task getting rid of the numberless infractions of the regulations, service and discipline. They were like nasty thorns that he could only remove by means of sternness and all sorts of reforms. One of these, which however was not due to him and was very galling to His Highness, was the suppression of the chasseur wearing a cock's feather and the footmen who walked on certain days before the ducal carriage with their gold-knobbed sticks. The Emperor of France himself had had something pretty lively to say about this "Gothic etiquette," and an order so thinly veiled had to be obeyed, however much it wounded the pride of the exiled sovereign.

Another mortification overtook His Highness a fortnight later. Three-quarters of his German household, his oldest and most devoted servants, left him, being home-sick, and returned to their native mountains of Wolfenbuttel. The Duke was more deeply pained by their forsaking him than he might have been perhaps by a great and cruel misfortune. He was greatly affected when they took leave of him.

"What!" he repeated in a shaken voice. "You will never see me again?"

The good people were at a loss for an answer. He ordered that they should all receive two years' wages and that Claribel's last friend, Frida, should be given a dowry of 3,000 florins. Baron Cramm, who also spoke of leaving, received a share of this manna, in proportion to the treatment he had had to suffer from Otto. That imp had even tried to toss him in a stable blanket with the aid of three grooms. After some talk, however, the Duke was able to extract from him a promise that he would remain in his service.

His desire to leave was merely a grimace; Baron Cramm had better reasons for not leaving the house. Who else would have spied on the Duke Charles? Who else would have sent a long report in cipher to Blankenburg every two months. The little tubby man with the doll's face, piping voice and innocent eyes had for several years been swallowing treachery and deceit like water. He had been in the pay one after the other of Berlin, Francis V of Modena, uncle and ward of the Duke Charles, Hanover, and Wilhelm. He would have grasped a red-hot iron rather than have nobody to sell himself to. Not that much profit was gained from his reports. They conveyed nothing beyond what everybody might know. They contained all the happenings of the household, day by day, even the most insignificant, but without any comment:

> *6th September.—God preserve Your Most Serene Highness! Here it is raining hard, to the great annoyance of His Highness. Having felt a draught during the night, he has ordered double frames to be fitted into his windows and his furs and muffs to be brought to the Hotel Windsor.*

> *14th.—I should have a good deal to say to Your Gracious Highness, if my pen were not too feeble to express my sentiments. I forgot that last Monday, Monseigneur went to Binder's to see his new equipages. They are chocolate-coloured with white borders.*

And so forth down to the P.S. which was usually:

I have nothing to relate to Your Highness regarding Madame Augusta Linden. The good lady becomes more of a recluse and lunatic every day.

An unexpected diversion for this lady in the midst of her shelves of old porcelain, and stuffed dogs and cats, was the appearance of M. d'Andonville with his inventory books, with which he could hardly cope. She called him "the finest figure of a man she had seen since that poor Lieutenant Thomayer." His task did not take more than a couple of pages in Augusta's rooms, but the large study used in common by Hans Ulrich and Christiane, gave him far more to do. Hans Ulrich had gathered together all that was most luxurious and magnificent in the Arts, spending on this collection whatever money his father gave him. The gilded, sculptured ceiling with its immense Venetian chandelier was adorned with medallions of antique Italian frescoes; the curtains and door-hangings were of pansy-coloured velvet, gold damask, and tapestry; the walls were hung with gorgeous old gold brocade, which formed a harmonious background to a great number of pictures, triptychs, gilded and painted wooden sculptures, enamel Madonnas surrounded with fruit, portraits by the great Masters in tortoise-shell and tarnished silver frames. There was hardly room to move among the divans, rare vases, piles of engravings and rare books, the grand piano placed crossways, the valuable furniture littered with quaint violins and cases. Every nook required several hours for inspection owing to the heaped-up treasures of bronzes, enamels, porcelains, laces, Chinese knick-knacks, rock crystal cups, grape-adorned goblets, a Nuremberg egg beside a carved Breton pebble, a wedding salver by Guido Fontana. . . . At the bottom of the room stood a glass case containing the last writing table used by Schumann, several manuscripts of Beethoven, and sundry other Romantic relics. The wall over the door was occupied by a crucifix in old oak, which had been picked up at Ausburg and caused M. d'Andonville to say: "What a great sculptor, that Inri!"; four fine

Florentine busts, filigree medals, and a thousand other charming nothings made up the great store of treasure.

In the midst of books and pictures and the profound peace of this wonderful retreat, the life of brother and sister was nothing but one long chapter of the ideal: smiles, tenderness and love of the beautiful. After the departure of the disturbers, they passed radiant days together refreshing their soul with song and poetry. Giulia Belcredi, who used music as the key to their apartment, usually closed to all the rest, happened at that time to be at the Hotel Windsor, where she remained a fortnight. Charles d'Este had suddenly remembered her and had capriciously come and taken her away. She reappeared at last, so pleased with her "dear lord" and her progress with him that she began to think the time had arrived for her to set to work.

The viciousness of her mind together with her long acquaintance with the most shadowy mysteries had promptly enabled her to realise whither the intimacy of Christiane and Hans Ulrich was leading them. For years they had been drowsing in the peaceful enchantment of their life together, and it only needed the touch of a hand to push them towards the abyss over which Giulia saw they were leaning, in order that those pure delights and joys might be changed into bitter torments and tragic disaster.

"When you are married . . ." the terrible woman had once hinted to Christiane in order to probe into her soul. She was delighted with the result of her words. Hans Ulrich was quite startled and went as white as his linen, while Christiane protested that she did not wish to get married. She would always be quite happy with her brother, her music and her books.

"But if your father ordered you to?" Giulia had objected.

"Ha! the Duke is certainly thinking of it!" retorted Hans Ulrich in a trembling voice.

And for several days after this outburst a sort of wild timidity set a seal on his lips. But Giulia was not at all rebuffed by his prolonged silence. In the company of Charles d'Este she was frivolous and indolent, but with the young people she was all

Shakespeare and Beethoven. She knew a good deal, judging works of art with taste and discernment and pretending to enter into the emotions of books as ardently as those two enthusiastic souls. It was Giulia who revealed to them Byron's sinister Manfred and that part of Schumann which they had always put off reading. She recited whole passages to them, such as the invocation to Astarte: "Hear me! Hear me, Astarte! My Beloved, answer me, I have suffered so much, I suffer yet so much!" and the scene between the brother and the sister's ghost. Brought up by her mother, Giulia had acted in London for a while, for her gestures and pathos were no less admirable than her singing. And she talked so often of certain tragedies of the time of Shakespeare, Ford's *The Broken Heart*, Webster's *The White Devil*, calling them masterpieces, that she filled Hans Ulrich and Christiane with an ardent desire to read them.

So one afternoon she yielded to their entreaties and brought them the volumes. She read to them the finest scenes from Marlowe's *The Jew of Malta*, Fletcher's *Valentinian*, and Ben Johnson's *Volpone*. She had a bold, virile mind and was fond of these unusual pieces, of which the blood, terror, swords, tumult and shouts thrilled her in comfort. The reading went on for a long while and each time Giulia thought of ending, Hans Ulrich and his sister protested, until the time came when they agreed that the next scene should be the last. She enfolded them both in a smile and cruel look, saying:

"Very well. It is your wish!"

And slowly opening her book like a woman who has made up her mind, she began without naming the title, saying only that the author was Ford:

> GIOVANNI.
> *Come, sister, lend your hand; let's walk together!*
> *I hope you need not blush to walk with me;*
> *Here's none but you and I.*

ANNABELLA.

How's this?

GIOVANNI.

I'faith, I mean no harm.

ANNABELLA.

Harm?

GIOVANNI.

No, good faith. How is't with ye?

ANNABELLA (aside).

I trust he be not frantic.—I am very well, brother.

GIOVANNI.

Trust me, but I am sick; I fear so sick, 'twill cost my life.

ANNABELLA.

Mercy forbid it! 'Tis not so, I hope.

GIOVANNI.

I think you love me, sister.

ANNABELLA.

Yes, you know I do.

GIOVANNI.

I know't indeed.—You're very fair.

She had read out this prelude in a low, icy tone, that hinted at some approaching mystery. Then she took a breath. A sombre red had come over Hans Ulrich's sallow face, as with head bent forward and palpitating heart, he eagerly awaited each line of the dialogue. Facing him, Christiane sat with a frightened look, her cheeks pale, her lips apart. . . . But Giulia's voice rose higher as she read these words:

GIOVANNI.

O, Annabella, I am quite undone!
The love of thee, my sister, and the view
Of thy immortal beauty hath untuned
All harmony both of my rest and life.

ANNABELLA.

Forbid it, my just fears!
If this be true, 'twere fitter I were dead.

GIOVANNI.

True, Annabella! 'Tis no time to jest.
I have too long suppressed the hidden flames
That almost have consumed me: I have spent
Many a silent night in sighs and groans;
Ran over all my thoughts, despised my fate,
Reasoned against the reasons of my love,
Done all that smooth-cheeked virtue could advise;
But found all bootless: 'tis my destiny
That you must either love or I must die.

ANNABELLA.

Comes this in sadness from you?

GIOVANNI.

Let some mischief
Befall me soon, if I dissemble ought!

ANNABELLA.

You are my brother, Giovanni.

GIOVANNI.
You My sister, Annabella; I know this.

Then Giulia paused and raised her head. The silence that followed was so great that one could have heard a pin drop. Ghastly white, Christiane was bowed in her chair. Heavy tear-drops gathered at the rims of her eyelids. Hans Ulrich had a wild, constrained look in his eyes and seemed to be thunderstruck.

Sunset-glowing clouds were dying down in the western sky; the birds had ceased their chatter; the pale silver crescent of the moon was rising in the upper heavens, and an unusual peaceful-ness spread over the world. Meanwhile Giulia went on:

ANNABELLA.
Live; thou hast won
The field, and never fought; what thou hast urged
My captive heart had long ago resolved.
I blush to tell thee,—but I'll tell thee now,—
For every sigh that thou hast spent for me
I have sighed ten; for every tear, shed twenty:
And not so much for that I loved, as that
I durst not say I loved, nor scarcely think it.

GIOVANNI.
Let not this music be a dream, ye gods,
For pity's sake, I beg ye!

ANNABELLA.
On my knees, (she kneels),
Brother, even by my mother's dust, I charge you,
Do not betray me to your mirth or hate:
Love me or kill me, brother.

GIOVANNI.
On my knees, (he kneels),

Sister, even by my mother's dust, I charge you,
Do not betray me to your mirth or hate:
Love me or kill me, sister.

ANNABELLA.
You mean good sooth, then?

GIOVANNI.
In good troth, I do;
And so do you I hope; say, I'm in earnest.

ANNABELLA.
I'll swear it, I.

GIOVANNI.
And I; and by this kiss, (kisses her),
Once more, yet once more. . . .

Giulia Belcredi stopped reading, and dropped her voice. She felt a slight pity for Christiane as she looked at her, while Hans Ulrich, pale and confused, fidgeted about on his chair. He wanted to say something. . . . His voice choked. A storm of tears, sobs, cries tore itself from his breast and he fled in order to hide them. . . . Christiane did not stir. Two streams of silent tears flowed from beneath her closed eyelids. Dusk fell; and under its cover Giulia Belcredi slipped furtively away.

For some time afterwards she spared Hans Ulrich and his sister the discomfort of seeing her again. She gave out that she was indisposed. And her retired, peaceful life, that seemed so abstemious in the midst of the pleasure that enticed her and so void of ambition in the midst of so much wealth, was in striking contrast with the noise and follies with which Emilia was at that time filling the house.

✳

The usual time of flowers and honey common to those kinds of liaisons had scarcely lasted in the case of Count Franz. At his first hint on the subject, Emilia had bridled with much bitterness and instead of forsaking her hats, plumes and grand airs had made them twice as extravagant. The poor victim shrugged his shoulders and merely murmured:

"What a Marphise!" or "What a Bradamante!" and admitted to himself, as he stroked his whiskers, that he had not known what he was doing when he put his head into that noose.

Emilia was now dreaming of marriage and called on the young man to act up to his promises. Though she had listened to them as though they had been airy nothings, as indeed Franz had spoken them, she now insisted on treating them as spoken in earnest and vowed that she had been deceived. She even declared she was pregnant, hoping no doubt that this would appeal to his paternal affections. She carried out a long comedy of joy, chattering without end about the baby and declaring beforehand that it would have its father's blue eyes and big appetite. But Franz kept so calm about it and showed so little faith in the story that she was at last convinced that he was not the kind of fibre to work upon. So having no further purpose to serve, the child disappeared as quickly as it had cropped up.

She was at a loss what to do next. It struck her that she might do well to entrench herself behind religious scruples. Franz was therefore treated with pouting and every evening when he tapped at her door he found it locked. But by virtue of talking so much about morality and simulating religion, she suddenly experienced in reality a painful revival of these scruples.

Trifles seemed to her like hydras. Prayers, fasting, maceration and the most austere practices were hardly sufficient to satisfy her repentance and fear of the devil. She made a tragic scene one day, throwing herself at the feet of Augusta and imploring her not to curse her. Augusta was quite taken aback and could only repeat:

"Aber! Aber! dear mademoiselle. . . ."

And in the end she mingled her own tears with those of the penitent Magdalene. After that, Emilia paid frequent visits to her. Augusta showed her how to discover the future by means of calculations and dots, caressed her, told her endless fairy-land romances, and from time to time gave her a feast of German cooking: cabbage soup, dumplings in spinach broth and invariably sausage stuffings.

Finding, however, that she was making no headway, Emilia had sudden fits of fury. She smashed her plaster Madonnas, tore her scapulars to shreds and roundly abused the Saints, saying that those stuffed dummies had no power whatever.

Franz's quiet manners did not afford him any shelter against her overbearing pride and insolence. Her voice could be heard from two rooms off, and did not lower its tone even in speaking of the most intimate things. The scenes took place three or four times daily. When she was exhausted she would get her maid to comb her hair for her, deriving much comfort from the operation. Her heavy silky hair emitted sparks in these stormy moments. Under these conditions she conceived extravagant ideas that sometimes made one wonder whether she was in her right mind. She madly imagined that Franz's resistance came perhaps from aristocratic pretentious. Under this impulse she addressed to Count d'Oels the following lines. It must be noted that in accordance with the fashion of Courts, the Duke called his chamberlain familiarly, "my cousin."

Count, they call me Luck-bringer, I want to bring you luck and restore you to health. This is what I will do for you: I am a Catholic, I will become a Protestant; that will bring you luck. Besides, I have so much magnetism in me, especially in my hair, that my presence in the same room will suffice to drive away your suffering.

*In return I beg you to do me a small service. I am
anxious to be the cousin of Franz. Adopt me as your
daughter. I only ask to bear your name. I fancy that
Franz will be on better terms with me, if I am his
cousin.*

*Believe me, dear Count, a good deed will bring
you luck. Think it over! A chance to win a soul for
your religion!*

EMILIA CATANA.

It is not hard to imagine the laughter that accompanied the
reception of this weird missive. Count d'Oels was in bed with a
serious attack this time and was not shamming. The gout made
him bitterer than ever, and he immediately sent the letter to His
Highness. Nevertheless, the good man was disappointed in the
result. Charles d'Este had too many domestic troubles to pay
any attention to this trifle. In fact, he was now hard at work
moving into the Beaujon mansion.

He spent the first days settling the numerous details of arrangement, and going round the house in the company of Arcangeli,
who jotted down everything his master suggested in the way of
embellishment. The Duke noticed that the windows gave them a
good view of the Arc de Triomphe and he sometimes laughed to
think that he, the grandson of the Prussian Generalissimo, should
live right opposite that magnificent trophy of the "Marseillaise,"
with its eternal challenge to his ancestor.

The arrival of Count Otto, whose apartment was ready for
occupation, brought fresh trouble to the Duke, who seemed to
show no less indulgence, even submission, towards the young
man.

This darling son now began to go about with an eighteen-
year-old underservant who answered to the nickname of "Saint
Amour." Otto had taken up this stable-lad for the pleasure of
playing the French horn together. Otto soon became very much

attached to him and even grew jealous. Saint Amour could no longer call his soul his own even in the smallest things.

Sometimes, just as they were about to go out together, his capricious tyrant would send him back; at other times, he overwhelmed him with abuse and made him shed tears on account of rivals. Kicks and blows were not infrequent, only to be followed by reconciliation. All of which was done so publicly that Count d'Oels, who was recovering from his attack, asked ironically one day whether that was the kind of Greek Baron von Cramm taught his pupil.

Small, slim, with reddish curly hair, Saint Amour struck one at first sight by a certain ugliness, but he had clear green eyes and a rumpled face revealing so much vice, promise and effrontery that he was worse than pretty. This Ganymede soon appeared with very costly neckties and smart clothes, plenty of money, pomades and rings. He was gluttonous and low-minded and seemed made on purpose to go about with Otto.

One after another the various works came to an end and for a whole fortnight the business of moving in went on. First it was the turn of La Belcredi, Count Franz, the chamberlains, in short, the main body of the troupe, and they were all not very well pleased with their new abode. There were so many different floors, stairs, nooks, turrets, communicating rooms with doors concealed by wardrobes, and in the midst of so much magnificence, great inconveniences and dark, unpleasant outlooks from the windows. Emilia even made some indiscreet complaints, which, had they reached the Duke's ears, would no doubt have caused him to withdraw the grace of being as perfectly unaware of her intrigue as he was perfectly informed of it, and of keeping her in his service. But for the sake of Claribel's memory, he desired to treat Emilia with particular distinction. He therefore gave her a regular footing in the household, appointing her like Augusta to be maid of honour to Countess Christiane.

The migration left the old house with only a few servants, who ransacked everything, Augusta, who desired to keep away from the fresh plaster as long as possible, and Hans Ulrich and his sister, who were happy perhaps to be alone. But their solitude was not to last long. An order of the Duke arrived, couched in such absolute terms that it had to be obeyed at once. They passed over to the new house and the old one was immediately put up for sale.

※

Next day about two o'clock, Charles d'Este summoned to his presence his four children, Giulia Belcredi, Arcangeli and his other household officers in full uniform. Placing himself at the head of the procession, His Highness showed them round the new establishment. They spent a long time in the gardens, the aviary with its collection of rare birds, and especially in the famous caves which were brilliantly illuminated. The Duke puffed with pleasure, held his head high and laughed loudly all the time. His laughter became almost a bray when Baron von Cramm accidentally knocked up against a panel in the last cave and set all the alarm bells going.

"Ha! Ha! von Cramm!" said the Duke. "I've caught you! You were trying to rob me!"

And brandishing his keys, he wept with laughter. Then he pushed open a door that was so cunningly contrived in the middle of the wall that it could hardly be discovered. A low winding staircase of forty odd steps led down to an iron door guarding the treasure vault. Within were iron safes fixed to the walls and protected with thick bars. They contained an immense sum of money: ducats, doubloons, pistoles with the effigy of Charles's ancestors, old guineas of every reign since the accession of the younger branch of the Blankenburgs to the throne of England, fredericks, louis, napoleons, that had gone through many a campaign with the Duke's uncle. All were stowed away in labelled sacks and piled up like a mountain of gold. One coffer alone was worth more than a million and a half in bars of silver and nuggets of platinum. The Duke delighted in opening several cases of new coins, minted during his reign. In a fit of generosity, he made a present of a good number of them to d'Andonville and Count d'Oels. The Duke was delighted with his house and went from one person to the other, radiant with joy and as though floating on air.

They returned to the ante-chamber, which was guarded by a couple of footmen and was very lofty, profusely gilded and resplendent. A fresh surprise awaited them at the end of the room. Joseph pressed a hidden spring. The wall opened, disclosing a glass-panelled cage, in which stood a gorgeous armchair on a velvet dais. Not only was much time and fatigue saved by means of this lift, but the Duke found pleasure in it for another reason. Having a puerile, ill-balanced mind, he adored these romantic mechanisms, while everything connected with machinery, the theatre and the extraordinary seemed to him like the outward sign of grandeur and luxuriousness.

They all sat down one after the other and the armchair conveyed them to the middle of a staircase, before a rather ugly door. The Duke mounted several steps through the middle of the wall, crossed a narrow ante-chamber hung with old tapestries portraying Italian cities, and lifted up a curtain.

"Messieurs," he said. "Here is my room."

Before them stood a gorgeous bed, gilt and majestic as a throne. Over it was a canopy of old, wine-coloured Genoese velvet, with plumes, furbelows and old gold embroideries. A richly gilt balustrade, breast-high, passed from one end of the room to the other, cutting off a good third of its length. In the room everything was bright and gay; gildings, paintings, sculptures, the most exquisite and costly ornamentations were scattered on all sides; the sumptuousness was excessive; the ceiling was of gold and silver; the walls were covered with a magnificent design, gold and purple, in massive gold relief; the marvellous Persian carpet was placed on a thick mat of floss silk; the floor, chairs, and furniture were all admirable and beyond price. Nature had been exhausted, all the arts and crafts had toiled for years on end in order to decorate that ceiling, those doors, those walls, so that this madman might strut about and lead his children and domestics up and down before them.

"But where is the safe?" Count d'Oels suddenly muttered through his teeth, expressing the thought that was in the minds of everyone.

Then with an unusually serious and majestic air the Duke led them to the far end of the vast room into a large open study at the foot of three steps. It was upholstered to the very ceiling in saffron-coloured silk and the Duke had to give all his attention to finding what he sought for. At last a peal of bells resounded; secret hinges and hidden springs were set in motion so artfully that in a twinkling of the eye the entire panel folded back like the sides of a screen and the safe appeared.

There were some exclamations of surprise and then the Duke manipulated the various secrets of the immense door, which bore the Blankenburg Horse Passant in enamel in the centre. Everyone looked on with a sparkling eye and earnest attention. Profound silence reigned as the Duke opened the last lock.

They started back instinctively; never before had such a dazzling, alarming spectacle met their gaze even in imagination. In the lower compartment, which alone was as big as a fair-sized alcove, piles of banknotes, hundreds of kinds of State, Town and Company securities, lying in disordered heaps, formed a chaos of amazing wealth that awaited the arrival of Mr. Smithson, who alone was capable of reducing it to order.

The species lay above in great piles of louis, some of which had tumbled down and formed a pool, from which the Duke drew his pocket money for the day. The immense upper part of the safe was reserved with jewels, plate and goldsmith's work, which were laid out with admirable pomp. It would have needed several hours of patience to count the gems, diamonds, ropes of pearls, invaluable settings from the treasure of former dukes, sacks of green velvet full of precious stones, curios and valuables.

But the most beautiful of all was the back, which was padded with flush-of-dawn satin and glittered with emeralds, sapphires, magnificent diamonds and great bands of marvellous rubies. The light emitted by this heap of gems was wonderful. Their arrangement formed a sort of mysterious sun, whose splendour astonished one's gaze. And in the dim light, before all those vast riches, the extreme silence seemed to proclaim what was occupying the thoughts of all present.

"In case of danger," said the Duke in a muffled voice, as he pointed to the gaping safe, "it can descend by means of weights and chains to the bottom of the big cellar."

Nothing more was said. They were all troubled and oppressed; the slightest word would have betrayed their uneasiness. It was useless for them to compose themselves: their faces revealed their feelings. Except for Otto, Ulrich and Christiane, who hardly saw what was before their eyes, the rest of the company could not suppress the expression of their anxieties whether by frequent changes of attitude, dark, haggard looks, the care to avoid one another's gaze or the sighs that escaped from one or the other as though by stealth.

D'Andonville was dumbfounded, his eyebrows raised in astonishment. Baron von Cramm was eaten up with envy and smiled with visible anguish. Even Franz no longer ogled Emilia with those understanding glances of his. A heavy silence came over the room. With his gleaming eyes fixed on the safe, Count d'Oels revealed in his face the avarice and covetousness that filled his heart. And they were no less visible on the face of Emilia in spite of her amazement. . . .

Then of a sudden Arcangeli and Giulia looked at each other as with a single thought. The Italian was strong and stiff, obviously pleased with himself for being able to keep his counsel in the midst of the general emotion. Giulia was even more detached, though slightly pale, with a sort of mental fire coming from the pupils of her eyes and piercing brows and bosoms. Their eyes spoke to one another of contempt, challenge and struggle, and then looked away. And Giulia vowed that one day those treasures would belong to her. Steeped in hope, cupidity, and selfishness, her heart, from having loved to excess, no longer found anything to attract it. . . . Those treasures would be hers. . . . And her gaze turned towards Ulrich and Christiane, who were sad and pensive, travelling perhaps in far-off regions. Then it settled in a strange manner on Count Otto who was yawning, his eyes fixed on the ceiling.

V

YES! it was now time to strike a decisive blow. After so much timidity, and so many unfulfilled desires, that arose only to be drowned in nonchalance and torpor, Giulia pulled herself together at last. She felt a thousand serpents astir within her breast. They gave her no rest. Night and day, even when conversing, Giulia dreamed of that great pile of gold and precious stones. The blaze of that gold remained at the back of her pupils. Her whole person took on a sort of new brilliance; her complexion became rosier, her manner livelier, her conversation delicate and gay. But behind all this simulated sweetness, which she used like an adornment to deceive all who came near her, the prima donna pondered frightful thoughts and infernal plans. She spent her days thinking over the obstacle of the Duke's children. She strained her mind to think out some devilish plot that would stealthily develop and encompass their ruin.

At present everything seemed propitious. She was firmly anchored in His Highness's establishment by dint of wit, complacency and flattery. Her growing favour was evident when the Duke distributed gold medals bearing his effigy with the ceremony of the inauguration of the house on the reverse. He sent one to Giulia together with a large cabinet full of costly trifles, and a small present of lace to Christiane. Giulia undertook to convey this present to Christiane in order to renew her relations with her and to carry on her espionage in the apartments of Ulrich and Christiane.

She had reason to be satisfied with the success of her cruellest hopes. Could anything have been more expressive of sorrow and pain than the sighs that escaped their lips when she read to them the moving scene from *'Tis pity she's a whore*. That day Christiane and Ulrich had imbibed a deadly poison which was beginning to infect them. With frowning brows and wild looks, they were seized by a sudden emotion as though they heard once again the terrible warning:

> *You are my brother, Giovanni!*
> *And you my sister, Annabella!*

which Giulia had read to them. Alas! how far away already was that delightful time, when their life flowed so gently and all their being was bathed in a powerful, chaste and sweet enchantment. Now something uneasy and mysterious was working within them and their inner transports were revealed only too well in their flushed faces, irregular pulse and the melancholy vapours which their enflamed blood sent to their heads. In whatever direction they turned they were confronted with an ever-present constraint and shame which came between them like a wall where previously they had lived so free and unconstrained. Whenever they sat next to each other or chatted, their mind seemed to drift away. They found it irksome to keep their gestures and looks in perpetual bonds. And their self-imposed silence and shifts not only were of little avail as a remedy but merely revealed the gravity of the evil and urged their subtle enemy to sweep them forward to catastrophe.

One morning about ten o'clock, Giulia was in the apartment of brother and sister when a footman came to inform her that "Monseigneur le duc" was waiting for her in the winter garden. During the last few days he had found it amusing to go there and watch the opening of the cases that had been filled at Wendessen during the debacle of June 25—at least the great part which Count d'Oels had been able to rescue from the rapacity of the Prussians. The spectacle usually provided His Highness with occasions for anger or mirth.

Giulia found the Duke in his dressing gown; Arcangeli had been pommading him, and feeling bored the Duke had called for Giulia. Outside, the rain never stopped pouring. The grey light falling through the arched bays left the great hall in dimness. Tiers of orange trees stood on all sides, while the floor was littered with vases and porcelain objects taken from the cases already opened. Some big red-shirted workmen were bestirring themselves lazily. The blows of hammers resounded. The Duke yawned with boredom and said he was going away, but Giulia, though yawning likewise, begged him to remain. The menservants were just about to tackle a final case, and Giulia had been seized by an odd feminine whim to know what it contained. It was as though she had a sudden, inexplicable presentiment.

The cover was soon lifted and Giulia leant forward, but was disappointed, while the Duke said, laughing:

"Oh, it's only music!"

She had already taken up one of the manuscripts and recognised at once the first act of *The Valkyrie*. In the confusion which reigned on the night of the flight, the soldiers had packed up all sorts of trifles, and these music-scores probably on account of their red morocco binding and coat-of-arms. All the parts were there, including that of the conductor with the pencil corrections and notes in Wagner's handwriting.

The Duke's mind went back to that fatal evening and the dazzling spectacle at the theatre, Sieglind and Siegmund on the stage, the universal expectation . . . and the messenger scratching on the door of the box. He had taken from his pocket a small malachite mirror and was examining his nose, which for the last fortnight had been getting red, much to his displeasure. Then with a forced grin, he exclaimed:

"Ah! The Prussians were not fond of music. I should have liked at least to see the act through."

A flush crept furtively over Giulia's features; her eyes sparkled with a sudden emotion. A dark, stealthy smile, which Gioconda-like she addressed to her most intimate thoughts, appeared like the sombre aurora of an infernal plan she had conceived. Still looking in the mirror, the Duke was applying white powder to his nose with a pad and kept repeating through his teeth:

"Yes! Yes! I should have liked to see the act through."

"*Cher Seigneur!*" said Giulia in a calm voice, as she looked into his eyes. "It lies only with you whether to hear it again. Your Highness has only to repeat here, far from all interruption, the performance that could not be finished at Wendessen."

"No doubt!" said the Duke gallantly, after a moment's silence. "I can see Sieglind quite well; with a Siegmund . . ."

But Giulia interrupted him:

"Your Highness will pardon me! I wasn't thinking about myself when I made the suggestion. I wasn't even thinking of any professional actor."

And mentioning Hans Ulrich and Christiane, Giulia warmly praised the effect they were sure to produce on the stage, and grew enthusiastic over their voices, which she declared to be as admirable as any:

"Such fine voices. There's nothing equal to them in any theatre at present; and I know what I'm speaking about, Monseigneur. . . ."

And pleased with the manner in which the Duke reacted to her suggestion of a performance, she became very tender and affectionate.

Twenty times a day she brought the question up, always singing the praises of Hans Ulrich and Christiane, always complimenting the Duke on the performance at Wendessen, where he had succeeded to the point of the miraculous, she declared, knowing well that success was assured if she played on that string with the Duke. Moreover, theatrical performances were the vogue in society at that time. People talked of nothing but masquerades, comedies, operas. The most princess-like princesses studied, declaimed, and played roles in their houses or in public, dressed like comediennes. Encouraged by Giulia, the Duke gradually got it into his head that to inaugurate the new house he must give a fête that would eclipse everything else and remain forever a model of gorgeous luxury and fine taste:

"Excellent! We'll give these imbeciles of Parisians, who hissed Tannhäuser, an unpublished act by Wagner. . . ."

And finding boredom in his *tête-à-têtes* with Arcangeli, whose star was on the wane, the Duke determined to carry out his resolve. From that moment the household talked of nothing but the opera, while Hans Ulrich and Christiane were the only ones who were unaware of the role His Highness intended assigning to them.

They seemed to appear less in public than they had done at the Champs Elysées house. Their room was exactly like the old one with the same sculptures and adornments, gilded ceiling, exquisite paintings and immense Venetian chandeliers, so that they did not feel they were in a new place. The Flemish triptychs, enamel madonnas surrounded by fruit, paintings by the old masters, the glass cupboard with Romanesque relics, the four Florentine busts, the same piles of rare books, stuffs, ivories, knick-knacks and precious trifles, the old painted harp in its corner, theorbs and archiluths lying about on the armchairs, were just as they had been in the old house. Their arrangement was finished towards Christmas after long disorder and reminded Hans Ulrich and Christiane of the bright and peaceful days they had formerly spent in those surroundings. Brother and sister had a sort of breathing space; the yoke that weighed their spirit down seemed to have been lifted somewhat. They took pleasure once again in reading. Music was heard once more. It seemed as though a filter of former delights, of that stream of tenderness and suavity that had once flowed in their veins, was re-awakening. One morning

Christiane rested in the arms of Hans Ulrich with her head on his shoulder till they became aware of an inner voice which they recognised so well:

> *You are my brother, Giovanni!*
> *And you my sister, Annabella!*

They turned pale and were roused from their dreaming. The scales fell from their eyes and they both became aware of the progress made by the cancer in their heart. They had fallen asleep on the verge of a precipice! In the midst of storms and tempests they had thought themselves secure! The days that followed were days of torture to both unhappy children. They tried to kill time with all sorts of occupations, and always at the mercy of their devouring uneasiness, went about in all directions, to the Bois, the races, and social gatherings. But these trivial remedies were of little avail against their sufferings. It was the source that had to be stopped, and that source was their heart. Christiane grew pale and thin. Her eyes grew dull and haggard, her face disfigured. Tears flowed from her eyes frequently, while Hans Ulrich, formerly patience itself, became irritable and nervous. The least noise, the scent of a rose, sufficed to disturb him. At night they were harassed by countless dreadful thoughts; something more violent stirred within their being and they were horrified at the monster they were nourishing within them. And when at last they fell asleep, they were afflicted by cruel torments in their dreams.

Meanwhile everything in the house around them was being got ready for the gala. The workmen were already erecting the stage in the Mirror Room, and each afternoon the Duke went to see the decorations in the atelier of Séchan. The conductor of the Lyric Theatre orchestra had undertaken to supply the musicians. The part of Hunding was to be taken by Doëry, the famous baritone of Vienna, to whom Giulia had written. Everything was turning out splendidly. The Duke was enthusiastic. Only then did Giulia remind His Highness that it was time to inform Christiane and Hans Ulrich of the roles they were to play.

But they both refused at the very first words, saying that they would not consent to sing in public.

The Duke gave way to a flood of imprecations. Was he then to be barred in his slightest intentions? Was he to be deprived of this little pleasure by the caprice of a child? So furious were his transports that Christiane gave way, while at the sight of her tears Hans Ulrich yielded to what was demanded of him. They had no other reason for their refusal but shyness of appearing on the stage. But might not the distraction serve to lighten the burden of those weary hours, that moved as on leaden feet?

It was Giulia Belcredi who undertook to instruct the Countess and her brother in their roles. She appeared in their apartment next day, gay, light, talkative and fluttering, going into raptures over the finished room and the scores of charming objects displayed on all sides. Some wax candles of the great chandelier had been lighted and their light revealed the smallest details of the pictures at the top of the walls. The candles were put out before the rehearsal began. Silence reigned on all sides with a sort of majesty. Giulia, now quite serious, was standing upright by the piano. A single lamp lighted the vast room. Giulia sat down at last, ran her fingers over the keyboard and then, before commencing, asked brother and sister whether they remembered the poem.

Neither had well understood the first act, which had been so brusquely interrupted, and Giulia gave them a brief account of it: Siegmund is given shelter by Sieglind; Hunding recognises and challenges him; the hero remains alone; he dreams; he feels his breast heave; Sieglind reappears; their avowals, the long duet, flight. In all this Giulia did not breathe a word of the still darker crime that blackened their adultery. She then struck a few chords, and Hans Ulrich began.

They recited the first duet and sang their part separately in the scene with Hunding. Like two chords in unison, one of which sounds when the other is touched, their hearts vibrated as they replied to one another. They rejoiced with full voices. Transports of love clothed their spirit with joy and light, and when they burst forth with the triumphal song of spring at the end, Christiane and Hans Ulrich seized each other's hand. Enthusiastic and panting, they went without a fault to the end of that wonderful page.

Then Giulia said, as though coming out of a dream:

"In the act that follows they turn out to be brother and sister, both of them being children of the god Wotan, concealed under the name of Walse."

Their faces turned extraordinarily pale and their hands opened and separated. Their enraptured look died out in a convulsive movement of their faces. A heavy silence betrayed the horror that filled them. Christiane had closed her eyes as on the evening when Giulia read to them the scene from Ford. Hans Ulrich gazed in a stupefied manner through the shadows at a portrait of Rembrandt in his old age. What demon, aware of the trouble of their soul, was taking delight in raising the curtain on it so constantly? Were their cruel torments pictured everywhere, and were the songs of the musicians and the verses of the poets destined to give them henceforth no other subject but that of the terrible phantom that pursued them? Brother and sister did not stir. They were filled with other flames, which their heart had not yet made clear to them. They could form no clear idea. And in the midst of this agony, they felt themselves sinking, not into any particular evil, but into an abyss of all the evils.

And next day, for the first time since their childhood, Hans Ulrich did not go to Christiane's rooms. Lying flat on a divan, he groaned and sobbed. He execrated all man-made codes and laws, dreaming of those kings of ancient Egypt. He wished he were dust. After these gloomy reflections, he gave way to spasms of rage that died down at last to mutterings, sighs, and long murmurs. He got up, rubbed his red eyes and paced up and down the room. His troubled head thought of nothing but the two quaint English lines, which he constantly recited:

'Tis good; though music oft hath such a charm
To make bad good, and good provoke to harm.

He tried to remember where he had read them. "Poor thing!" he kept repeating, as his mind reflected on Christiane. He felt she was more to him than his own heart, that her sufferings were more than his own; and at the thought of his sister, his eyes brimmed with tears.

A thousand demons tortured his mind. He passed the following days in this state, at times dull and silent, at others so frenzied that everything in his body threatened to break. He threw out all the clocks, because their ticking irritated him. He groaned because he appeared ugly in the mirrors.—"I want to go away! leave her!" But his strongest resolutions vanished into the air. Alas! the more he reflected on his secret, the more he realised that his life was bound up with it; and crying, rolling on the floor, foaming at the mouth, he ceased from these furies only to lie flat on his back, dishevelled and open-mouthed like a dying man. . . .

And yet he was astonished at not having to suffer more. "What! was it nothing more than that?" The words, passion, torment, despair, had always impressed him in books with a crueller and bitterer meaning than this little spasm of the nerves, this slightly more rapid beating of his heart. And Hans Ulrich became angry with himself; his repose was loathsome to him. He called to suffering, embracing it desperately but never able to find his fill.

Nevertheless, he had to dress himself on the evening of the fifth day, and however cruel the effort was to him, drag his sick body and tortured soul to the apartments of the Duke, who had asked for him. Christiane was already there. The Duke presented her with an enamelled watch in the shape of a lute, and gave Hans Ulrich a case of pistols, in order to soothe their tempers.

They did not raise their eyes, but the harsh tone of their voices, their sighs and slightest movements found a reply in each other and were magnified to the point of pain.

All was silent around them. Caesar was asleep at the Duke's feet; Giulia was talking about Karl Doëry who was unable to leave Vienna. They felt a growing temptation to look at each other, if only for a moment. At last Hans Ulrich turned his head. She was wearing, hanging from a velvet band around her neck, a medallion of their old nurse, Margareta Bracholz, who had watched over their childhood at Herrenhausen and Blankenburg. Their hearts melted at the remembrance of those forgotten days. Hans Ulrich started up on the point of crying out, rushing forward— and something sweet and strong that seemed to well up from their heart, filled their throbbing breast.

From that day they no longer struggled against the stream, but abandoned themselves to their fate. Hans Ulrich returned to Christiane's rooms. They took up the rehearsals again, letting themselves go without fear in the passionate songs of *The Valkyrie*. Giulia, who was following their course step by step, ceased from pouring more poison into an already mortal wound, and visited them rarely, being sure they could no longer escape from their unholy fate.

They were subject to reveries, furies, all the violences of passion. Christiane gave up praying. The hair on Hans Ulrich's head turned grey. Their idleness, nonchalance, delicate foods, the pretended tendernesses of the operas that softened their heart, all the fume-breathing poetry which they drank in and which mounted to their head, the luxuriousness around them, all these things conspired to lead them to the brink of the abyss, till the moment when their conscience, after being long forgotten, suddenly awakened and darted in their eyes so violent a flame that it was like a flash of lightning shattering all. They fled from each other in horror. But they were scarcely alone when they felt a hunger to see each other again. And no sooner did they see each other once more than they were overwhelmed with torments, a gloomy depression and confused, ardent thoughts. They came to hate each other and say hard things. Often as they sat together, a sudden aridity would freeze them for hours, while neither of them could produce the slightest affectionate thought. Hans Ulrich would have given anything for one of those effusions, in which his heart had formerly seemed so uplifted. Wild and indifferent to everything, Christiane and he were pitiable. They had recourse to Nature, but the fields, forests and sunshine were no more a joy to their eyes. They took refuge in Art, but they bore within them an enormous emptiness, wherein neither music nor poetry could enter any more. Like frozen, shining water that in a moment is turned into mud, their former occupations changed into a dark nothing as soon as they reached out to them. Devoured by an insatiable infinity, their very love seemed to flee and fade away in their soul. "Christiane doesn't love me!" Hans Ulrich repeated in despair. He wanted to kill her and himself. And each moment of their life, each beat of their pulse, each flash of their mind, was now more intense a torture than ever.

The days went by with great speed, and the Duke was so impatient that he seemed to push the hours on with his hands, running hither and thither and getting everything ready. The material machinery was almost finished. Karl Doëry was to be replaced by a baritone from the Lyric Theatre. After a second flattering letter from His Highness, Wagner granted the necessary authorisation. Three hundred armchairs were set in rows in the hall and nothing more remained to be done except fix the day for the general rehearsal, which the Duke wished to see and which fell on Saturday, the 21st of January.

Christiane and Hans Ulrich tried on their costumes in the afternoon. His was a simple leather jacket, while hers was a long white linen tunic with a gold fastening for her hair. Giulia came to fetch them about eight o'clock. All three of them went down to a brilliantly-lighted small room that was behind the stage and communicated with Christiane's apartments by a secret staircase.

"Oh Heavens, Countess!" said Giulia. "You have forgotten your earrings."

They were a new present from the Duke, a pair of gold-mounted dandelions; a rough jewel which His Highness had had chiselled for Sieglind.

"You will find them in the writing-desk," said Christiane to Hans Ulrich, who went after them.

The room was deserted and quiet. Two large lamps shed their light around it. Hans Ulrich opened the curious ivory and tortoise-shell cabinet. As he was about to close the drawer he suddenly noticed his pistols at the bottom, for Christiane had secretly taken them away from his rooms lest he should commit some rash act.

He opened the silver case, adorned with the Horse Passant like all things that come from the hands of Charles d'Este; and went to examine the fine weapons in the light of one of the lamps. The silence around him suddenly struck him as being extraordinary. Confused, deep memories surged in upon him, while his heart sank in a vague, unbearable suffering. And looking madly about him, the young man went on loading one of the pistols.

"Ulrich! Ulrich!" cried Christiane from below.

He started up, pushed the drawer back into the cabinet, and hurried downstairs.

"The March of the Blankenburg Hussars," which the orchestra was playing in the hope of a royal gratuity from the Duke, announced the arrival of the company in the hall. The Duke led the way, giving his arm to Giulia Belcredi. She was bare-shouldered and wore a diamond necklace and a magnificent gold and white robe spangled with diamonds and pearls. After the Duke and Giulia came the two bastards, Arcangeli, Count d'Oels smothered with medals, and the rest of the household. At the tail of the procession was the enormous ox-blood-coloured suit enclosing the perspiring form of M. d'Andonville. The Duke sat down in an armchair in the front row. He placed Giulia on one side of himself and Otto on the other, a little to the rear.

The orchestra began the prelude. A storm rumbled. Then the curtain divided in the middle, disclosing a dwelling with massive beams, a huge rough-hewn door and a roof supported by a giant ash-tree, in the side of which gleamed the hilt of the sword promised to Walsung. Ulrich—Siegmund—made his entrance; Christiane started the first notes of Sieglind's song—and in the midst of the stern calm which they tried to affect, they both felt their hearts invaded by memories of the time when they played children's comedies and dramas together at Herrenhausen.

"Cher Seigneur!" Giulia whispered in the Duke's ear during the applause that greeted the end of the scene. "See how well the Countess plays her part!"

Standing motionless in a corner of the scene, as wild-eyed Hunding made a gesture of surprise on perceiving the stranger, Christiane wrapped her brother in a deep, dark look. She loved him! Oh, she loved him! What was the use of struggling any longer? . . . The enormous chandeliers blazed above the empty hall, that stood already prepared with its rows of chairs. Applause followed applause almost without ceasing. Yes! it was all very well to applaud them, the unhappy creatures! It was their very heart that they were playing; those songs with which they were amusing the ears of the uncaring, were no less than the very cries of their passion. A flood of tears welled up to her eyelids. Since the gods themselves, since Wotan drove Siegmund into his sister's arms, could there be any crime? . . . And with her gaze plunged into the tortured depths of her being, Christiane continued her sombre reverie.

"Bravo! Bravo!" exclaimed the Duke, applauding loudly as Sieglind withdrew from the scene with solemn gait.

Night came down on the scene. Hans Ulrich was now alone by the dying fire. The gentle symphony of the orchestra did not reach his ears; a thousand fancies rose up before his mind, already abandoned to its evil. A door opened. It was Sieglind.

She had sent her husband to sleep by giving him a sleeping-draught. She came in order to show Siegmund the sword embedded in the ash-tree. And as they passed across the vast stage, in whose darkness Sieglind looked like a white phantom, it all seemed to Hans Ulrich once again nothing more than a dream.—But did he really know whether he was asleep or awake? The world appeared to him as through vague, dim eyes, jutting out from the depths of his soul. He wondered whether suffering and living was anything else but a slightly more excited part of a gloomy, continual sleep. But there rose upon the air a melody, as strong and heroic as the spring. The enormous door sprang open with a crash. The whiteness of the night flooded the room. Then, in accordance with the poem, Hans Ulrich enfolded Christiane in his arms; and the beat of his heart was answered by the beat of one that was full of him. Their voices rose in unison, followed by the silence of ecstasy, wherein nothing could be heard but the restless murmur and palpitating rumble of that beautiful night of spring. It was all love and torments of love; and from the topmost heaven the shining, milk-white moon poured over all a vast love-compelling philtre. The forest was alive and sighed. The brooks swelled with tenderness. The enfolded lovers at the far end of the scene shook with thrills. Instinctively they moved forward to sing at the proper moment. And the flowing, passionate music, ever increasing in warmth and fire, enkindled, intoxicated them.

Hesitations, scruples, remorse, all seemed to slip like a burden from their soul. They sang, and sang again. In that song they cried out to each other all that they had been unable to say before. They sang their triumph and adoration, panting with the superhuman transports of their love. They cared for nothing else. Taking three steps, Hans Ulrich drew out the sword at a grasp and brandished it. Then lifting his lover in his arms, he fled in haste, and the curtain fell.

The lights in the chandeliers went up, and the Duke passed with his suite into the winter garden. He summoned Hans Ulrich and Christiane to him as soon as they had changed their dress. Supper was served. It consisted of game, fish, fruit and various Rhine wines, with which His Highness carried out the toasts. Then in order to help Christiane to recover from a slight fatigue, the Duke proposed going into the garden and seeing by torch-light the frozen waterfall of the rock-garden. This amused the company for a while, but the increasing cold drove the Duke back to the house. Hans Ulrich and his sister walked last of all along the snow-covered path. Then, without uttering a word, they went upstairs to their study.

She sat down in an armchair. Hans Ulrich stood by the window, looking very pale. The full, sad moon seemed to gaze at him like a living eye. And looking at the endless stars one beyond the other, he vaguely thought of the infinite depth of the universe. A sudden start ran through him. Christiane had risen. Her light steps behind his back terrified him as though Death itself had walked towards him. Sombre snatches of a dream came back to him. He seemed to see the burning candles, a coffin hovering about, and himself standing upright with his eyes fixed on his bare feet. His heart was beating enough to break. He felt she was behind him, perhaps looking ghastly in death. Mad with terror, he turned round and they came face to face. With a shudder she threw herself into his arms and their lips met.

Towards half-past four in the morning, two shots woke the household with a start. Giulia, who had just got into bed after seeing Hans Ulrich leave Christiane's apartment, slipped on a dressing gown and ran to the Count's room. Extreme confusion reigned there. The doors were open and the servants were running to and fro. Count Ulrich had fired one of the Duke's pistols into his chest and finding himself still alive, had blown out his brains.

VI

A GOOD number of people came and wrote their names in the visitors' book at the house of mourning. There were just as many yards of black cloth as strict propriety required. As for grief, the Duke had never loved "the son of the serf" As he called him, so no time was lost on weeping, and once the funeral was arranged and the servants dressed in black, there was no further question of Hans Ulrich or affliction. Moreover, the terrible tragedy had a ridiculous contrast in the farce that came after it.

On the evening Franz came home from the interment, he discovered Emilia had flown. He questioned the chambermaids. They told him, with much hesitation and exchange of glances that after many tears and cries following the scene at luncheon. . . .

"Yes! Yes! After!" interrupted the Count, who knew that the deluge was due to a fresh refusal to marry.

Mademoiselle had suddenly ordered a carriage and told the coachman, it seems, to drive to a railway station. Franz sent for Arcangeli, but the dear brother declared he had seen nothing and knew nothing.

"Come now, Giovan, tell me where your sister is!"

Holy Virgin! did he keep her in his pocket! And losing his temper, he cried out against such suspicions, protested his ignorance and even railed against Emilia with very little delicacy.

Next day, however, he came to the Count fairly early and after a wordy preface informed him that Emilia had fled to St. Germain. He had just received a short note.

Franz set out immediately, having nothing in heart and mind but to see his mistress again. He counted on the help of one of his closest friends there, the Marquis de Courson, a lieutenant in the Hussars, in carrying out his search. But just as he was stepping out of the carriage, he suddenly wondered whether the Marquis's house might not be the place of refuge of his beloved Helen. The young man had, in fact, shown much attention to Emilia on many occasions and she had been gratified by it. Besides, the desire to be sought after and to rouse Franz's jealousy might have had as much to do with Emilia's flight as that lean and lanky de Courson with his yellow, ugly, pimply face. Franz went and thought about it in the avenue of the Terrace and found it all quite likely. He visited the château, prowled about the approaches of the marquis's house for a while, but soon retreated for fear of a public scene with Emilia, if she happened to come out. He went and had luncheon, and then returned to Paris, firmly persuaded that he was being played a trick.

He went to bed early and spent the evening talking over the escapade with Louis, his valet. On awakening, he found a letter from the fugitive, which shed on the affair all the light that was required.

Francis,

> *You came here today to get information. You did wrong to go back without seeing the Marquis, as I am in his house. I came here to beg him to give me shelter for a few days, till Sunday. You know that I did not want to remain your mistress and offend the Virgin and the Saints. . . . But it's no use repeating all the reasons.*
>
> *So if you have not made up your mind to marry me, I shall be the Marquis's mistress on Sunday. I swear to you on my bended knees and by the soul of my father that nothing has happened up to the present.*

Should you refuse to have me for your lawful wife,
give up all relations with me from henceforward.
Adieu! I await your reply. Think it over. My resolution
will not change.

"Tra, la, la, la, tra, la, la," sang the Count between his teeth. And that was his only wrath against the insolent alternative which Emilia offered him. His merriment was all the greater when he received a letter from the Marquis de Courson, in which the latter pleasantly told of Emilia's sudden appearance like a bolt from the blue, and related about her sighs, transports, lamentations and the pistols which guarded her virtue, and that, seeing no way out of the grotesque scene, he had gone to lodge at a friend's, leaving the lady for courtesy's sake mistress of the battlefield.

It was a useless victory, however. In the forsaken house, Emilia grieved to see so much precious time wasted. Losing patience, she wrote a letter, but Franz sent it back with the following words below her signature:

The manner in which you have behaved does not de-
note a person who is quite proper.

Whoever knew the Count with his fondness for propriety, would have realised that he could not make a graver reproach. Giovan, who arrived a few hours after, declared that all was lost and that obstinacy would only lead to an irreparable rupture. A last bit of comedy made Emilia write a desolate letter; after which she blew into her hand to dry her tears and left St. Germain. She installed herself in the Rue d'Orléans, near the Bois de Boulogne, where Giovan gave her board and lodging for the time being, though she was like another millstone round his neck.

The time of Giovan's favour with the Duke had now gone by. His amusing actions and the buffoonery which he brought to the most serious actions had lost their savour and were *vieux jeu.*

"Well, that's all right, my poor Giovan!" the Duke would mutter languidly. And the tone became day by day more imperious and bitter after the strange adventure at St. Germain. Arcangeli's green-apple neck-ties, low, narrow, puny mind, garlic odour and even his coral ornaments began to tire the Duke and make him cross with everything his jester did. The Italian seemed to be resigned. But his heart bled in secret at so complete a reverse. He had been the one and only man in the house and good for everything, from attending to His Highness's intimate needs to re-conquering the Duchy together after dinner. Yet now he was restricted to the dry, silent, embarrassed performance of his master's toilet. Or if he risked a jest, the Duke stopped him with an icy glance and returned to his figures or the lawyers, who were at that time his only and not very pleasant company.

The troubles that now assailed him, had to do with the house itself. At first he had been delighted with it and sent magnificent presents to both architects, but before paying their bill he thought he would verify their charges. He was astounded by the amount of cheating, and being anxious to get to the bottom of the matter, had the inventories, leases, memoranda, contracts, and the book of receipts and expenses brought into his study, where he spent the mornings in Mr. Smithson's company fathoming his own most abstruse and profound arithmetic.

When he visited Giulia, his head was still full of it, and being bored with etiquette and pleased to see Giulia doing her best to amuse him and brighten up his table and apartment, he got into the habit of lunching with her *tête-à-tête*. They both had their own menu. Hers was very abundant, for she loved eating and all sorts of dishes. The Duke took very little and always the same—a little fruit at the beginning of the meal, especially melons and figs, capons, roast and boiled pigeon and game, and every day a little pastry with cheese stuffing, caviare or poppy-seed; but everything was done with so much gravy and spice, that there was small wonder the Duke extinguished all this fire with torrents of beer. There was never any salad or venison, rarely fish, which he thought insipid; and just a little dash of liqueur or very old brandy after the meal, while he dabbled with his jewel-caskets, which Giulia went to fetch for him.

It was the time when he had undertaken to draw up the *Official Catalogue* of his collection of precious stones. He was aided all along by Van Mospes, an expert jeweller, who had once sold some trifles to Giulia and had been introduced by her to His Highness. Whoever entered, saw the Jew, strewn over a high chair, his big eye fixed on a diamond, his face all livid, bunched up and looking very much like a frog; and always in front of him was his eternal pair of scales, of which two enormous humps in his chest and back looked like the case. Meanwhile the couch from which the Duke dominated the assistants was smothered with more than twenty millionsworth of stones of all kinds, diamonds, rubies, enormous turquoises, emeralds as big as a Victoria plum; and in the light of the candelabra the motionless, bearded Duke, his fingers and breast ablaze with myriad fires, looked like a stage-king on his dais.

All this trouble of verifying figures and weighing diamonds was due to the Duke's desire, after Hans Ulrich's death, to put his fortune in order and make his will. The result of all his labours was to leave him with a score of unpleasant lawsuits, for, getting tired of the job, the Duke decided to dispute all the lot of the contractors' charges. But what were the few hundred thousand francs in dispute compared with the monstrous amount of money revealed by the Will? Five million were bequeathed to Christiane on her marriage and another five million at the Duke's death; to Count Franz, fifteen million; and the remainder, almost three hundred and thirty million, *id est*, as the precious draught explained:

> *Our castles, our domains, our forests, our mines, our salt mines, mansions, houses, our parks, our libraries, gardens, quarries, diamonds, jewels, plate, pictures, horses, carriages, porcelain, furniture, cash, stocks,*

*banknotes, and particularly that part of our fortune
which has been taken from us and retained by sheer
force, since 1866, in our duchy of Blankenburg.*

All these the Duke bequeathed to his darling Otto, who was
to pay a few legacies to be designated in the codicils.

✳

When the will became known there was a good deal of murmuring and uneasiness in the house. As nothing exact was known
and Count d'Oels found pleasure in disseminating contradic-
tory rumours, everyone was afraid lest his own piece of the cake
should have been bitten off by his neighbour. Even Augusta
faced the peril of cold draughts in order to go and beg Giulia
to continue to think kindly of her. This was because Giulia
seemed to occupy as favourable and radiant a position with His
Highness as anybody had ever done. Same apartment, same bed.
The Duke never left the young woman's company. They had become very affectionate and twenty times a day Giulia took her
"cher Seigneur's" orders as to what she was to wear or do.

The child of caprice, he liked her on account of her exquisite
refinements, delicacy and reserve. While he was at work with Mr.
Smithson, she would read or embroider. Her nose was hardly
ever off her wool. Amid all the heaps of figures with which His
Highness insisted on filling his will, she saw immense lands, few
debts, an El Dorado of money and gems, Christiane and Franz
to be provided for, and Otto no doubt to be treated with favour;
but all that would not go very far; there would still be many fine,
splendid millions left. And believing herself established in the
height of favour, she seemed to be giddy with hopes.

The will was made known one day towards the end of March.
The ceremony was carried out in the rather theatrical style which
the Duke was fond of. Entering the great Tapestry room one
evening after dinner, he advanced towards his assembled house-

hold, took his youngest son by the hand and slowly looking round the silent company, told them that all his titles, honours, possessions, and the Duchy of Blankenburg would go to Otto, who was to succeed him; then walking a few paces to the other end of the room, he called Count Franz. With excuses for the smallness of the sum, he informed him of the fifteen million he bequeathed to him, and mentioned the excessive share allotted to Otto:

"But one cannot do with less, my dear children, when one has to keep up one's rank. . . ."

After which he seized Franz by the shoulders and leaning on him so as to make him bend, begged his two sons to embrace each other in his presence and to remain true friends after his death. Then he embraced them himself, and the whole of the little court swarmed eagerly around them with congratulations.

"And what about me, *cher seigneur*?" said Giulia an hour later, as she drew off her rings. "Won't you give me anything, then?"

He looked at her. She was smiling in her familiar enigmatical way. The Duke was about to drink a glass of chicory water according to his habit every evening. "Here you are!" said the Duke teasingly, and Giulia took a long draught of the medicine, which was no doubt less bitter than her disappointment.

That was all she got in the month of March, which she had hoped would turn out rich and fruity. But far from showing the least concern, she increased in gaiety and attention in His Highness's company, to the grave displeasure of Arcangeli.

"Go on, wretch! Do your acting and beware of tumbling!" he murmured, shrugging his shoulders, for his own rapid disgrace showed him the stick always ready to fall on others. "No, it can't go very far. She'll fall and break her nose, the insolent creature!" concluded the buffoon, as he watched his rival in the gallery of the seasons, where His Highness had placed him. It was a hard penance for him to see her enter the Duke's apartment a score of times daily, always self-possessed, rather matter-of-fact, and looking graceful and unconcerned. Only now and again dig:

a glance in the mirror betray some secret hope, as though the haughty sorceress had smiled to herself at finding something in her eyes and handsome face that assured her of achieving her designs and confounding her enemies.

For the past week Count Otto, who had been almost always out of the way before, began to frequent his father's apartment. He came early and took a big breakfast, surrounded by his bitches and feeding them with the scraps. In this way he had audience with the Duke, who was still in bed and appeared to be delighted with the procedure, though all he gained in the long run from this sudden outburst of filial affection was the unpleasant odour of a saddle. He thought himself lucky if the darling youngster indulged in only half his extravagances and moderated his usual oaths when Giulia chanced to take a morsel he wanted.

She was the only one, however, who had any influence over him and could try to bridle his dreadful temper. The entire household trembled before Otto. He was master over all through his father's predilection, and wild like those animals that seem born only to devour. Even his amusements breathed of the tyrant and the untamed. With his yellow, spoilt complexion, his fat, shaking head, and a sort of red soul, so to say, that blazed in his bloodshot eyes and red hair, he resembled, according to Count d'Oels, the lurid sulphur flames of hell, with which the damned are tormented.

"Yes, a demon, a real demon!" His Highness would say, not without pleasure; and one day his chamberlain ventured to remark:

"Indeed, monseigneur, when Satan enters his body, it will be the devil who will be possessed and made more of a devil than he is already. . . ."

Charles d'Este laughed heartily at this joke for many a day as soon as d'Oels crossed his sight. A son like that made him feel young again. He seemed delighted to gaze upon him, even forgetting his cellars, which had just been finished and were as magnificent as a drawing-room. The Duke had spent 200,000 écus on their construction. In the light of the gas-lamps, which made the stuccos, gildings and marbles shine with incredible splendour, the menservants were busy arranging endless bottles in a sort of oak dovecote that reached as high as the ceiling. There were also cellars, arranged like libraries, for the Bordeaux, Burgundies,—the best in Europe, according to the Duke— Champagnes, foreign wines, the rarest liqueurs, and finally a cellar for the Duke's beer, which was brewed especially for him at Pilsen in Bohemia. Otto and Saint Amour found much pleasure there, drinking their fill and breaking bottles. There was singing and shouting; toads were blown up with gunpowder, dogs were baptized and set on, and a whole catalogue of horrors. Their extravagances led to physical reaction, and the Duke felt some alarm, spending the afternoon at the bedside of his beloved son in the company of Giulia.

One evening when Giulia was alone with the Duke about half an hour after one of these long visits, she was greatly surprised to see a figure in a masquerade costume suddenly enter, and to recognise it as Otto. She cried out, but after a moment's hesitation at the door, he rushed forward, repeating, "Oh, the fine bed! the fine bed!" and jumping on it in a sort of frenzy. Then he went over to the astonished singer and begged her to put right a fold that had become disarranged. He was wearing long, floating, green streamers surmounted by deer's antlers and a weird head-dress that gave him the look of an Acteon.

"Are you going to Monsieur Aguado's?" She asked, for a fancy-dress ball was to take place there.

And turning round, the young Count embraced her without a word. She fell backwards and for a second one saw her lemon-coloured silk stockings.

"Have done!" she said, defending herself against his kisses. . . .

The terrible thing was that only five paces away was a half-open door with a few marble steps leading to the room in which the Duke was taking his bath. She kept turning her eyes towards the door. Her strength was forsaking her, when the Duke called out by chance:

"Giulia!"

And the unexpected sound of this voice put the young Count to flight, while His Highness sat in his bath without realising what had happened.

The young Count turned elsewhere for consolation. His vices had palled on him and now he exchanged them for worse. Everything seemed licit to him. He would have frightened any-one in a wood with his cadaverous paleness, wild, leering look and the frightful twitch that kept jerking his face forward every minute as though to vomit his evil spirit. Every night he had to be picked up and carried to bed, dead drunk. He woke up about midday and there followed the weirdest possible proces-sion of ruffians, rogues, pimps, musk-scented matrons, coach-men. They stood in a circle around him. Their voices chanted his praises. They pressed him to come and see, in the usual style of the trade:

"A new picture or two of rare value."

For twelve or fourteen hours on end, the Duke's horses re-mained standing outside infamous houses. . . . Otto ended by staying there for weeks at a time—so that His Highness was able to avail himself of the vacant apartment for a few days in order to accommodate the Princess of Hanau, a poor, Romanist relation, who was suddenly left without clothes or money owing to her luggage going astray.

Neither she nor the Duke had seen each other for almost eighteen years, and His Highness, who in his youth had shown a little inclination for his cousin, was a long time recovering from his astonishment at finding "Sophie so much changed." She was astonishingly thin, and so tall that she almost gave one a fright when seen at a distance. She had an enflamed-looking face and long witch's teeth. In spite of this, she was the soul of honour and straightforwardness; a lively spirit, full of penetration and natural graces, and burning with a love of good works, which had led her to give away much of her possessions in order to feed the poor and build hospitals. Good works, alms, prayers at home and at church, rare visits in society, for which she had an inclination rigorously held in check, formed the tissue of her life. And so much piety and virtue, maintained without fail during the whole fourteen years of her widowhood, had always somehow obliged the Duke to show a particular respect towards this relation of his. Indeed, when Christiane was a child, she had once spent a whole summer in the company of the Princess in a sort of convent built by the former Counts of Hanau in the heart of the Italian Tyrol.

Christiane, therefore, was the first person Princess Sophie inquired after, and was inexhaustible on the subject of her niceness and gaiety in the days gone by. She must have grown up very beautiful and graceful.

"Ah! she has changed a great deal!" said the Duke with a certain unconcern.

But sooner or later they would have to meet, so towards the evening the Duke and the Princess went together to Christiane's apartment.

The bedroom was empty. There was no one to announce them. They went back through the silent gallery. The carpet covered with wax-droppings reminded the Duke of Hans Ulrich's death and the burning tapers of the catafalque. They opened the wrong doors but managed at last to find the great study with the piano. But the profound silence and the sight of Christiane stretched out on a couch with her eyes shut so perplexed the Princess that she hardly ventured beyond the threshold.

The Duke coughed. "This is our cousin of Hanau whom I bring to you," he announced.

Christiane turned round without saying anything, and showed that she recognised the visitor with a look of gentleness and affection that went to the good woman's heart. Her livid, set countenance had something wild about it. The Duke told her that the Princess was going to live in Paris. She had got up and stood without uttering a word in reply. The tears she was trying to keep back trickled from her eyes.

116

"Look how nice it is here!" said the Duke looking round, for he had never seen the room before.

She closed her eyes and was silent. A barrel-organ was playing in the distance. The evening sky was growing paler, that sky so often watched by Hans Ulrich through those same window-panes. He was dead, he was dead . . . he was asleep in the darkness . . . and there would be no end to it.

✳

That evening as the Duke, after undressing, was having his feet brushed according to his custom by Arcangeli (the only function left to that fallen grand vizier), a note was brought in by Count d'Oels. It had just arrived from the Tuileries. "From the Emperor," said the Duke, hastily unfolding it. His Majesty begged the Duke that they might have a serious conversation together; "and I should like very much, if it is possible, for you to fix it for tomorrow, Friday, afternoon." To which the Duke replied "Yes" and went to bed wondering extremely, especially as a post-scriptum begged him to bring some of "his fine diamonds" with him.

He went to the Tuileries about half-past two, but His Majesty was at that moment receiving the Austrian Ambassador. A chamberlain begged the Duke to go into a little study overlooking the garden. The room was empty and the Duke amused himself, as well as he could, by looking at the antique bronzes and medals that adorned two high windows. Nevertheless, he found the time long and kept pulling out his watch every minute.

"Ah, I've got you!" said the Emperor agreeably, as he entered. And he immediately asked the two footmen of the ante-chamber whether Mr. Babinet had arrived, and ordering that he should not be disturbed except on the savant's arrival, shut the door and bolted it.

"But, Sire, what is the matter then?" the Duke asked with astonishment.

Taking him by the arm and leading him to a table loaded with a copper apparatus and glass bells, he told him that he had desired to show him what could be done in the way of colouring diamonds. It was Mr. Babinet who had first interested him in the subject, and had mentioned the name of His Highness as that of one of the best connoisseurs of precious stones and most likely to be interested in the matter. Whereupon the Duke most courteously expressed his grateful thanks. They then proceeded to look at the Crown jewels set aside for the experiments. Some of them were in small cases which Napoleon took out of his pocket. He placed them one after the other among the papers, atlases, and models of infantry equipment which littered the writing table. Then suddenly he asked in his soft voice:

"You have many relations, Monseigneur?"

"Ah, Sire!" exclaimed the Duke. "Might they all be at the bottom of hell!"

His Majesty twirled his moustaches, as though somewhat surprised at the remark, and there was something so icy and serious in his silence that the Duke changed colour.

"What is there then, Sire? Tell me! I am ready to hear everything."

The Emperor indicated an armchair to him, and placing himself at his table before the Duke, explained to him by way of preface, that he had very powerful enemies. The Duke began to fidget in his chair; but His Majesty went on to warn him in outspoken terms that he would have to be careful with regard to his conduct, as he was being watched. He told him that things were moving towards a climax and that, as usual among relations and allies, a plot was being worked up against him. Finally, the Emperor mentioned the name of his uncle and former guardian, Francis V, Duke of Modena.

"Him! the beggar!" exclaimed His Highness in a sort of transport. . . .

Whereupon the Emperor cut him short and turned to another subject, asking him if it was true that he had spent 16,000,000 on the Beaujon mansion.

The Duke's answer was incoherent and more like the out-bursts of a man who is indignant and wants to storm. After allowing him to plead his cause for a while, the Emperor told him that however much he regretted informing him of such unpleasant things, he could no longer hold them back. He knew from an undoubted source that the Duke's family was intriguing against him, and pretending to fear that so many prodigalities, the construction of that mansion, that violent outburst of law-suits, and scores of other queer actions (though this adjective was not used) might indicate some derangement of His Highness's health. There was talk of setting about the task of putting an end to such a state of affairs. Francis, Duke of Modena, was at the head of the coalition.

"And I have reason to believe," continued the Emperor, laying stress on his words, "that he has taken steps to bring together a family council in order to have you placed under his wardship."

"Ah! Sire! Pardon me!" said the Duke, standing upright, his face purple. And he began to pace up and down the room, breathing heavily. . . . "A coward! a tyrant! a thief," he stam-mered, choked with rage.

Yes! he was a thief! Had it not been proved at the time of his shameful flight, that Francis V had taken pictures worth five or six million belonging to the State? He was an incapable and wicked old man. He himself, Charles d'Este, was his superior by right, as head of the elder branch. . . .

And losing his temper, he allowed himself to be carried away on a torrent of invective. The Emperor sat at his great, littered writing table, looking very pensive and taking chocolate pastilles from a jar before him.

"Yes! no doubt!" he said after a while. "It is all very annoying, extremely annoying."

For a fairly long while the Duke continued raving and pacing up and down the room. After a considerable silence His Majesty looked at him earnestly and said that there was something fur-ther to be said. He had desired to get to the bottom of the matter and know all the possible effects of such a decision. He had been told all about them, and that once the decision of the family council was transmitted to the Minister for Foreign Affairs, it would be handed on to the Imperial Procurator.

"But, Sire!" the Duke interrupted. "In France. . . ."

"In France," rejoined the Emperor, "as in Italy, Switzerland, Russia and in any country where you have possessions, Francis V will put in a claim on the revenues of your property, in virtue of the act of sequestration, and obtain a judicial order to have them handed over to him."

"Sire!" said the Duke. "We shall go to law."

"No doubt! That is what I expected," replied the Emperor, shrugging his shoulders. "You will go to law . . . will you win? It appears that the decision of the family council can be upheld as a genuine personal statute, that follows you everywhere. And the Minister of Justice did not hide from me the fact that this doctrine was quite likely to be accepted by the tribunal."

"But it would be monstrous!" the Duke protested. "But, Sire, I'm not a fool!"

"Have you no means of taking action against Francis V?" continued the Emperor without replying. And he rose from his chair, looking at the Duke with gloomy eyes.

Mr. Babinet had already been announced a good while. Having delivered himself of his burden, the Emperor went and opened the door, calling the savant from the threshold. The first few moments were spent in the greetings and compliments of the visitor. He was very bent and hoary with a very big head and grey trousers; he had just come from visiting Her Majesty the Empress.

"I will be with you in an instant, permit me!" said the Emperor; and taking Charles d'Este aside he went on with the interrupted subject and asked him in a low voice what he had decided to do.

"Sire," said the Duke, "I've just thought of it. I still have in my possession some papers in connection with my wardship.

They can be very embarrassing to my dear uncle, and since I'm forced to do so, I will make use of them. If Francis V attacks me in Paris, I will have him condemned in Florence."

"It would be better not to go to law, Monseigneur, believe me," said the Emperor.

And the firm tone in which these words were spoken reduced the Duke to silence. The Emperor drew him into a window bay and talked to him for more than a quarter of an hour regarding the inconveniences and dangers of a lawsuit. Then, getting nearer and nearer to the Duke's ear, the Emperor led up no doubt to his political and confidential reasons, which he developed at great length. With his nose against the window pane, from which he could see the sentinel with a beaver bonnet marching to and fro below, the statue of Diana the huntress just opposite and the green trees of the Tuileries beyond, the Duke kept changing his posture every minute like a man who is full of rage but dare not answer; and no noise was heard in the sun-lit room except that low whispering and the muffled steps of the savant, who had begun to fix up his instruments.

"Not to go to law!" the Duke suddenly exclaimed aloud.

Then after a short silence, lifting up his head and sighing, he asked: "What shall I do then?"

"There's only one thing to be done," replied the Emperor. "That is, to negotiate."

"Negotiate!" exclaimed His Highness in bitter tones.

"The Duke of Modena is in Rome," His Majesty continued. "Send him a negotiator in whom you trust. He will frighten the Duke who is miserly, and will threaten him with a lawsuit, and if the papers you mention are of any real importance . . ."

"Most certainly!" the Duke interrupted.

"Very well! The good fellow will be only too happy not to breathe a word about the request for restriction, provided on your part that you give up bothering him."

And as the Duke made no reply, the Emperor went on: "Think it over. Take your time; you will give me an answer presently."

They then went back towards Mr. Babinet. And His Majesty, with the Duke a little to the rear, watched the pneumatic machine which the savant put into motion. The Duke broke the silence by asking whether a picture by Karl Muller, a Virgin on the right of the bookcase, was not a Raphael. They then spoke about various indifferent things, which led up to anecdotes about the Court. And His Majesty, in a cheerful mood, asked the savant about the reception at the Academy, which had taken place the day before. But Mr. Babinet declared with a smile that he had been unable to get into the hall, as the crush was too amazing.

"And did they talk a lot of evil about me?" asked the Emperor with a pale smile.

Whereupon the savant replied in a modest, restrained voice that the Orleanists let themselves go on the subject of the Marquis de Mascarille (who, as everyone knows, wanted to put Roman History into madrigals), but that these gentlemen were trying to turn it into epigrams. And this allusion to the speech pronounced by the new Academician who, in discoursing on the Caesars had aimed his criticisms at Napoleon, brought a smile to His Majesty's face.

The first experiment was a short one. Under the action of an electric current, the diamonds were filled with light and sparkled with a myriad of multi-coloured fires, while Mr. Babinet explained everything in a chatty way that was very remote from academic pedantry. The two sovereigns understood and enjoyed a secret pleasure in the matter, and Charles d'Este asked the savant whether science would be able to fabricate diamonds someday.

Mr. Babinet reassured the Duke, adding as he tied up the window curtains in their green velvet loops:

"If I had that knowledge in my hands, I would take good care not to open them."

There was a little silence. At last the Emperor, glancing at the melting pots and instruments which Mr. Babinet was setting out ready for further experiments, suggested to the Duke that they should go into his inner study while waiting. It was a recess scarcely big enough for more than four or five persons at a pinch, in which Napoleon had a desk, some chairs, and books, with which only his most private household officers were acquainted, as he explained to the Duke. Two miniatures by Isabey hung on the walls, one representing Queen Hortense at the age of fifteen, fair, smiling, blue-eyed; the other, Prince Eugene, with a doll-like, curly head, whom the Duke Charles declared he had much resembled in his childhood.

His Majesty said in a low voice:

"I felt very sincerely for you, Monseigneur, in the cruel loss you recently had."

The Duke hesitated somewhat. Then, thinking that the Emperor was referring to Hans Ulrich, he muttered the words "dreadful misfortune"; for it had been put about, in order to conceal the suicide, that the Count had accidentally killed himself while cleaning his pistols.

"You still have two sons," said His Majesty.

"Yes, Sire."

"I am sorry," said the Emperor, taking a batch of papers out of a secret drawer, "to have to complain to you about one of them; but judge, Monseigneur, if it is possible to do otherwise."

It was a police report concerning Count Otto. The Duke read it at a glance. His son was accused, or at least strongly suspected, of causing a woman of a certain class to be burnt alive by some sort of sinister game, which had led to a very strange outbreak of fire in her house. And the report contained such a profusion of details of Otto's ferocity and monstrous de-bauches, that His Highness changed colour, while the Emperor said in his gentlest voice:

"Count Otto is well-born, Monseigneur, but he has been badly whipped."

"Oh, Sire!" Exclaimed the Duke. "My son and I have a lot of enemies!"

"However," continued Napoleon gently, "it would be advis-able for Count Otto to travel and go away for a while."

As the Duke appeared anxious to object to the proposal, His Majesty immediately cut the attempt short, declaring in a masterly tone that Otto should have shown more respect for himself on account of his high birth. It was only because he was the son of His Highness that one had consented to close one's eyes for so long. The scandal of his behaviour could no longer be shielded by his name and dignity. In a word, the Count would have to leave.

"Very well, Sire, I will obey," said the Duke in abrupt tones. "Or rather," he added, at a gesture by the Emperor, "I will follow the two counsels Your Majesty has kindly given me."

Three days later, Count Franz set out for Italy. However disinclined the Duke may have been to entrust any mission to those of his own blood he had not been able to find anyone else for ambassador. Arcangeli being very tired of trivial occupations, which kept him in a state of suspense and ever on the verge of disgrace, begged to accompany the Count as interpreter; which His Highness granted, in order to get the Italian out of sight. The day after their departure, Emilia took a train for the south. The same day Otto left, having been informed of the Emperor's wishes by his father. He received the order without regret and the same evening laid a wager that he would go from Paris to Vienna in thirteen days on Bellua, his favourite mare. He got into the saddle at the appointed hour, and a group of his friends accompanied him to the Trône gate. There he shook hands and went off at a gallop.

VII

ON the forty-first day after his arrival in Rome, which was a Tuesday and the feast of St. Victor, in whose honour the distant bells were pealing, Arcangeli woke up at five o'clock with a start and saw Emilia opening the shutters of his garret, and a blue-coated waiter of the Hotel Manni standing before him with a letter in his hand. It was a telegram from Charles d'Este to Count Franz, which had arrived in the night and commanded that Giovan should leave Rome at once and return to Paris.

He sat upright on his mattress and cried out: *Viva Garibaldi!* His disgrace was at an end and he was now saved, brought back from the depths. Had not the old soothsayer Cucurani foretold that he would never die in disgrace?—And while Giovan polished his boots, his foot planted against the wall, brother and sister recalled the surprising things that the old sorceress had told them: the exact details, the day, hour and place at the Campo di Fiori, where Franz met Emilia a week after his arrival, his silence during the following days, the gradual return of his love, his attempts to be admitted to her presence, even the very words he used when he had begged Giovan to go and live with his sister at their old mother's house in order to be closer at hand to assist him in his suit.

"Ah! gracious Virgin!" said the young woman, suddenly bursting into tears. "Now I shall be all alone! You're going to leave me! He-he-he, how unlucky I am!"

"Come now, silly!" he replied vivaciously. "You know quite well that everything is in working order and that our good friends don't require any more of Giovan in order to finish the comedy."

And this was perfectly true. The mere sight of the skirts of Emilia, whom the young man had suddenly encountered at a street turning, had sufficed to sweep him off his feet. Passion will always spring up afresh, so long as it is not rooted out entirely. And Franz, being guileless like the dove and tired of hovering about and gathering passing favours, forgot all his former grievances and did not even find anything suspicious in the presence of Emilia in Rome, once he had conceived the secret hope of regaining her for his mistress. It was a simple thought at first, which grew in his imagination and soon filled his mind day and night. The negotiations, however, were making slow progress. Napoleon was secretly pulling the ropes with regard to Francis V through the Roman Curia. The young Count was unoccupied and languished with the heat and boredom. Filthy streets, a leaden sun, nights of mosquitoes and bugs, coarse people of Nature relieving themselves alongside the houses, an abominable oily taste in the food, such were the things which the celebrated city held for Franz. Everything seemed to him unpleasant and ridiculous: manners, shop-signs, costumes, even the Coliseum, which was "smaller than he had imagined it." His only resource was to receive long visits from Giovan. And even Giovan was serious and sombre, and wiped his brow in a gloomy way. He had been rejected; what was the use of insisting any longer? The unhappy woman was heart-broken. . . . After these declarations came oppressive silences, deepening sadness and repeated yawnings, till at last the Italian got up and went away, taking with him a love letter from the Count to Emilia or a request for a meeting with her next morning in some garden or church. Such was the man who had formerly been so smart and proud of being in Paris!

One day as Franz was coming down the steps of San Clemente, he caught sight of the buffoon in the distance, kneeling in the midst of some triangles of lighted candles. There were exactly forty-one, the fatal number of his days of exile. He continued praying and beating his breast until he had completed the recitation of forty-one Our Fathers and forty-one Ave Marias.

The young Count went up to him and said in a plaintive tone of voice:

"You're going away, Giovan, you're forsaking me, though I have nobody to rely on but you!"

He was wearing spats and blue trousers and looked so well turned out with his side-whiskers and the little spaniel under his arm that Giovan thought of the bespatted, fashionable travellers who used once upon a time to throw him coppers on the road to Castellamare.

"Come, *Signor Inglese!*" he said jestingly. "Have courage! *Eh! Pardieu!* you won't die of it yet!"

And leaning towards the Count's ear, he added: "Let your father know at once that you still have need of me for three or four days . . . highly important business . . . negotiations in hand . . . His Highness's interests . . ." and he held him by the elbow, stopping him at every step. At the door of the church, where Franz took the leash off his dog, they noticed coloured placards on the walls:

Frizo is not afraid of Patrizio.

Patrizio is not afraid of Frizo.

These were the challenges of two jugglers, who were very popular with the Roman rabble at that moment.

"And I'm not afraid of Frizo or Patrizio, signor count," said Giovan, frisking about and tossing his hat into the air. "Before three days are out, Emilia and you will be like a pair of turtle-doves."

Almost the whole of the following week he was to be seen here and there in frequent conversation with Papal officials, speaking under obscure porches to mysterious priests, always on some business, and making as many signs of the cross and genuflexions as there are churches in the Eternal City. At last, having settled everything and generously greased the palms of his acolytes, and after assisting at the interview between Emilia and the Count, Arcangeli left for Paris, his head still full of the great toss of the dice his sister was hazarding in Rome, but his nose already turned towards the Beaujon house and the way in which he was to make sure of his new footing in the Duke's favour.

He made no stops, gulping down the leg of a chicken at two or three station buffets; and about nine o'clock one Wednesday, a dusty, cheerful Arcangeli, humming cavatinas, passed in front of the gold Genius of the Colonne de Juillet, who was certainly less alert and throbbing with life than that deuce of a man.

Monsieur d'Andonville was almost staggered out of his senses. He was standing at the top of the house steps enjoying the peace and calm of the court of honour and apparently admiring his ox-blood-coloured suit in the polished marbles and jaspers around him. Suddenly he caught sight of a broken-down, mud-bespattered cab with a split trunk tied up with a piece of string on the box, and two or three carpet-bags.

"What! You!" he exclaimed, recognising Arcangeli.

"*Hé oui!* it's me! it's me! Ah! good day to you!" replied the Italian. And taking off his black felt hat adorned with a peacock's feather, the brazen-faced comedian waved his greetings to the hospitable façade of the mansion. But his eyes alighted on Giulia who was looking out of a window.

"*Mala bestia!* " he called out, spitting contemptuously. . . . And with a slightly clouded countenance, he went up the steps, making loud inquiries about the health of His Most Serene

Highness, while a bevy of menials, among whom was a gigantic negro in Turkish costume, came forward to show consideration for him.

"Count Otto . . ." replied the Norman, who retired, giving place to the secretary for supplies.

"No! No!" protested Arcangeli. "Pass first, Your Excellency. . . . But what's the matter with these *coglioni*? . . ."

"Count Otto wired to the Duke yesterday. . . . After you, Monsieur Arcangeli."

"If they look at me like this . . . I won't do anything about it, Monsieur d'Andonville."

"One hundred and twenty-five thousand francs," the worthy chamberlain ended up, flickering his eyelids and clicking his tongue. "Half a million in two months! Ah! Ah! Ah! Living is pretty dear in Vienna! . . ." He looked round and dashed towards the kitchens, from which loud cries were issuing: Ho! wait a bit, you rascal! . . .

"The Nubian is unbearable," he said on his return, as he wiped his brow. "But here comes the faithful Joseph. The Duke has sent him for you."

Arcangeli was carried off like a Mercury in the famous sky blue machine at the prologue of an opera. He felt rather anxious at the thought of appearing once again before that capricious Jupiter. When he got to the ante-chamber he stopped. He was trying to pull himself together, when he heard the voice of his master through the door:

"The brave child!" the Duke was saying. "So you see, Ulmann, when he arrived, twenty-five Austrian Officers went as far as Linz to meet him, in order to show their sympathy towards the son of the Duke of Blankenburg."

"They are talking about Otto," thought Giovan. "Ulmann? . . . no doubt an employé of Monsieur de Rothschild." And lifting aside the heavy door-curtain, he rushed forward, crying out:

"Ah! Monseigneur! Monseigneur! what joy!"

"Shoo!" said the Duke, throwing him an imperious look that nailed the buffoon to the spot and left him thoroughly astonished. All his staging of the scene was upset; no embracing, no sensibility, and the Duke haughty and phlegmatic as never before. Seated in a big armchair, and looking very serious with a light bonnet of green cashmere on his head, the Duke was considering some thick bundles of bank-notes lying before him, while a big, curly-haired, stolid man was rapidly counting them with his thumb and throwing them in packets to his right.

"Yes!" said His Highness gravely, taking from the side table a pile of newspapers full of Otto and portraits of his horse:

"*The mare Bellua, that accomplished the journey from Paris to Vienna in thirteen days. . . .*

"Verify them, Ulmann, verify them," said the Duke. "Baron James told me yesterday that there were a lot of false notes circulating in Paris at the present moment."

And recalling a recent article on Otto in the *Entraineur*, the Duke made a note of it in order to send a bit of jewellery to the editor in accordance with his custom. As he was writing, he noticed Mr. Ulmann stop, recount one of the bundles and finally throw it aside on his left, like a man sifting chaff from good grain. Ho! what could that mean? His Highness stood upright. A second packet soon went to join the first, then a third, a fourth, one after the other.—Ah! a thousand thunders of the deuce! so the notes were no good! . . . and bristling up, drawing his trailing robe of flowered damask closer about him and shuffling along in his yellow leather slippers, he started pacing up and down the room. But when, for the fifth time, that nasty Jew tossed aside with an insulting gesture a further bundle of notes, the Duke was no longer able to restrain himself. Standing right in front of Arcangeli, who looked as though he wished himself underground, he said to him in a voice broken with fury

"Begone, vile rascal! I drive you out!"

Arcangeli thought he would collapse with dread, but went out without saying a word. Meanwhile, having counted the last packet, Mr. Ulmann had risen.

"So there were some false notes?" said the Duke in a dry voice.

"False! ... on the contrary they are very good," replied the other placidly. "But I have separated them according to the series."

Astonished beyond words, His Highness ran to the door and cried out in a loud voice:

"Arcangeli! Arcangeli! come here! I'm delighted to see you back again!"

Then dolorously lifting up his green cashmere bonnet and revealing his almost bald pate, he exclaimed:

"Ah, Giovan! your master is very much changed, my child!"

The bathings, perfumings, and steamings of His Highness resumed once more their course on the following day with Giovan as grand master. An end had really come to his disgrace, and the doors that had been closed upon him during Giulia's triumph, were thrown open again. Or rather, the medal had turned over. To his extreme surprise and utter delight, he realised that better than all his efforts to cast out that abhorred Sultana, the machine was working of its own accord. A vague voice seemed to go through the household proclaiming openly the downfall of Giulia; and the acts seemed to confirm it. There were no more *tête-à-tête* luncheons; the Duke's capricious humour had upset the stools; cajolery and loving tenderness were now distasteful to him. If they remained together for a moment, the Duke's uneasiness became obvious. He yawned and was at a loss to find something to say.

"Look! there goes Sophie's lover!" he would say at last, as he stood at the window and with the same dull jest every morning greeted the appearance of Father Le Charmel, the confessor and spiritual friend of the Princess of Hanau. They were often to be seen together in the orange plot situated just in front of Otto's apartment and forming in the midst of the gardens a sort of thicket of vases, statues and flower-beds terraced just above the great water-piece. Christiane also dragged herself along with them sometimes, looking very black and mournful in the light of the dying sun; and the Duke never failed to make a few scoffing remarks on the port wine birth mark that disfigured the Dominican's cheek.—"What a mug! a fine lover to tame women in that way!" It reminded Giovan of a similar envy on the part of Father Sotto-Cornela, one of his good friends in Rome, and made him think of the nets that had been spread there in order to trap Franz. And he began to have very bad nights, wondering impatiently what was happening in that city.

On Tuesday, 12 August, as Giovan was going out at half-past nine in order to get some scented water and pomatum at Félix's, a messenger from the house ran after him, crying out "Stop! Stop!" He handed him a telegram, which only contained the fairly enigmatical words:

Have a Mass said for success,

and the name of his sister at the end. In order to settle his doubts, Arcangeli rushed off to the somnambulist fortune-teller. It was time enough. The farce in Rome was taking place at that very moment exactly as the entranced woman described it: an Empire room with red window-panes, Emilia standing upright, with her face flushed (at which the sybil cried out how greatly she resembled Giovan), and a man at her feet, who appeared to be in the act of supplication.

"Poor Franz!" Arcangeli grinned. "Oh, I know what you're being told: 'I don't want to be damned. . . . Let's go and see a priest;' in short, the ordinary procedure before a nice little clandestine marriage in the Roman manner. . . ."

The scene changed indeed. Great joy! Franz had consented. . . . Emilia was embracing him . . . running . . . going out with him. Then a third character made his entrance, in the person of the good Father Sotto-Cornela, who was following the couple through the streets. Then, minute by minute, in spite of her being very tired, Dona Estefania described the Mass, just as Arcangeli had himself assisted at it many a time in that obscure little church of the Trastevere quarter, the dim nave, the people kneeling around, the flickering wax-candles. Suddenly a bell tinkled. The priest at the altar held up the wafer. Emilia seized Franz's hand and whispered a few words to him:

"My Francis, I take thee for my husband."

"Emilia, I take thee for my wife!" And abruptly the curtain fell. Giovan had seen all he wanted to see.—"Ah! a good bank-note will settle this!" Franz was saying to himself in Rome at that moment, being sure that such a marriage was null and void. The marriage had in fact taken place, just as Dona Estefania had described it, however inexplicable her witch-like knowledge of it may have been. And Arcangeli, on his part, went back to the Beaujon house and laughed merrily over the Count, for the most holy Council of Trent had foreseen these secret unions and declared them sacrilegious.

Giovan had to invent an excuse for his long absence, as his master liked to lock up very jealously everything that had the honour to come near him. The fear that his hairless pate made him ridiculous, turned the Duke into a very sullen-looking man. He had tried everything, brought together savants and doctors, exhausted ointments, lotions, restorers. Conversation from morn till night always came back to that sole topic, to which Arcangeli made evasive replies, taking great care to use a circumlocution in order to avoid the detested word "bald." As the Duke remained gloomy and only exclaimed from time to time, as in a spasm of suffering, that he felt too disgusted to wear the hair of some verminous dead person, the celebrated Monsieur Felix thought fit to make a suggestion.

"If hair wigs are so unfortunate as to be repugnant to Your Most Serene Highness," said that illustrious man from Toulouse, "let Your Highness try silk ones!" Whereupon he drew a few out of his case, and turned and twisted them about on his pink porcelain model-stool.

"Not for the present!" replied the Duke, who felt the piercing eyes of Giulia fixed upon him.

Had she ever deigned to take the slightest notice of all this matter? It was no doubt beneath her; she played the majestic, the disdainful; and the Duke could only breathe at last when he was back and alone with his pair of acolytes. Nevertheless the looking-glass did not make the poor man happy. He kept looking for his physiognomy, his brow, his eyes, and all his vanished features. Besides, how could one change one's style of hairdressing and vary its arrangement according to one's pleasure?

"But I should always be the same, my good Felix," exclaimed His Highness mournfully.

"Have courage, Monseigneur! I will find a way! . . ."

And a day or two later, Monsieur Felix arrived, looking very proud and triumphant. He merely asked to have all the portraits of His Highness that had ever been made.

So for a couple of days a great search was made in the lumber-rooms and cupboards. The result was the discovery of fifty-four likenesses of the Duke in oils, marble, busts, medallions, miniatures. . . . The carriage was packed with them and sent straight to the hairdresser's. A number of old Italian masters, chiefly Carraccis, were discovered at the same time. They had belonged at one time to the picture gallery of the Elector Anton Ulrich. Madame Sophie took charge of them and they were placed on tile walls of Otto's apartment, where she continued living until her little house at Passy was properly furnished.

What surprised the Duke most of all were some enormous cases filled with masquerade costumes, which Arcangeli discovered. For several days the apartment looked like the dressing-room of a troupe of comedians. It was littered with all sorts of garments, and get-ups, Tartars with drooping moustaches, Moguls, Chinamen in saffron and blue satin, a quartet of gilt Turks with gigantic cardboard heads. The Duke was transported to the days of his youth and the long conferences he used to have with Herr Pforzheim, the Court mask-maker, and was so deeply interested in this resurrection of his past that the great Felix begged permission to take a cast of his face.

"But what the Deuce are you up to?" exclaimed the Duke at last. And it had to be revealed to him that they intended making thirty wax models of his head for the purpose of bearing thirty different wigs. Such was the mystery that Giovan and his companion warmly explained to the Duke, as though it was the cauldron of Medea and destined to elect his complete transformation and rejuvenation. The enameller had even brought, as a sure bait, several wax masks of the previous year, which had been ordered for the famous ball given by the young Prince Radziwill. People had put on two or three masks one on top of the other, so that when they took one mask off, the onlookers were deceived, thinking the second mask was the real face. The Duke took great interest in them, especially one representing a young, fair, pink-faced woman with a lively, capricious and pleasant look. He ended by asking who she was.

"One of my best clients," replied the hairdresser, unconcerned. "She looked very charming at the ball. . . ."

"Will you tell me her name, imbecile!"

"But it's la Renz," Felix replied, looking up as though astonished, from placing one of the masks in their compartment-case. "Is it possible, Monseigneur! Your Highness doesn't know Mademoiselle Lyonette?"

And both artful fellows cried out their surprise, for Giovan, too, was acquainted with her, having met her, no doubt, at the enameller's. And he proceeded to sing her praises and describe her graces and wit so passionately to the Duke, that the latter declared he was in love with her already and laughed heartily for the rest of the evening over such an astonishing discovery. Giovan himself laughed still more when he was alone at last in his room. The bait had taken indeed; Giovan's great undertaking was now well launched and on its way to success. After a good many ups and downs, he perceived a sure hope of driving Giulia away and providing his strange master with a mistress of his own finding. He would be quite capable of keeping the new favourite within the traces. They would both govern together, or rather, he would govern over her; and he would come at last into his own. . . . "Amen! so-be-it!" thought the buffoon, as he got into bed.

Next morning, the Duke seemed little disposed to enjoy Arcangeli's friskiness and merely ordered him to read out aloud the *Gazette de Florence*, one of the papers from Italy, which were being taken in since Franz's departure as ambassador.

"Giovan, take this and begin here," said His Highness, pointing to a certain place, where it was written:

A MARRIAGE IN ROME

"At the words 'We have gone over. . . .'"

"I have already read the beginning of the story," said the Duke to Monsieur Félix, who had started fitting him with a wig. "It's about a fool of a foreigner . . . the paper doesn't give his name. He no sooner arrives, than he falls in love with a coquette. She keeps him on his knees and makes him despair, and in the end he marries her, just as my father married Ghigelli."

"*Aï! Aï!*" thought Giovan, his heart throbbing as he suddenly saw the smoking bomb he had loaded. And in an outburst of joy and expectation, he sprang on to the window-sill and sat on top of the cupboard, saying that he could be heard from there better than anywhere else.

"Very well! are you going to begin?" said the Duke.

"*We have gone over,*" Giovan droned. "*We have gone over the field of the preliminary facts; we have seen how the credulous foreigner allowed himself to be dragged into the clandestine marriage, which was to ruin him. On August 13, about three o'clock in the afternoon, an agent of the Roman police called and arrested the young man, who was taken to the prisons of the Holy Inquisition.*"

"What had he done then?" asked Monsieur Félix, staggering back with his pair of little scissors in his hand, for he was cutting His Highness's beard.

"*The intrigue is easily understood,*" Continued Giovan in a screaming tone of voice. "*Almost immediately after her return from the church, the young lady, or one of her accomplices, went and denounced herself and her dupe. In point of fact, a clandestine marriage is a sacrilege, a profanation of sacred ceremonies, which the Council of Trent anathematised and declared punishable with physical penalties (ch. 1, section 24 of the Acts of the Council). The unhappy man was faced with an inflexible religious authority that rules over souls, and the convict-galleys awaited him, unless he consented to marry the woman. Such was the only alternative: marriage or the galleys!*

"*On the morning of August 14, the young man was placed in a padlocked carriage, escorted by the Pope's police-agents. In this nuptial procession he was taken to the church of St. Augustine. The carriage was unlocked and the prisoner was dragged in silence to the sacristy. His audacious mistress was there. He was told that he was free to choose: he could either marry or go to the galleys!*"

"Well, did he go to the galleys?" the Duke asked with amusement, while Giovan gave a mock rehearsal of the marriage scene in the middle of the room.

"Worse than that! The cord was tied round his neck!" Cried Giovan. "United, blessed, and bound before our Holy Mother the Church!"

And so great was his triumphant joy that he almost revealed the secret of the whole story to the Duke; but nothing was yet clear, and who could be certain that the marriage had been properly backed up with all that was necessary to make it valid? So moderating his first impulses, Arcangeli confined himself to grinning up his sleeve at the strange luck which had even given him the power to make fun of the Duke to his very nose.

The following day Arcangeli received a long letter from Emilia confirming and giving details of what he already knew. Everything had gone off quite well without a hitch and the farce had hardly begun before it was ended. The details were amusing. There had been contestations, lamentations, protestations on the part of Franz behind locked doors, and brandy to bring him to in the church of St. Augustine; but at the dénouement, the style had changed. It was so obvious as to who was manipulating the affair that the scales must have fallen from the Count's eyes, however little cunning he possessed. In fact, the Mass was no sooner over than the newly-married husband had got into a hackney cab and had left Emilia on the spot, saying to her with annoyance in his voice:

"I shall never see you again!"

"He'll knock at her door in a day or two," thought Giovan, shrugging his shoulders. It was not on this account that he felt uneasy, as indeed he wrote to his sister together with a whole plan of behaviour, but on account of having to break the news of the marriage to the Duke, who would not fail to let loose a torrent of fury on his back.

As it happened, His Highness was pestered several days running by dreadful fits of bad temper for no earthly reason. The members of the household exchanged terrified glances; everybody had his own surmises, even Baron von Cramm who ventured to speak to the Duke about Count Otto and the immense amount of money which that beloved son was running through in Vienna. It was well for him that he was still nimble and could get out of the way pretty quickly. Cheated in that direction, the Duke's fury turned towards Giulia, who, the last five or six mornings, had not even paid the Duke the compliment of going to visit him at the hour of his waking up.

There was a terrible scene, and the howling and stamping resounded throughout the whole house. At last the riddle was cleared up, and it became known through Mr. Smithson, who arrived next day, that the Duke's terrible rages were due to the loss of several of his law-suits.

Arcangeli spent a whole day in the joyful hope of seeing his rival driven out at any moment. He never ceased singing the praises of Mlle Lyonnette, and the Duke grew more and more indignant with Giulia and her incredible insolence. He ended up one morning by giving a formal order to Giovan, who expressed great astonishment, to go and call Giulia to his presence. Giulia's splendid haughtiness had, in fact, revived in his drowsy, surfeited soul what little affection he still retained for her.

The look of joy on Arcangeli's face as he went to the favourite's rooms can be left to the imagination. Though it was still very early in the morning, the doors fell open at the Duke's name. Giovan advanced quietly, greeting the cantatrice as soon as he caught sight of her. The interview remained in his mind forever after as something of a mystery.

Giulia was at the far end of her boudoir, sitting on a divan with a writing-pad on her knees and a pen in her hand.

"Whom is she writing to, I wonder?" thought Giovan, as Giulia folded up her papers.

He thought he had seen the word "Vienna" on one of the envelopes, but he knew very little about her great number of friends in that city.

It was now Giulia's chance to recover the Duke's favour, but instead of rejoicing over the change, she seemed hardly to condescend to accept the Duke's advances and even appeared to frown on them.

She would sit at the end of the room (usually beside the last of the three porphyry tables situated between the windows and loaded with vases and jewels), looking indifferent and silent, giving no answer except to what was definitely a question, and apparently absorbed in the contemplation of the silver equestrian statuette of the Elector Otto Ludwig, or the little silver temple with its silver-gilt figurines representing the princes and princesses of the House of Blankenburg. At the other end of the room the farce went on around the sofa on which the Duke sat enthroned in Turkish fashion. Giovan frisked about, sighed, rolled his eyes, and talked of the divine Lyonnette every moment of the day. She had said this, she had done that. And what hands! What dimples! What personal charms! He made no secret of his visits to her now. "But not so much as that!" He added, hooking his front tooth with his thumb-nail and looking quite miserable.

However cruel Mlle Lyonnette might be, he did not fail to produce her portrait at a timely moment one day when His Highness was yawning and complaining of his loneliness. And the miniature revealed a most charming smile, a face that seemed to have been made by the Graces, and something piquant, roguish and capricious that filled one with surprise and delight. So much so that being snubbed by Giulia and hearing nothing but "Lyonnette, Lyonnette," and "Lyonnette" all the time, the Duke soon began to take an interest in these everlasting litanies and ended by conceiving a desire to see the marvellous creature.

One afternoon, when amusement in the Duke's chamber was at a low ebb, Giovan proposed, as though on the spur of the moment, that they should go up to the new terrace and watch the carriages driving to the Bois. His Highness had taken it into his head a few weeks previously to have some alterations made to a gallery on the ground floor, thereby creating three or four small rooms and an Italian terrace adorned with flowers and orange-trees in tubs. From the terrace a fine open view of the Place de l'Arc-de-l'Etoile could be obtained. Accordingly, some lorgnettes were taken there, as well as a folding chair for Giulia. But the Duke showed little interest in the unknown faces that passed by, and amused himself like a schoolboy with throwing balls of torn paper into the next garden. Suddenly Arcangeli cried out as though with the greatest surprise:

"Why, it's her! There she is! *La Madonna del mio cor!*"

And he wafted hand-kisses into the air, while Monsieur Félix raised his hat.

"Is it Lyonnette?" the Duke asked, hastening to the balustrade.

He found her even more delicately and singularly attractive than he had imagined.

She was alone, with a footman, in a light carriage lined with mauve satin and drawn by three small ponies in silver harness with rosettes and ribbons, and she was driving them at full trot. As she passed, the Duke took off his fur-edged bonnet to her, holding it beside his ear. She looked up from beneath her large, plumed, muslin hat, made a half-curtsey accompanied with a charming smile and disappeared like the wind, while the Duke exclaimed:

"Where the deuce has my jester been to find such a pretty woman!"

"Yes, she is charming, quite charming," said Giulia, behind him. "And Your Highness is quite right."

The Duke turned round. She spoke with a profound peacefulness, standing upright with her hands clasped and smiling so strangely that the poor Duke blushed with embarrassment. The immense western sky was yellow and green; Giulia was leaning on the balustrade and gazing into the distance. Was her tranquillity just a blind. Was it a sinister mind that she concealed behind that peaceful, gentle countenance? Or was she really indifferent to this new caprice of her master and pursuing a mysterious objective that would be revealed later on? She had risen very high in fact, being the official mistress of the Duke Charles, and could very well hope to achieve still more with a little patience; but the highest ambitions, once attained, immediately become steps in the ladder to something higher still. Perhaps the Duke's age and corpulence seemed to Giulia a rather perilous basis on which to found her fortune. Perhaps, in that sumptuous, brilliant life, she had already glimpsed the fatal end and was trying to withdraw. . . . But who knows? Who could penetrate the secret of her heart?

September, that year, was admirable; a clear sky, beautiful sunshine, a most pleasant temperature. The Duke had the terrace decorated in Chinese fashion with porcelain and lanterns. Every day he went there in order to see Lyonnette drive past; and neither of them failed to keep up that tacit and regular rendezvous.

From the street, His Highness could be seen with his two acolytes, drinking and eating in the open air amid flower-pots, cushions, sofas, and furniture varnished in red and gold. Sad Christiane and Madame Sophie had been obliged to take refuge from the rollicking laughter at the bottom of the garden in what was called "the Copse"—a thicket of horn-beams arranged and planted after the manner of the famous Wendessen maze.

They wandered round the place in the company of Father Le Channel, passing through the arcades and cloisters of verdure, under forsaken porticos, along gloomy colonnades, round mournful fountains overshadowed by motionless cypresses, with sleeping nymphs reclining on the backs of dolphins. Questions of piety and subjects of controversy lasted for a short while, though the priest and the princess made no longer any secret of trying to convert Christiane. Besides his knowledge of the saints, the celebrated Dominican had the knowledge of men. Altogether different from Princess Sophie, whose extreme loftiness of mind and spirituality sometimes left one out of breath, the priest continually sought to incline Christiane by means of earthly things: a flower, tree, or bird gave him a subject to talk about and the means to get to the hearts of his listeners. She nodded her head in reply: "Yes, Father," or "Yes, Aunt," and trying to keep a peaceful face before these two black phantoms. In this manner they walked about the green, moss-grown paths with slow steps until they stopped at last at the foot of one of the enormous vases, or at a stone seat in a horn-beam thicket. The priest or the Princess would then read aloud, from the place at which they had left off the day before: "My fifty reasons for returning to the religion of my forefathers," the famous apologia published by the Elector Anton Ulrich of Blankenburg, when he recanted the Reformation. Christiane tried to understand, but her heart was in the Highlands. "Ulrich! Ulrich!" She saw him again, everywhere. The least resemblance brought him to her mind. It was so he used to place his hands, so he used to look. But where had he gone, that friend of every hour? Why had he forsaken her? The world seemed to her hazy and bedimmed. Things passed before her mind like a muddy, lurid stream. . . . Evening came. The notes of the Angelus sounded from a neighbouring chapel.

"Hail Mary, full of grace. . . ."

And crossing herself, Christiane said the prayers together with priest and Princess. What did she care about all these practices, rosaries, crucifixes, medals, which she docilely accepted. All three walked back towards the house, Christiane a few paces ahead. In that solemn evening hour, she seemed to feel her dead brother's hands upon her heart. It was wrung with deeper anguish.—"Yes, I hear you! I hear, poor soul! Be at rest, forgive me!" And at these heart-breaking memories, her very soul seemed to melt away. . . .

Meanwhile, the day was drawing near when Monsieur Felix was to deliver the busts of the Duke. His Highness decided to go and inspect them at the enameller's workshop. He had been boxed up in the house so long that to go out was a sort of adventure, which amused him like a child. The day before, he selected from his wardrobe the clothes he was to wear, green tweeds, lilac gloves and tie to match, and the ribbon of his order. It was no easy task for Giovan and Monsieur Félix to deck him out to his liking, when the great day dawned at last. The Duke could hardly keep on the ground with impatience, scolding and hustling his people. And he almost believed there would be no end to the thirty yards or so from his house to the hairdresser's place in the middle of the Champs Elysées.

"What is it then?" said the Duke, as he mounted the broad staircase decorated with flowers and statues. "What was it that d'Andonville mumbled to me just now?"

"He had a letter for Your Highness from Count Franz," replied Arcangeli, whose heart was beating somewhat faster.

The Duke passed through the door and the same instant Arcangeli and Monsieur Félix slipped away, so that when the Duke turned round he found himself alone.

He heard the sound of a cough and the rustle of clothing and at the same moment Lyonnette appeared from behind a screen. The silence and mutual embarrassment lasted a good minute. She was wearing an attractive dress of turquoise blue velvet with a green satin skirt, embroidered with brownish green velvet flowers, and a pair of earrings as big as nuts, being the royal present which the Duke had sent beforehand. He noticed that she was wearing them, and he began in a rather uncertain voice:

"So Monsieur Félix has spoken to you, Mademoiselle?"

"Oui, monsieur!" replied Lyonnette, correcting herself immediately with:

"Oui, Monseigneur."

"But where the deuce are my busts?" said the Duke in order to avoid a pause. And he began to walk round the room with his nose in the air.

The walls were lined with seventeen large double-doored cupboards in white and gold with gilt carvings. The oval ceiling was decorated with bas-reliefs, paintings and emblems relating to the art which Monsieur Felix practised. His Highness made a few laughing remarks about them, while Lyonnette explained that each flower painted on the white and gold panels corresponded to the flasks inside the cupboard. So the busts could not be there.

The Duke discovered them at last behind a curtain that might have been taken for the draping of a window. They were all there, thirty-three in number, standing on their stucco pedestals on a sort of dais and roped off with a gold cord. And in the half-light of the little study, the whole collection of wax-figures, striped with blue veins and reflected on all sides by a host of mirrors, looked more like the curiosities of some quack at a country-fair than respectable bewigged busts at fifty louis a piece.

"By all means, Felix is the first artist in Europe!" the Duke exclaimed enthusiastically.

"Ah! . . . They frighten me!" said Lyonnette, as she went into the Flower Room. She realised that she had once more omitted to say "Monseigneur."

"Don't take it amiss," she said. "You know, it's just my light-heartedness."

They both smiled and looked at each other. She was standing with her arms raised, taking off her fur toque, while he pulled her by her dress and gazed at her beautiful fair hair, which was of shining gold with silver shimmerings in the sun-light. Then he suddenly sneezed.

"May Heaven bless you!" thought Lyonnette, "and make your nose like my thigh and your chin like my heel!"

And complaining of the cold and its early arrival that year, she went and stood before the fire, slightly raising her skirts. She was wearing flesh-coloured stockings. The Duke caressed her ankle without saying a word. He was wondering all the while whether his wig would fall off.

"*Ah! mon Dieu!*" said the young woman, as she sank on to the sofa. "I had no idea Your Highness wanted me to come here for such attentions. . . ."

Arcangeli, Félix, Charles d'Este and Lyonnette returned to the house about four o'clock. They filled the carriage, without counting a couple of wax figures, which His Highness insisted on taking with him—No. 13 in a blue frock-coat and No. 25 with the yellow diamond epaulettes; and as there was a hamper of pastries in the carriage, Arcangeli and Lyonnette were about to enjoy a little snack when the Duke's voice was suddenly heard to exclaim:

"Oh! oh! three pots of jam for Hildemar! If only the imbecile had not allowed himself to die!"

His Highness was going over the register of food bills, which d'Andonville had left on the seat just as the horses were starting. Encouraged by the laughter of the company, Charles d'Este continued half-aloud:

> "*29th.—Dinner for His Highness's staff . . . 114 fr. 70*
> *Sweetmeats ordered by H.H. . . . 20*
> *Trout for the Countess Christiane . . . 14*

"Ho!" exclaimed the Duke, breaking off. "Here's my daughter eating fish on Fridays like the Papists."

And turning over the page, he gazed open-mouthed and haggard at the register, as though he had discovered a venomous scorpion. His neck swelled with fury, his eyes bulged out of their sockets; and rushing out, as the carriage drew up before the steps of the house, he ordered the first man-servant he caught sight of to bring Mademoiselle Belcredi to him that very instant.

"Where, Monseigneur?"

"Here, triple brute, in this hall!"

And His Highness slammed open the door with such violence that the armouries standing symmetrically on either side rocked on their wooden base and a feather of the horrible mask hanging from Montezuma's helmet broke away and fluttered to the floor. At the same moment, Giulia appeared at the foot of the stairs, as did seven or eight footmen attracted by the unusual din.

"Is it true, madame," the Duke asked from one end of the room to the other and without giving her time to come close, "is it true that you were served last month with fourteen jugs of my beer?"

"Monseigneur," said Giulia, "recover your wits, I beg you."

"She insults me!" the Duke cried out, bursting into so terrible a fury that he not only made Giulia tremble, but Félix, Giovan, Lyonnette and all the congregated domestics as well.

He let loose a deluge of hard, contemptuous words and insults upon Giulia, who, white and still as a statue, had neither time nor opportunity to utter a syllable.

"Outside! outside!" he howled frantically. "And may you never be seen again!"

Then, suddenly making up her mind, with a superb look of contempt, Giulia Belcredi went out in silence.

"Bon voyage!" muttered Giovan, as he frisked up the stairs behind his master's back.

It was not until late in the evening and during his toilet for the night that the Duke opened his son's letter. Count Franz announced first of all, as a sort of honey-cake, that his embassy had fully succeeded. After that came a rather short, disjointed story which made out that the arrest, imprisonment and marriage were all the work of Francis V, who had taken his revenge on the poor Count in this way. The letter ended with protestations, plenty of humbleness, and the request to be allowed to return to Paris with the wife.

"The imbecile!" exclaimed the Duke, shrugging his shoulders and taking no trouble to get to the bottom of the imbroglio.

The clock struck.

"Monseigneur, go to sleep!" said Lyonnette, who was dodging about in her chemise and reciting in a child's tone of voice:

> "*Il est minuit.*
> *Qui l'a dit?*
> *Jésus Christ.*
> *Où est-il?*"

VIII

NO doubt Giulia Belcredi had only to pull the ropes she held in her hand in order to bring Otto back to Paris. Forty-eight hours after the weird scene at the Beaujon mansion, on Saturday the last day of September, about the middle of the afternoon, a young man, who had just had time to change his travel-stained clothes and swallow some broth and an egg, turned up at the Grand Hôtel, where Giulia had taken rooms. Though he had travelled day and night without a stop, Otto would have inwardly desired not to meet Giulia.

She rose to her feet with a cry.

"Ah! it's you, Otto!" she stammered.

He stood silent before her, feasting his eyes upon her in a sort of intoxication and waiting for her to speak to him. She was dressed in white with lace and ribbon trimmings, adorned here and there with nosegays of fresh roses. He gazed entranced at the roses, the dazzling dress, the eyes, and hair of his mistress, even the least of her features. He thought he could love Giulia for ages on end, and engrossed in pictures of delight, the young man did not stir. The silence at last woke him up. He tried to pull himself together and said in a vague sort of way:

"Yes, I left as soon as I got your wire. I would have come from no matter where. There was nothing to keep me."

"What about Mademoiselle Schlosser?" Giulia asked.

"Schlosser!" Otto exclaimed, blushing and going very pale in turn. After a heavy inculpating silence, he tried anxiously to excuse himself. How could he really be in love with Mademoiselle Schlosser? She was such a stupid creature, always weeping, ugly and thin, a perfect grasshopper. Ill at ease and annoyed, he accompanied his words with excessive gestures and spoke in a sort of spasm. During the journey, he had found the most touching and tenderest phrases. But fearing lest he might not succeed in unbending Giulia and being excited at seeing her once again and affected by the heavy odour of jonquils and roses that filled the room, he felt his thoughts scatter and all his efforts fail. And the sight of Giulia, sitting dreamily beside the fire and throwing into the flames old theatre scores, letters and faded bouquets from the box on her knees, made the young lover still more ill at ease. So much so that he was beginning to say just the opposite of what he evidently intended, when a chambermaid put her head into the room and asked to know at what o'clock the trunks were to be taken down.

"Are you leaving the hotel?" the Count asked.

"I've taken a small furnished house, 7 Rue du Puits-qui-parle," Giulia replied.

And tripping over to the door, she whispered something to Laury, who went and gathered up some tippets and muffs that were lying under the chairs.

Otto had also risen and was standing by the window looking out at the teeming street, the trim shops and countless vehicles that passed along one after another under the rainy sky. In spite of the sadness, he tried to assure himself that the moment was one of the happiest and most beautiful that he would ever know; and furious with himself, he endeavoured to rouse his emotions. He felt ready to weep, ready to do all sorts of unusual things; and as Laury had at last left the room and Giulia was replacing the papers in the box, Otto suddenly went up to her and slipped his arm round her waist.

"Aren't you hungry?" she said. "Won't you have something to eat?"

Then, bending towards the fire, she began to shake the box in the grate, holding the pile of scores with the tongs so that none should fall away. In the meantime the young man covered the back of her neck with kisses. Otto's heart had suddenly dried up; he stood there like a log before her. And Giulia likewise was dumb as a statue, her eyes fixed on the fire, where a last faded bouquet was flaming and crackling. Its green satin ribbons were painted by the famous Dalbono, of Milan. A strange smile passed over her lips. . . . What long-forgotten memory did the bouquet revive in her? Was it the day when the Duke had found her in the midst of costumes and crowns? . . . Their eyes met, and giving the young man a kiss, she sank into his arms.

Otto's legs were shaking when he came down the stairs; he had an empty feeling of horrible disillusionment. So love was nothing more than that! Nothing more than with any other woman! Like a child astonished after eating the coveted fruit, Otto doubted whether it had all been real. All those ravishing delights of his long reveries, that love which had smouldered three years in his innermost being almost without his suspecting it, those passionate letters written in darkest secrecy, his desires and emotions, all had come down to that sad, short embrace and the dreadful emptiness he now felt!

"And I thought I loved her!" he said to himself.

He was heartbroken, and wept bitterly. He could never remember how it came about that, after wandering round the theatres and cafés, he found himself one morning in a certain notorious establishment. He spent a couple of days there in complete abandonment to his terrible, wayward temper. On the third night, as his troubled imagination kept filling his mind with the same thoughts, he felt once more how happy he would be to see Giulia again. It was a peculiar, irresistible sentiment of affection; all his violent sufferings of the preceding days seemed to him nothing more than a dream. He could hold out no longer. He called a cab and drove to the Rue du Puits-qui-parle. The weather was cold. Paris was asleep. The moon was full. Looking up at that motionless golden wheel in the sky, he was filled with so lively and impatient a reverie that it seemed to endow him with the happiness he sought. Arrived at the door, he rang, knocked and called until Laury came at last to let him in. He went across a square court and mounted a wooden staircase. Giulia, just awakened from sleep, appeared before him. . . . Passionately they threw themselves into each other's arms.

Oh, the happiness! the happiness of being in love! the elixir of life that makes everything new! fountain from which the heart drinks and spreads over the whole world like a torrent rushing on its course! No sooner did the lovers catch sight of each other than they were lifted above themselves in a sort of enchantment. Never had the sunlight seemed to them so brilliant, or the sky so calm and splendid! They found delight in a flower, a cloud, a grass, the humblest things around them. Their simplest actions were imbued with an extraordinary joy and impulse. From their eyes flowed a spirit that enlivened the universe for them. Even the ragged, grimy quarter in the shadow of the Pantheon, the weeds in the cobbles, the washing drying at the windows, and the little narrow Rue du Puits-qui-parle with its tumble-down hovels and old garden walls, seemed to them the most beautiful places they had ever seen on earth. And when they perceived from afar their low door in the wall with the old written notice stuck over it:

FOR LETTERS AND OTHER MATTERS
APPLY TO M. SPITZER, NEPHEW,

which neither Otto nor Giulia ever dreamt of tearing down, they felt a light shine forth within them, revealing the depth of their love.

After a lapse of two days, their afflictions were renewed more closely. Their spirit rejoiced in tying its knots once more. Their hearts were overflowing and they could not do enough to prove their love for each other. They ran about the house, following each other, calling, embracing, talking tenderly for the pleasure of saying "thou" to each other and enjoying the new delight which that familiarity gave them. But though only a few days had gone by since he had left Mademoiselle Schlosser in Vienna, his lips repeated the same words of affection, the same thoughts and phrases as he had used towards her. And very soon he was calling Giulia by the same loving names as he had used with regard to the dancer, so limited are man's resources in trying to express the infinite feeling of his heart.

Anyhow, what did it matter to him? What did any other woman matter to him since he possessed Giulia? Neither of them had ever had their equal. They felt there was nobody like them in the whole world. And hour by hour, if one may say so, they both formed of each other new ideas, embellished by their senses and imagination, like spiritual idols which they set up for worship in their innermost heart. "How sweet you are! how nice you are!" the boy kept repeating to Giulia. He longed to obey, bow down and be the slave of his mistress.

Yet his humility in love only increased his pride with regard to the rest of mankind. A joyfulness, a fearful force, flowed through his veins. He would have liked to cry out, strike, bite, smother lions; yet the eyes he turned towards Giulia never revealed to her but infinite gentleness. He could not help smiling at her, admiring her, touching her shoulder or hair, even in the presence of the workmen, who came to do up the little apartment.

It consisted of three rooms on the first floor, which was reached by a wooden staircase against the wall with a couple of railings just like the stairs of a country loft. The entrance led into a passage with the three rather poorly furnished rooms opening off it on the right and left. That was all the house contained apart from a few box-rooms, a small attic and the kitchen on the ground floor. As Giulia had taken the house in a hurry and occupied it at once, very little had been made ready. Not a lock was in order; the keys of the rooms were all mixed up, and at night there was only a wretched candle or two to make a light, while Laury went to fetch some oil. In that shadowy light Otto sat pensively before Giulia and contemplated her devotedly. In the falling dusk, the room grew yet more dim. With trembling fingers he caressed the pale cheek of his idol, and the sweetness of the sensation stirred his heart and inundated his spirit with a dawn-like brightness.

But the falling plaster and the hammering of the workmen disturbed them exceedingly. Giulia discovered a key to the ground floor and the two lovers went there in order to unpack some cases of old Polish arms which Count Dzalinski, one of Otto's new friends, had sent him as a present. And they ended by staying there altogether, although the two rooms had been excluded from occupation until after the sale of the former occupant's belongings which were stored there.

On all sides, dust-covered and hung with cobwebs, stood skeletons of men and beasts, plants, birds, metals, all sorts of freakish productions, a monkey and cat born with wings, medals, urns, mummies, trees of black coral, and over a hundred flasks, filled with a transparent liquid, in which were reserved scorpions, tarantulas and serpents. In the midst of this weird collection the lovers spent many a precious hour, worshipping each other devotedly. "How I love you, dear treasure! How I would like to die for you!" was Otto's constant refrain. The very name of the Beaujon house, where he would have to present himself if only for a few moments, brought a frown to his face. To leave Giulia for an hour seemed to him like a bitter poison. She was sweeter to him than life, more necessary than his right hand. Whenever he caught sight of her from below leaning on the wooden railing, he was filled with ineffable emotion. Even the rustle of her skirts sufficed to waken all his sensibilities. A fever of love seemed to melt his heart like wax; he became silent, rapt in adoration. Motionless and vibrating through and through, his spirit was soon plunged in a peaceful, infinite happiness, in which each separate joy was swallowed up, even as the pale stars are blotted out by the sun. His being was entirely filled; there was no emptiness in him—till the brimming fullness overflowed at last in sobbing, weeping, depression, and most often of all, in fits of rowdiness and extravagant mirth.

Especially after meals, when he was satiated with meats and wines, his brain would seethe with frenzied thoughts. He would run about on all fours, neigh, roll on the beds, belabour the skeletons, lift up the furniture in a way that made Giulia fear lest he break his chest, howled, whirled and played all sorts of tomfoolery, though nothing was able to deliver him from the hot and heavy demon that oppressed him. He had Bellua brought to the house. The horse had recently arrived under the escort of the groom Lajos and was temporarily stabled at the Bernard-Pelletier manège, not far from the house in the Rue du Puits-qui-parle. He then began to perform all sorts of wild follies, such as jumping out of a window on to the mare's back, and a score of similar dare-devil tricks. Though he listened to music with a sort of rapture, he derived no soothing benefit from it, but was moved to tears and sighs so powerfully that it literally stifled him. His coat had to be unbuttoned and in this state he had to be laid on the bed; and the daily storms accompanying those early days of October put the finishing touch to his disorder. Nothing else was capable of subduing his furious outbursts except going out into the garden and standing naked under a sheet like a corpse and being drenched with the torrents of rain from that black and sulphurous sky.

Meanwhile slight money difficulties began to warn the young man that it was time to go to the Beaujon house in order to have his pockets filled again. The few hundred napoleons which was all that had remained of the million so swiftly eaten up in Vienna, had somehow melted away. Small clamorous debts kept worrying the lovers. And, since the cup would have to be drunk sooner or later, Otto and Giulia drove in a hackney cab one evening to the house of the Duke. They let down the blinds and filled the cab with flowers in order to brighten it up and make it sweet-smelling. Ensconced in either corner and engrossed in their thoughts, they hardly exchanged a word till they reached the Place de l'Etoile, where Giulia was to remain hidden in the carriage and await her lover's return. He came back almost immediately. The Duke was not in Paris, but staying near Fontainebleau at the Château de la Roche-Brûlée; so Otto had been informed by M. d'Andonville, whom he had met at the foot of the stairs.

"At la Roche-Brûlée!" Exclaimed Giulia pensively.

"Indeed," replied Otto. "There's nobody at home except my sister Christiane, and Emilia, Franz's wife. I've just been told that he's married to her."

What strange whim had induced the Duke, in spite of his usual fondness for gorgeous surroundings and material show, to go and bury himself in the depth of solitude like a shepherd, who delights only in hollow caves, rocks and fountains? The very first evening made the petulant Lyonnette wonder where he had got the strange idea from. In the midst of constant yawns, she had tried blacking her nose with a piece of burnt cork for the sake of amusement. There appeared to be so little with that old enamoured bull snorting around her, and those moss-grown stone gods in the garden. And what a fine pair of lovers too! . . . Her imagination began to stir. Her thoughts flew back to her dear women-friends, whom she had not seen for three days. She longed to show them her new splendour and fortune. Accordingly she wrote and asked Anna Deslions and Julietta Barucci to come and see her. When the two princesses arrived, Lyonnette went in and told His Highness. "All right, my dear, invite whomsoever you like," he replied. Whereupon letters began to fly about, telegrams flashed one after another, and by the end of four days, la Roche-Brûlée was filled with all the richest and most elegant of the ladies of middle virtue in Paris.

The dapper château with its flags, jutting balconies, and red bricks, shone gaily in the sunshine. In the background was a thick, massive wood stretching several miles and teeming with deer.

It was there that Lyonnette and her companions wandered about all day long, while the Duke walked alone in the vase-adorned garden, his footprints being removed from the red sand of the walks by gardeners with rakes, as soon as he went indoors. Dressed in multi-coloured hoods, green-collared capes, violet and white-striped robes and crowned with plumes, these nymphs ran about with their fringed sunshades, chatted, wrangled, threw flowers at one another, devised a thousand games, laid wagers as to who should gather the most heather or mushrooms, or roguishly hid themselves among the giant ferns in the thickets; and their shouts amid the damp, silent paths would suddenly set in flight a black crow, which would soar aloft on its heavy wings and disappear cawing.

"Hark! There's Flora singing again!" they would exclaim.

And this joke, which they always addressed to Mlle Van Bloemen, of the Opéra-Comique, produced roars of laughter that resounded throughout the peaceful park. They were autumn days with damp mornings of white haze, which the afternoon sun filled with long shafts of reddish light. The atmosphere, still tepid and soft, hovered between warm and cold. The surface of a stretch of clear water was sprinkled with dead leaves. And the freshness of the dense trees, the infinite peacefulness of that beautiful spot far from the madding crowd, where nothing was heard but the babble of the brooks, the murmur of the pine woods, and now and again the swift gallop of a deer in the distance, impressed even the brainless heads of those doll-like creatures and made them stand agape with admiration before the charming views and perspectives that changed at almost every fifty steps—till at last Mlle Fougerette drew her vanity box from her pocket, or flighty Gabrielle Odry regretted there was no carousel to ride on.

One afternoon, as they were coming back from their forest jaunt, the wicker trap which Lyonnette was driving overturned on the edge of a path of heather and wet sand. No damage was done beyond spoiling the frills and fancy bits with which that beauty was rigged out. There was plenty of laughter for the rest of the way and Lyonnette used the whip very briskly on the little Shetland ponies in order to get back to the château as quickly as possible. She went immediately to the Duke's room, where she had left all her dresses and attire. She was changing her dress in front of the clear, crackling fire and playing all sorts of childish pranks with Pepa Sanchez and Giovannina Flor, who were assisting her as maids, when the door suddenly opened and Otto appeared on the threshold, red in the face, perspiring, and covered with mud, for he had run all the way from the station at Montigny.

"Isn't my father here?" he asked in a husky voice.

"There's an awkward fellow for you!" exclaimed Lyonnette angrily. "What does he mean by entering people's rooms like that!"

Her sparkling blue eyes, her upturned nose, the curled locks, which she shook with impatience, and the deep flush that red-dened her cheeks made her look like the most roguish Bellone that had ever been surrounded by Cupids, Games and Pleasures. She was only half-dressed, and Otto saw her in all the mirrors with which the room was full, her arms and neck bare, a silver medal on a silver cord hanging over her firm, slight bosom; and her mauve-blue satin corset stopped short of her charming, deli-cate, infantile shoulders.

"Ah! you are Monsieur Otto!" she added in a gentler tone, recognising the young man from the numerous portraits of him in the Beaujon house. "Oh no! he's not here, the old mad dog!"

She was walking up and down the room, and her light petticoat of white lace fluttered about her, revealing her pink-stockinged legs. . . . He had gone to Fontainebleau with his ape of an Italian and the other man, the old mummy with eyes like burning coals.

"My father is not here?" exclaimed Otto, taken aback by the unexpected mischance.

"No! no! when they tell you so!" replied Lyonnette, slipping on a bodice. "I ought to know, I think, since he wanted to take me with him. But what does that old Solomon, that old Cossack, want to do at the château de Fontainebleau? Is it just to go and see the things they stole from us in the days of the first Emperor?"

She became more and more petulant in her language and really believed that Charles d'Este was a Cossack, or at least "from one of those countries over there." She stopped, smiled at herself, curtseyed before the looking-glass in which she caught sight of herself full-length, and touched the charming pits of her shoulders and neck, saying one after the other:

"Salt . . . Pepper . . . Mustard. . . ."

Then, leaning on the arms of her two companions, she began to hop and sing:

"Ha! the old werewolf! I laugh at him! Ha! fireworks this evening! Ha! we'll have some fun! Ha! you'll be there, Monsieur Otto! Ha! we'll dance together!"

But a pin pricked her, and a drop of blood appeared on her finger. In a fit of childishness, she smeared it on Otto's cheek, saying:

"Now you're my cousin. . . ."

Whereupon all three women laughed and hastily slipped away.

The day was drawing in; the sun was setting. A motionless purple colour hung over sky, river and park. Alone in the room, Otto felt drunk with sadness.—"Giulia! Giulia! dear happiness!" He felt drawn to Paris by a desire to see her again and fold her in his arms. He could resist it no longer. And uttering a husky cry, he began to break open the massive mahogany writing-desk in which his father kept his money. Smashing the lock with an iron fire-dog, he felt his anger appeased. He was rather ashamed at heart of having seen Lyonnette in such a state of disorder.

And ill-at-ease in mind, he was torn between a fit of rage against Lyonnette and a transport of adoration towards Giulia, so that almost stifled with sighs and emotion, he cried out:

"Oh, my love! my darling love!"

In these moments he had to go to the open window. It was a long time since the evening had been so beautiful. The western sky beyond the pond called La Petite Mer was striped with orange and turquoise, over which floated a great number of golden clouds. And by the side of this stretch of water, in which the gorgeous archipelago of the sky was reflected, under the dark red foliage of the trees, the ten women were having a peaceful meal on the grass with flasks and pies served by menservants in a red livery.

It was already night by the time the writing-desk was opened. Otto struck a match and took some bundles of bank-notes, ten or twelve piles of louis, and left only the silver. Then he made off through the forest. His heart was full of cries for Giulia, his far-off idol. He would stop and lean his burning brow against the bark of a tree. A noise behind him made him turn suddenly round. A couple of bitches which he had once cared for, had escaped and overtaken him:

"Miss . . . Turlu . . ."

And bending down, Otto stroked them affectionately. Tears welled up in his eyes; a damp air, smelling of mushrooms, penetrated and chilled him. The still park was asleep: not a light, not a sound. Suddenly he felt afraid and fled. He did not breathe freely until he saw in the distance the red lights of the Montigny station.

Nevertheless, even as a subtle perfume sometimes loses all its fragrance before anyone becomes aware of its escaping, Otto had emptied and exhaled his spirit all that day in vain longings for his absent mistress. When he was with her once again, he found none of the emotional transports he had imagined. Their conversation flagged, and though they were both anxious for details, they waited painfully for each other to begin:

"What stockings have you got on?" said Otto. She was wearing green spun stockings with close black stripes. All was silent; the stars were shining; the loving couple stood in a reverie on the wooden balcony among the plots and tubs of the little garden. He asked her whether, in the event of his dying first, and she saw his ghost, she would be afraid of it. She was at a loss for a reply, and stroked his hair, murmuring:

"Child . . . child . . ."

"I shouldn't be afraid of you," said Otto bitterly. And very pale, his eyes fixed on the orb of the moon, he felt his heart sink, even as beneath a mighty sorrow.

He did not sleep that night. Feverish and sitting up in bed, he drank continually from a jug of water into which he threw lemons cut in halves. He tossed and turned about unceasingly. His thoughts were made up of all imaginable follies, passionate transports and remembrances, and above all, he complained angrily of her having called him "child." . . . Alas, he was only too well aware that he was little more than a child to her and that the difference in their ages separated them like an abyss. And pacing up and down the room during the misty morning that came after that feverish night, the pride-wounded young man indulged a host of thoughts in which he kept bringing to mind how little fuss Giulia appeared to make over him.—She was never forthcoming, never came a step forward to meet him. When he made that bargain with the Fontenay florists for the supply of fresh flowers during the whole winter, had she ever spoken a word to him about it? And what was more exasperating, as soon as ever he went near her, than those everlasting questions as to whether he had scented his hands or washed his mouth! . . .

"Down, Turlu, down!"

And close by the wall, he suddenly stopped in front of a cabinet containing scores of knick-knacks and Saxony shepherds, which Giulia was fond of collecting.

"It's she that has childish fancies and not I," he thought.

And the whole week long, he strove to belittle her in his own eyes, giving her pretty nicknames and imagining her as a little girl. The short days and misty season kept them at the fireside; she lay on the sofa, which was covered with heavy pink satin embroidered with scarabs and flowers, while Otto sat on a cushion at her feet. At first he talked to her in a dry, constrained manner, putting in a word of affection here and there and then lapsing into silence, till at last, under the influence of her beautiful eyes that poured so much light and gentleness upon him, his ill-temper melted and his secret sorrows faded away:

"I love you, I love you, heart of mine!"

He felt drawn, as by a divine power. It was during these after-dinner moments that Giulia somehow put the last touches to the young man's education, for Love, the great book written from within and without, teaches the things of the world as much as it rules the heart. However violent, impetuous and terrible Otto had been until then, it was not long before he came forth from that abyss a tamed and patient lover, obedient to Giulia. Being fond of perfumes, she imbued the young man with the love of them by pouring bottles of scent on his hands and hair. She accustomed him to take the utmost care of his person. His yellow complexion grew clearer, his green eyes became less wild-looking. The inner glory of loving and being loved gave to his outward appearance a certain look of gracefulness and politeness; and it appeared even in those little acts of lovers' playfulness, as for instance when she sometimes slipped a rose or sprig of white lilac into his collar and commanded him not to take it off all day for love of her; a splendour of something more than joy and passion would light up his face.

On All Souls Day there was a terrible hurricane that blew off the top of a neighbouring house and littered the garden with broken branches, slates and glass. Otto and Giulia spent the evening side by side, listening to the fury of the gale and making no other movement except to press closer to each other from time to time. "Dearest!" he said to her amid the clouds of incense with which she had perfumed the room, "How I love you! How beautiful you are! . . ." And his eyes closed of their own accord; he would have liked to be blind and deaf in order that nothing might come between him and his ravishment.

With a strange smile she replied: "I am less beautiful in Ondedei," meaning perhaps some rival of her youth.

The words wounded him. It seemed to him as though his adoration was ignored and mocked. It made him shy, and never again did he tell her that she was beautiful.

Nevertheless, he was a prey to uneasiness and melancholy; a ceaseless sadness made up the tissue of his days.

And for all his coming and going, and ceaseless walking about the house from top to bottom, he could not find a place to suit him. The window panes shone like crystal; the garden walks were so trim that Giulia roamed about them in satin slippers; the polished furniture gleamed in the wax-rubbed floors. Yet in the midst of this tranquillity and happiness, the young man was harrowed by sombre thoughts. Often, as he lay on a couch, he pretended to kill himself, pointing the loaded pistol or placing the knife upon himself. Once in a sort of frenzy, he gave himself a blow and wiped the drops of blood that flowed from his thigh with his pocket handkerchief, finding a bitter pleasure in being alone, helpless and, as it were, forsaken. . . .

A life of gloom and despair set in. His affections began to languish. They became like a flitting flame, that failed to grow and was soon extinguished. Everything seemed to pass away from him like a murky smoke. His delight in Giulia faded away. Yet he loved her always; but his hands were powerless to caress her, his eyes without life to admire her, his mouth without warmth to kiss her. What was the matter with his heart? Poor wretch! why wasn't he happy? And unable to fathom the mystery, he would remain motionless for hours, his elbows resting on the table, his head lowered between his hands, and his face as pale as dusk.

"Giulia! Giulia!" was his constant sigh.

He endeavoured to revive his passion with a host of remembrances, and sometimes a fleeting image returned to his embrace for a moment. But his being was devoid of spontaneous emotion. If his reveries were no more, his love had likewise dried up. And yet, the less he loved, the more his heart sought instinctively to rouse itself, and wearied itself with exaltation and efforts to recover what it had lost.

✳

Strong drink came to his aid. The heating vapours of alcoholic beverages puffed out his breast; his jaws trembled; his whole being swooned with joy in a sort of inward spasm. He began to long for these moments and procured them every day, when dining with Giulia. The wine enlivened his spirits and he felt lifted beyond the impulses of passion as much as the latter surpassed the rest of his sentiments.—"Ah! how I love you, my treasure! I could put my very heart beneath your feet!". . . His face livid and perspiring, he swayed in his chair, saying softly to himself: "I'm drunk." His emotions grew stronger, and he felt himself deeply in love, sighing, sobbing, laughing. He kept saying to himself within:

"O my love! my treasure, my dearest life, my only good! O my joy, my light! You are my only one, my all. I love you, love you, adore you. . . ."

Nevertheless, even all these ardent phrases failed to express Love as passionately as he felt it. His emotion was far beyond all human words. So he imposed silence upon his spirit.

And in the ecstasy that followed, his eyes had never been so keen and penetrating, nor his senses so responsive. A gesture, the twinkling of an eye, transmitted to him by a sort of contagion even the least perceptible state of Giulia's feelings. He lived and breathed in her. And as a man who falls into the sea, sinks deeper and deeper, so Otto plunged and sank deeper into the blissful happiness, with which his spirit was surrounded—until the time came when the wine-fumes faded away and Care knocked at his heart once more with its heavy hand.

Sometimes, during one of these moments, he would take Giulia by the waist and they would stand in front of the mirror, looking at their reflexions. She was serene and mysterious, smelling a rose which she twirled with the tips of her fingers, while he was pale, with red hair and brutal jaws, and wearing a Hungarian jacket with black tassels; never any red or blue, not even in his neckties, which were either bronze, green or big black bows.

"Talk to me, tell me something," she murmured at last.

But he had nothing to say to her; he knew only one phrase: "I love you!" And anything else annoyed him.

Ah! did she then love him so little that she now had to be amused, chatter, show off her charms in his presence! He began walking up and down the room once more.

"What are you thinking about?"

"Me? . . . Nothing."

"You're angry with me."

"Oh, no. . . . I assure you."

Then once more his measured steps up and down the room.

Besides, what could he say without running the risk of exposing his ignorance or being picked up in his mistakes, as usually happened; for his primary education had been so much neglected by that wretch of a von Cramm that he knew almost nothing about the most commonplace things of morality, religion, science or contemporary happenings. He stamped his foot and stopped in front of the window. The sky looked icy and the falling snow was being whirled about by the wind. Nature looked half dead. The spectacle was so much in keeping with the young man's low spirits that his whole being seemed to dissolve in weakness. Never had he felt so gloomy, so wretched. His imagination offered him nothing but languor and troubles. He thought that he might perhaps get rid of his boredom by going for a walk, and as the feast of St. Genevieve was at hand, he went out with Giulia. They strolled about the religious fair which is held once a year in front of the church of St. Etienne. But the inquisitive looks to which his beautiful mistress was subjected, annoyed and enraged him.

The idea that she did not love him sank deeper into his consciousness day by day. How often already a haughty glance or a cold word from Giulia had tugged at the very roots of his affection. Could anything be more eloquent of contempt than her way of never getting up or advancing towards him whenever he entered? What a contrast with Mademoiselle Schlosser, who was always so tender and so anxious that she watched at the window for his coming long before he appeared! Poor girl! He could see her again in her lace night-dress picking raspberries in the garden and pretending not to know he was just arriving, because he had forbidden her to watch at the window. When he was ill, she had nursed him without a murmur or sign of disgust, showing him a mother's compassion in all her actions. She loved him; that was the mystery.

"And Giulia does not love me!"

Alas! the closer he came to her, the further-off she appeared to him. He would have liked her to shut herself up within the circle of his own thoughts and love nothing but their love; but from hour to hour the gulf between his heart and Giulia seemed to grow ever wider. She fled from him, withdrew herself from him. His mind, for all its keenness, lost itself in the haze that surrounded her. She was to him a goddess both known and un-known, a wonder both present and far-off, a star, carried within him and yet inaccessible. In vain he loved her, so to say, beyond his heart; in vain he lifted up and carried his heart forward in pursuit of her. He could never reach the dim point he saw afar, where his mistress beckoned to him. And the only thing he could make out of her was that she was incomprehensible.

One evening when he returned from the stables where he had been to visit Bellua, who had been unwell for several days, he went up noiselessly to Giulia's room. The door-curtain was pulled back and the dying embers in the grate cast a steady purple fire-light on walls and ceiling. And standing on the threshold, he gazed in so great an ecstasy at the livid nightfall, the dark foliage of the garden and the shadowy furniture, that he did not think of going forward.

Suddenly he caught sight of Giulia. She was lying face down on the bed; and the dreadful sighs she heaved from time to time, made the intervals of silence yet more sombre and mysterious.—"Ah! I would like to die!" She murmured' half-aloud. Otto's hair stood on end. Staring hard before him he was afraid to move and stood listening to the thumping of his heart against his breast. After a while Giulia raised herself on her elbows and exclaimed, as though talking to somebody:

"Don't think I'm cold!"

Then she sank back on the bed. A strange sadness invaded Otto and overwhelmed him so completely that he stood there for a good while like a man out-of-breath. Had that plaintive sigh been addressed to him?—Cold, alas! He felt indeed that she was by no means cold, but athirst for violent, superhuman emotions, which their passion failed to give her. What, then, did she conceal in the immense depths of her heart? Was she not destined, like other women, to possess the great treasure of love? And while bemoaning her ill and detesting the emptiness and tedium of her heart, could she not rise above it, by dint of her desire, and yield herself up to the infinite that attracted her? . . . Who could know? Who would reveal to him the secret of that mysterious heart? . . .

Notwithstanding the exuberance of their passion, Otto realised that he could never claim possession of Giulia entirely. To reach the depths of her being he would have to remove the final veil that made her such a mystery to him. No pleasure could fill the immense empty space that separated him from his mistress.

He woke up with heavy eyes, drowsy and uncertain of himself. The flames of the candles burning in their sockets, flickered against the wall and made him blink, while the mirrors with which he had adorned the ceiling, reflected his upturned, frightful, purple-red face. His mind teemed with jumbled ideas. Bending over Giulia, who was asleep, he said to her softly, as though talking to a child: "You love me? tell me, you love me?" But he found her as mysterious as ever. He began to have doubts. Perhaps she was unfaithful to him? A host of suspicions and painful reflections prevented him from going to sleep. He kept turning over in his mind her simplest utterances. He wanted to persuade himself that no faithful woman existed, and he felt tempted to go and break her writing-desk open. But as soon as she woke up, Giulia put his heart to rest with her voluptuous gaze, so that for all his daily struggle, the unhappy lover was still left in a state of perplexity.

What exasperated him most of all were the long, deep sighs she heaved from time to time. Moreover, his lacerated heart seemed to court suffering so that he might be able to accuse his mistress. Whenever he went to embrace her, he remembered what she had said about Ondedei, and with bitterness in his heart he repeated the words: "No! no! there are women more beautiful than you. . . ." And thinking incessantly of Mademoiselle Schlosser, he could only compare her behaviour with that of Giulia. His eyes were always watching the one whom he loved, and he expected Giulia to offer him constant sweetness, gaiety and pleasantness; and though he demanded all this of her, he was astonished that she should expect the same from himself. They had violent scenes, which soon became a habit with them. At every opportunity he threw home truths at her face, and as the quarrel grew more heated, he overstepped all bounds with his resentments, shoutings and furies. Sometimes, in the moments of silence, they could hear Laury playing the zither in the Tyrolese manner in her room, and the notes would die away in the air with a crystal-like tremor. . . . Exhausted and haggard, he went out into the street, running about as though he was looking everywhere for relief and asking where Death was. In the falling dusk he walked about the deserted streets, where the flickering gay light danced on the snow. His breast seethed with anger, and he still kept calling her rude names. At last his rage suddenly abated and he assured himself that she would be the greater loser if he left her.

One night when he was wandering about in this manner after a violent scene, he suddenly began to walk in the direction of his father's house, vowing aloud that he would return to the Duke and never see Giulia again. The house was all asleep, the courtyard wrapped in silence. With his brow pressed against the railings, he gazed at the gloomy statues holding aloft their flickering gay lamps in the background. "This time she can keep on waiting for me!" he thought. And the idea of Giulia being anxious gave him a pleasant feeling of bitter-sweet revenge. Three o'clock struck in the distance. Nothing stirred; the air was sharp and cold. The rumbling of a carriage aroused Otto from his thoughts. Great was his surprise when he saw the cab draw up at the gate. A man got out and rang the bell. It was his brother, Count Franz.

"Hi! Hi!" called a voice, and a swarthy head with big black side-whiskers appeared at one of the windows of the cab. "Don't forget that the big stakes will be played for at the Circle tomorrow with de Poix and Caussade. . . ."

"So my brother has become a gambler!" Otto reflected with astonishment.

Even the best laid plans, though devised with all possible art and experience, sometimes engender troublesome consequences. This was certainly the case with Franz and Emilia. However happy-go-lucky the young man may have been, he felt a very keen disgust for his marriage. And although as a result of his accommodating nature, he had made it up with the Italian, their quarrels and fleeting reconciliations soon proved that Franz had not got rid of all his resentment. However, when Emilia left Rome, she found she was in the family way and she greatly hoped that the birth of the child would lead to a mutual reconciliation and settlement. But by the bad luck of the deuce, they met Romero, the celebrated gambler, at Monte Carlo. It has never been revealed by what astute means this ugly, dark, audacious, little adventurer, who had plenty of intelligence and outward show, managed to get Franz into his power and infect him with his vice. Did he merely guess at the dangerous inclination, whose seeds were in the young man's soul? Ought one to believe that the bait with which he seduced Franz was the sum of 85,000 francs, which he won at roulette the first night? However that may be, nobody ever caught the passion more violently. And when Emilia at last grew suspicious, it was already too late to oppose this mastering passion with tears or reason.

How far away already were those brilliant days when she used to ride out on horseback with her skirts tucked up so as to show her leg, and at night slept with her hands tied above her in order to have more beautiful hands! Since her return she seemed to have changed quite as much as Franz, not only in face and carriage, which her pregnancy had spoilt, but in spirit and behaviour also. It would have been hard to discover any vestiges of the smart rider of former days in that elongated figure of a woman with untidy hair under a bonnet, dirty, indolent and big at the waist. She shut herself up in her apartment, which was in a state of great disorder, and spent the whole day there, wandering from one armchair to another, when she was not decking out a statue of the Madonna with lace and flowers in company with Teresina, her Roman maid. She had remained very Italian in all her ways and had no other remedy for her sorrow and desertion but lighting candles in honour of the "bambino" and mumbling the rosary. She spent hours in this way every night, keeping Teresina close to her and waiting for Count Franz. The monotonous Hail Marys, the light of the candles, gradually sent the two women to sleep. They would wake up with a start and Emilia would begin to weep and wail. She could not understand how things had managed to turn out in such a way against all appearances. She thought that since she had passed over everything, Franz ought to have no further cause for complaint against her.

As for Franz, he made no complaint. His one care seemed to be to avoid her in order to give her no chance to discuss a matter he abhorred. When he came home in the early hours of the morning, he took off his boots in order to slip without noise down the corridor past Emilia's bedroom. During the daytime, their meetings never lasted more than a quarter of an hour, and in that time she gave way to such a flood of tears or show of temper that he took offence, seized his hat and went out. She always hoped to reclaim him, but the sort of insensibility which made him feel no grudge, prevented her also from getting any hold over him. He made no reply and let the outpouring pass. And as time went by without bringing any change, Emilia's tears and sorrows increased, while her frame grew thinner.

She wrote home to her mother, begging her to send her some secrets of superstition, prayers to be recited three times and believed to be of unfailing efficacy. She consulted fortune-tellers in company with Teresina, but the cards always predicted an "early bereavement." She sewed up in a small satchel various magical knick-knacks to form a charm; but once the scapular was finished, the question was how to harness the Count with it? And the satchel had to lie unused. On the stroke of midnight next day, she threw four packs of cards into the flaming coals, saying:

"I curse you, hearts!
"I curse you, spades!
"I curse you, clubs!
"I curse you, diamonds!"

Franz, however, continued gambling. If only she had found somebody to back her up! Arcangeli made no other reply to her complaints but a shrugging of the shoulders. Franz's mother,

Augusta, who was growing stout and beginning to look like a whale, besides becoming more cantankerous and visionary with age, refused to accept the situation and never stopped talking about the impudent marriage. And even Christiane, on whose support Emilia had relied, insisted on keeping to herself and shutting everybody out of her room.

It was only at this period that she began to feel the most distressing effects of Hans Ulrich's loss. Till then, her sorrow had been a sort of shock and like a long, frightful dream, in which there was little attachment to life. Suddenly the unhappy girl came to herself with her heart pierced by this sword of grief. Too strong to die and too weak to forget, she was condemned to live. She was to drag her expiation forever with her, and her eyes were filled with darkness and phantoms. Hans Ulrich was always before her mind, at the table where she read, in the inglenook when she sat by the fire, at her side when she went for a walk. The spectre obsessed her, yet she could not make out the face. It was just a vague form. When she dreamt of Hans Ulrich at night, she could only distinguish the back of his head.

Boredom overwhelmed her; remorse was killing her. The slightest noise, the weather, the long days, everything depressed her. Leaning back in her big armchair, she dreamily watched the glowing embers of the grate, the gloomy, cloud-covered sky, the backs of the fringed curtains; then she would start reading again. But however deep the abyss in which she strove to bury her thoughts, her heart remained as sorrowful as ever. Sometimes a cord on one of the rare lutes and violins that adorned the walls would snap with a long moan and Christiane would be startled, looking about her in all directions. Unaccountable terrors would take hold of her; she feared the ceiling would fall down on top of her and that one of the heavy enamel bas-reliefs over the doors would break away and crush her. She would shudder and move away in a cold sweat, after which she would upbraid herself for holding on to life.

But if she died, what would be her fate?—"I am damned!" she kept repeating to herself; and hell seemed to open out beneath her feet. She felt all its horrors, the burning fire, the shrill cries of the damned, and the fearful depths of the darkness and the furnace. She thought of the demons, wishing she were one of them, because they were only the executioners, and the torturers suffered far less than the tortured. Often Father Le Charmel and the Princess of Hanau chanced to arrive during one of these moments; and overcoming her bewilderment, Christiane pulled herself together with a terrific effort. On the priest's advice, she tried to raise her soul upwards to God, but her frightful thoughts gave her no truce.—Her sin was too great, there was no mercy for her! And since she would be damned, she could sin without fear and assuage her soul as much as she desired. And giving no further heed to the exhortations, she let her thoughts drift back to Hans Ulrich, evoking his beloved likeness, recalling all the most passionate episodes of their love, the duet of Sieglind and Siegmund, their kisses and all the strange terror and delight of their transgression.

Nevertheless, amid all these crises and sufferings, the great work of her conversion was going ahead. Day by day, her heart inclined more and more towards a religion that was full of a consoling suffering and a sweet sadness that softened down all evils. A ray of hope began to slip into her soul. Although persisting in regarding herself as a reprobate almost without hope of salvation, Christiane knew that there still remained to her, as Father Le Charmel said, "both her own great misery and the great mercy of God." And this thought filled her with a joy and warmth that deeply moved her. Poor soul thirsting for pardon! How she wept at the tender words of the priest quoting St. Augustine: "*Veni, columba te vocat, gemendo te vocat.*"[1]

"Come to us," he said, "come to the Church, my child. She is a dove that moans for you and tries to draw you by moan-

---

1 "Come, the dove calls you, moaning it calls you."

ing. . . ." But though she was not so wretched in the daytime, her nights were dreadful. She had hardly tasted the sweets of a first sleep, when she would wake up with her mind full of Hans Ulrich.—"If I breathe his name, I am damned!" she said to herself. She clutched at the bedclothes, panting, her face buried in the pillow. Then sitting up, she cried out:

"Hans Ulrich! Hans Ulrich!"

She sat motionless, listening to the beating of her heart. . . . And a voice kept saying to her: "I am damned; I am damned." Till at last the unhappy creature fell into a swoon that left her without colour, warmth or respiration.

But it was not this that brought her to the feet of the Lord. She was won over by something much more pleasant; by the hope that the punishment might not be eternal, that not all sinners were damned, that souls, who were not so much guilty as weak, only went to Purgatory. The day when Father Le Charmel expounded to her the true Romanist teaching on this subject, Hans Ulrich's sister became converted. Her heart was filled with a spontaneous, happy belief. Since her brother was not damned and she would be able to share herself with him and the Lord, her mind was soon made up: she would consecrate her life to the task of redeeming Ulrich from their crime. She would enter a convent. What more had she to do with the world's great vast ways that led only to perdition? It was far better to seek a refuge beneath the right hand of the Lord. Moreover, the Beaujon house was already becoming uninhabitable on account of the everyday scandals and follies of the Duke.

It has never been quite settled why His Highness fell out with Lyonnette. The coldness is said to have arisen on account of a kennel groom to whom the nymph showed remarkable kindness. Or was it because the Duke was fed up with the impertinent peals of laughter, with which she treated him to his very nose, as soon as ever he started talking? It is all very doubtful. On the other hand it was as clear as daylight why Count d'Oels came one fine morning and informed His Highness that he was going to marry Mlle Lyonnette.

"What! You're going to leave me as well?" exclaimed the Duke with great feeling. . . .

Whereupon the chamberlain raised his eyebrows most sorrowfully. Everything had drawn him towards the marriage, which had occupied his thoughts from the very day Lyonnette entered the house. He was attracted by her fortune, and considered the difference between being at the mercy of the Duke and being lord and master in his own house.

Perhaps, also, he took into consideration that such a marriage was rather scandalous. Accordingly he bided his time, and played the passionate lover. Finally he proposed the bargain. The beauty was to have full liberty and in no way change her life, except that she would have a status in society. At first, Lyonnette laughed at the proposal, but thought it over afterwards. Though d'Oels, with his evil eyes and dark face, would have frightened her in a forest, she did not find him disagreeable in her own house. As old Irma said:

"He looks very grand seigneur, my dear. . . ." Besides, how funny it would be! After all, he was no uglier than Prince Alexeiev or the marquis of her friend Giovannina Flor.

True, he hadn't any money-bags, but she was rich enough for two. With the title glittering before her eyes, it was not long before she swallowed Count d'Oel's proposal as though she was gobbling up a strawberry. For the sake of form, she hesitated a couple of days or so, gloating over the forthcoming sensation and His Highness's wrath. Finally she gave her consent with an inward eagerness which she masked with an air of condescension. Such was the love story of Count d'Oels and the pretty Lyonnette.

✳

Charles d'Este returned to Paris towards the end of November, thoroughly vexed. The kitchen boys, grooms, coachmen and menservants forsook everything on his arrival in order to crowd round his landau and shout hurrah. They were all Italian rascals, with whom Giovan had filled the house in his master's absence, and who were all strangers to His Highness. The scene-setting delighted him, but next day, being bored at the sight of so many gobbling rascals around him, the Duke announced he would not keep any table, and so much a day was given to the menservants to go and get their dinner at the pothouse.

He was possessed by the demon of misanthropy and was eaten up with anger, bitterness and grousing. From the very first days he started fresh lawsuits and bickerings. The quarrels relating to the construction of the house were soon augmented by others. Being bored with his life, the Duke had very soon mastered the jargon of the law. Everything became a subject for chicanery. Every day the ante-chamber was full of whiskered folk. Rich as he was and spending a million or more a month, the Duke was more put out over a few stolen louis than any poor wretch would be. In fact, he even went to law over an account for seven francs which his secretary owed the laundress. On several occasions, His Highness deigned to appear personally at the law court and give his evidence himself, first against his breeches-maker, for "defects of outfit" against his saddler and coach-builder, and finally against an unfortunate blind man whom his horses had nearly crushed to death.

"Let the award be settled in relation to the coachman," said the Duke. "I only come on behalf of my servant, paying for him if he's unable to meet his obligations."

When the damages were fixed at 15,000 francs, the Duke complained a whole week long that he was being ruined, that they were taking advantage of his being a foreigner, that he would die in the gutter, and so on.

Moreover, he was at the time of his life when he might easily have gone off his head altogether. The various extravagances to which the Duke had given himself up for so many years, had become his daily habits, and all sorts of weird ideas seemed to come to him from nowhere. After giving audience in bed to a host of lawyers, and sometimes to Van Moppes and Monsieur Felix, he would rise about four o'clock and begin dressing. There was great hesitation in the little *Salon des Bustes* in choosing what was most in keeping with His Highness's state of mind, projects, caprice, and the weather, clear or foggy. After this operation, the Duke would settle in his armchair in the Mirror room while Arcangeli solemnly proceeded to reproduce on his master's face the colours painted on the cheeks of the wax figure. Then, having been brushed, and had his necktie and skin corset adjusted, his face looking hard set in its coating of paint and plaster, the old spark would get into his landau and drive off with a dash. Very often when driving down the boulevard, he would draw up at a fashionable pastry-cook's, and consume plenty of fruit, dragées, and sweetmeats, mingled with glasses of ice-water, and all the while he would urge Baron von Cramm or Mr. Smithson to do likewise. Sometimes he sat at a table in the front window of the Maison d'or. He was not at all annoyed by the crowd that gathered to gaze at him. On the contrary, he liked to hear what was said in admiration of his clothes and diamonds on the other side of the window. And it was almost a comedy to see him brighten up under the astonished gaze of the passers-by.

His violent manners grew worse, and it was feared he might be seized with a fatal attack at any moment. One evening he got into his carriage and ordered the coachman to drive at top speed. The horses dashed off. . . .

"Not so fast!" His Highness cried out.

And the carriage immediately slowed down.

"Faster!" the Duke called out. Then once again he stopped it, repeating the process four or five times. Finally he sprang to his feet, brandishing a pistol (he was always stuffed with daggers and revolvers).

"Foot it! traitor! . . . brute! . . ." he roared. "Get down, or I'll break your head!"

And in the end, the carriage went to the theatre at the slowest pace, being driven by the groom, whose teeth chattered all the way.

Majestic and aloof in a box by the stage with a beverage close at hand, the Duke now appeared nightly on show, and visitors from the provinces were bidden to look forward to seeing him, as the Persian or the Man-orchestra. His fiery eyes, immense nose, bright red face, black, lifeless silk wig, and sparkling diamonds tickled the women to laughter, while the men never tired of looking through their opera-glasses at the creature accompanying him. She was loaded with jewels, dressed in flaming satins, and sat a little to the rear of him, having the order not to speak except when spoken to by him.

"Why, it's Esther Debloutz, by Jove!"

"What! Has he done with Léo?"

And in truth, for nearly six months there was such a constant succession of dancers, adventuresses, horsewomen and comediennes at the house, that it was no small task to know what name had to go down in the weekly accounts of pensions and wages. Not that Venus tyrannised so much over His Highness. The poor man merely wished to have a mistress who would show off his riches, like a mannequin, and complete his household.

She had her own staff of menservants, coachman, attendants, and her own table. One of the Duke's carriages was set aside for her use, and d'Andonville attended to her in the capacity of major-domo, a function assigned to him by the Duke. In spite of all these advantages, the job very soon palled on all the women who took it up. Though she might be out of sorts or suffering from headache and depression, the favourite was expected to be merry, laugh, amuse the Duke, sit up late, talk, dine and sup, never show cold or heat or any inconvenience, tell naughty stories and all the chitchat of Paris in order to keep His Highness amused, without any mitigation of etiquette or the task. When one or two took it into their heads to swoon or feel giddy, the Duke had them brought to with bucketsful of water thrown into their faces, and sacked them the same day. Happy were they whom His Highness got rid of decently, giving them sums of money, usually in the shape of moth-eaten securities that could only be collected by a lawsuit or at the risk of bankruptcy.

He grew more and more wrong in the head. His pride, the radical vice from which all his other vices sprang, became more insolent than ever. He obstinately refused to call on the Emperor on New Year's Day and almost came to refer to him quite simply as "Buonaparte." Formerly so polite that he used to take off his hat to every woman, even to the female gardeners at Wendessen, he now boasted of having openly snubbed the ex-Queen Isabella of Spain by turning brusquely away in a corridor at the Opera House. His life was nothing but a mixture of the most ostentatious grandeur and the lowest ignominy. He lived aloof in his picture-gallery admiring the portraits of the kings and emperors, his ancestors, except when he fooled about with Giovan and the servants, or pestered his mistress. Yawning and bored to death, he was at his wits' end to find something to do. Fed up with everything, the old miser found no more joy even in looking at his treasure store.

"Bah! I'll sell my diamonds someday," he would reply, whenever Van Moppes expressed his admiration.

His mistress for the time being was a rather pretty adventuress, called Miss Sinclair. She had flashing dark eyes, a beautiful complexion and short curly hair that took one's eyes off her snub nose. The proud prince sank so low as to take meals with her and all sorts of shady rascals, trainers, ruffians, and swashbucklers, who never failed to pocket some of the plate. The luxurious table-fare was prepared in the Duke's apartment, with the aid of cooks from Potel or the Café Anglais; and Miss Sinclair and the Duke himself sometimes tried their hand and floundered about the ovens. There was no end to the drinking, smashing of crockery and full-throated singing, and, though once so sober, the Duke drank his fill every evening. When the company could do no more, they went to bed and the feast began again next day.

Everything in the house was upside down. Creditors came in streams. The menservants fought among themselves. Thefts went on wholesale, and one night all the gold fringes in the Tapestry gallery were found to have been cut off. The investigations that followed merely led to the discovery of a host of other thefts, which nobody seemed to have noticed. As a measure of safety, the silver mirrors, jewellery and knick-knacks displayed on the various tables, were put away; but as soon as the first surprise was over, the carelessness began all over again. The wind whistled through the broken window panes in the vast rooms; dust lay in heaps in the corners, which were black with cobwebs; the bathroom taps, never properly turned off, flooded some of the drawing-rooms more than once. On the other hand, the Duke's extravagance became more and more subtle and seemed concentrated upon himself. He even took it into his head to be jealous of Miss Sinclair and dressed her up as a man each morning and put moustaches on her! . . . In a word, the neglect went so far that one day the Duke had no shirt to change into on rising, and in the evening his carriage stood pretty well ten minutes at the door of the house, neither porter nor footman being there to open the door to him.

Next day, on waking up, the Duke wrote a couple of lines to Miss Sinclair, requesting her to leave. He sent the note by a footman and refused to see her any more. Thereupon he rang for Arcangeli and ordered him to go and look for Giulia.

"But, Monseigneur! . . ." stammered the poor devil, half stunned by the unexpected cart-load on his head.

"Hold your tongue, rascal!" His Highness enjoined. "I know quite well that you don't like her. But listen and bear this in mind. I entrust you with the job of reconciling me with her, and if you fail, I'll turn you out."

And he would have carried out his threat, for he was very fond of these theatrical turns, and became as passionately attached to people as he had treated them to his dislike but a few days before. Accordingly Giovan made no mistake, and however much he disliked swallowing the medicine, set seriously to work to find out where Giulia was living. To begin with, he went to the Grand Hotel, and in doing so put his nose on the right scent, for the little house in the Rue du Puits-qui-parle had been let to Giulia by Mr. Tripp, the general agent, personally.

The poor house, once so peaceful beneath its mantle of ivy in the shade of its chestnut trees, had for six months known nothing but cries and moans. "Oh, I hate her!" Otto kept saying to himself every moment. But in the midst of his worst fits of fury and his most violent resolutions, he felt like a comedian banging about the stage but not believing in the story he holds forth. Weak and loathing his weakness, broken-in, but with a rebellious heart, he went perpetually backwards and forwards from hate to love and from love to hate, at one moment ravingly anxious to put an end to it all, and the moment after, hoping for less stormy and fairer weather. In this persistent state of indecision, he passed from one illusion to another, although the hot-headed youth would never admit it. "She's only a woman, after all!" he exclaimed, shaking his red head furiously. And in order to belittle Giulia in his own mind, he began to count up all his amorous affairs. Though he counted them on his fingers, pausing at each name, they all seemed to him more remote than phantoms. And at the least glance in the direction of Giulia, he could not help thinking that the sufferings he endured on her account were worth more than the happy hours he had spent with the others.

Meanwhile the young man's health, which had somehow been maintained by a strong vitality, threatened to break down at last. He began to have headaches, attacks of giddiness and constant looseness, so that he grew thin almost before one's eyes. Then the trouble attacked him in the throat, and for several weeks it looked as though an operation could not be avoided. Sitting alone by the bedroom fireside, where the infusions and potions ordered by the doctors slowly simmered, he felt bored to death. Every trifle annoyed and irritated him. If Giulia happened to start singing in the little drawing-room, no matter how soft and beautiful the music was, the sound of it so close disturbed him. He was now jealous of Laury, the chambermaid, and thought that Giulia showed too much confidence in her; but at the same time he was thinking of going up to the maid's attic one fine night. Laury's supple figure, snub nose and perky yellow eyes that followed him about like a pair of wasps, filled him with disorderly imaginings whenever they were alone. And he fancied that by this means he was taking his revenge on Giulia for her cold and disdainful behaviour.

Through leading such a lonely life for so long, the lovers found their hearts invaded by an extraordinary silence. The whole outside world dwindled away. Their restless spirit, turning upon itself, seemed by a perpetual moving to settle down at last; and filled with a single thought, they no longer looked at things except by the light of the torch which passion lights for lovers. They could not leave each other even for an hour. As soon as they were apart, they each held out their arms towards the image of the other; and they no sooner came together, than they started quarrelling and beating each other once more. It was she who returned first. In order to feel some emotion while she was wheedling him and to avoid being cold and hard, Otto tried to fill his mind with the picture of Giulia lying dead, and kept telling himself that perhaps he might have to carry her to the grave someday. Tears came to him at last and, as they moistened Giulia's robe, the hearts of the loving pair were softened and overflowed with mutual appeals.

"You demand too much," said she.

"And you don't trust me enough," said he.

And thus they complained tenderly of each other, entering into a deep and intimate consciousness of their mutual wretchedness. . . . Heart-sick and restless, consumed by never-ceasing chagrins, disillusioned and weary of the life they were leading, no longer having any faith in their love, athirst for the Infinite, hungry for a happiness that ever eluded them, in spite of all their troubles, disgusts and never-ending quarrels, Otto and Giulia loved each other in an inexpressible way.

One afternoon of early June,—Otto recalled afterwards that they had that day been reading together the trial of Madame Lafarge, for, being tired of *tête-à-tête* conversation, they sometimes borrowed books from a neighbouring library,—the loving couple were leaning over the railings of the little balcony at the top of the outside staircase. A storm was just ending. Vast black clouds were hurrying over the western sky and from their midst came repeated rumblings, while the opposite part of the sky was lit with a bright golden colour and appeared beautifully serene. Nothing was heard nearby, except the rustling of the dripping foliage. The wet sand under the chestnut trees was covered with pink petals. Giulia was about to go down and lift up her amaryllis plants that were bent in two by the downpour, when a big landau, resplendent with copper and steel, came out of the Rue des Postes and drew up in front of the little garden.

Giulia gave a cry:

"The Duke!"

"My father!" exclaimed Otto, staggering back towards the doorway. "What does he want with us? Don't open the door!" . . . He was thinking of the seventy-five thousand francs he had taken from the writing desk.

"Oh, come!" She said. "What makes you think like that? Go and shut yourself up in your room. . . . Go down and open the door," she said to Laury, who came in. . . . "But don't let them see you, Otto. You see quite well that the Italian is looking upwards," she went on eagerly.

Meanwhile the Duke and Arcangeli were already mounting the stairs at the other end of the corridor. She pushed Otto into his room and kissed him passionately. Then, putting a finger to her lips, she went out and closed the door.

Left all alone, the young man heard the startled cry she gave as she entered the next room.

"Well, yes! It's me!" said Charles d'Este, whose voice Otto recognised. "It's I who return to you, Giulia, since you disdain to return to me."

"Monseigneur!" exclaimed Giulia. "Monseigneur, I cannot listen to you."

She blushed, and with a strange impetuosity, made a show of going away.

"Come, Madam!" said Giovan. "A little patience! please consider . . ."

"Be off!" she cried out to him, stepping back abruptly, for the rascal had been so bold as to take hold of her arm.

"Madam! . . . Madam! . . ." said the Duke, obviously embarrassed.

"Well! what have you come here for?" she exclaimed. "What else did I get from you, Monseigneur, but insults? Your dog, your horses, your lackeys were better treated than myself! . . ."

Her lips were trembling with fury; her face, pale and haughty, breathed implacable hatred. And Charles d'Este merely shrugged his shoulders in a most pitiful manner, while he toyed with his gloves.

After Giulia had calmed down a little and a long pause had ensued, during which Arcangeli never left off making signs to his illustrious companion, the Duke opened his mouth once more. He began by protesting his respect and love at great length. It was because he realised the wrong he had done, that he wished to set it right. His repentance was sincere; since her departure he had not passed a single day without thinking of her and cursing himself. Getting more and more excited and as though carried away by the pathos of the words that fell from his lips, he cried out that he was a fool, that he was not worthy to possess her, and grovelled in all sorts of self-reproaches.

"But I implore you to be kind, I beseech you to make it up with me. . . ."

And with a look of appeal he waited for her to reply.

"Don't entertain any hope of my becoming your mistress again," said Giulia.

Whereupon His Highness began to reason with her.

"Never! Never!" she cried out in a sort of fury. Then, with a groan, she threw herself on to a sofa and covered her eyes with her hand, weeping like a woman who has no more strength with which to fight.

Astounded at the effect of their intervention, the Duke and Arcangeli withdrew into a corner of the room and waited while Giulia tried to quell her emotion. They were also very much perturbed and touched by the sight of so much violence. At last Giovan broke the silence and said in a conciliatory tone of voice that it was quite useless to talk in that way and that one ought to give one's reasons without any noise. Then, turning to Giulia, he said:

"Come, Madam! Your anger was quite justified. . . . Monseigneur! You were wrong in this matter; very much so, I assure you."

"Look here, Giulia," said His Highness, going forward a few steps. "Are you going to refuse your hand to me?"

She appeared not to hear anything and made abrupt gestures, as though to keep the Duke away. Gradually, however, her bodily agitation died down, and the deep sighs ceased to make her bosom heave.

"Now," thought the Duke, "now is the time to fall at her feet. . . ."

And drawing up a cushion, he dropped on his knees upon it, while Giovan exclaimed:

"See, Madam, how His Highness loves you; see how he makes up for his wrongs!"

"Ah!" replied Giulia, "I see how deceitful men are."

184

"Yes!" Exclaimed the Italian playfully. "We're cunning rascals and we start telling lies before we get our first tooth."

"After the lesson I've had," Giulia went on, "is it likely that I should allow myself to be taken in by your words? . . ."

Whereupon she rose languidly, and there was a long silence, His Highness also having risen. At last, the Duke ventured to take Giulia's hand and raise it to his lips; Giulia made no protest.

But with her eyelids half-closed and her eyes half-turned towards him and looking very proud, she smiled at him with that sphinx-like smile of hers, at once sweet and icy, with which she masked her most terrible resolves. Finding her at last at the point to which the Duke wished to bring her, the Italian clapped his hands and cried out in a happy tone:

"It's all right, Monseigneur. It's all settled. Ah, we handsome men! There's no doubt we're what the women like most of all."

After that, they all spoke a good deal with a wealth of questions, repetitions and explanations, such as occur after a long absence. Charles d'Este kept pacing up and down the room by the light of a candle which Giulia lighted to chase away the gloom of nightfall. He was dressed in a sort of frock coat caught in and pleated at the waist, a pair of trousers with a green velvet stripe down the side, a shiny black wig and a flood of lace at the coat-front.

From time to time the Duke broke away from the torrent of useless words, and came back to his point, the return of Giulia:

"Your apartment is all ready. I shall wait for you there from tomorrow."

"Very well, I consent, Monseigneur, on one condition," she replied at last.

"Well, what is it?" the Duke asked.

Giulia leant forward and whispered in his ear. Then, as he looked at her in amazement, she added laughingly:

"You can take it or leave it, Monseigneur. I want to know whether you will obey me in the future."

"Ah! The embargo is too cruel, Madam," said His Highness gallantly.

"Thirty days! That isn't at all long," she replied. . . . "Come, *cher Seigneur*, make up your mind. Swear!" she said teasingly.

"Well, so be it!" replied His Highness. "I swear, Giulia."

The talk went on a little longer and the Duke forced Giulia to accept some cases of jewellery, which he had in his pocket, as the sweetmeats of the settlement.

Soon, as the evening wore on, His Highness rose and took leave:

"The blue carriage will come and fetch you about three o'clock tomorrow, my dear."

He went out with Giovan. The horses snorted and the carriage wheels soon clattered over the cobbles. The bell of a neighbouring convent kept clanging in the dusk. Filled with an immense sadness, Giulia stood with staring eyes at the open window, listening to the sound of the wheels in the distance and to the gloomy knell resounding over the deserted gardens.

When she turned round, she saw Otto before her. He was standing in the doorway, pale and terrible. And that short moment of silence, in which they heard the green candle on the piano burn and palpitate in the night air, was the most terrible that Giulia and Otto had ever experienced in all the course of their sombre, chequered life. "You won't do that?" he stammered. "You won't go back to my father?"

"I'm going tomorrow," she said.

"Ah! . . . ah! . . ." he groaned two or three times, and then threw himself so violently on Giulia that she stumbled and they both fell to the floor. She tried to free herself, to take away the hands that were tightening about her throat. He called her by a coarse name in a fiery, concentrated voice, while he struggled with indescribable rage.

As his grip tightened on her, she suddenly bit him savagely on the right hand.

He cried out, let go his hold, and staggered to his feet. At the sight of his bleeding hand, he began to chatter with his teeth, like a man who feels very cold. Suddenly he burst into tears.

The night was dark and peaceful. From time to time thick clouds passed over the luminous cusp of the moon. Ten o'clock sounded in the distance. The heavy scent of the acacia came in through the open window. . . . There was a very long silence, and then a star shot across the sky. And as though in a deep dream, Otto perceived Giulia, pale and white as a ghost, raising her arms and adjusting herself in front of the looking-glass.

"Yes, I'm going back to the Duke," she said at last, in a low voice. "But for a whole month I shall keep to myself, and nobody shall cross my threshold. I made the Duke give me that promise."

"A month . . ." he said, palpitating. "And after? . . ."

"Ah!" she said, looking in the mirror at the necklaces which His Highness had given her. "Who is ever certain of living more than a month?"

"Giulia!" he cried out. "Giulia! . . ."

They said no more, pondering their thoughts in silence. She was pale and sad, with her hands crossed, while nothing in her stirred except the sparkling fires of the diamonds that trembled on her cheeks.

He sat with his head in his hand and his elbow on his knee, astounded and hardly able to control the tumult of his feelings, while he kept repeating stubbornly: "I'm mad! What have I been thinking of?" But in his heart of hearts, he was thinking that he was faced with the alternative of losing Giulia forever or keeping her eternally; that no doubt she was getting tired of their poverty and hidden life; that if the Duke were to disappear, he himself would be the lord and master of that amazing fortune. . . .

"And a crime like that, committed for her sake, will attach her to me, put her under my power."

Besides, would he be the first to risk such an adventure? . . . and the stream of thoughts flowed constantly through the mind of the pale young man.

"Yes, in his milk, or his fruit," Giulia suddenly exclaimed from the depth of her meditation.

A thrill passed through their frames and, waking from their dream, they looked at each other in amazement, already accomplices and criminals, with a sense of horror scorching their souls.

IX

THE five days following Giulia's return to the Beaujon mansion were filled with happenings that require a sort of diary in order to make them clear, so precipitately did they follow one after another. To begin with, there was the unexpected reappearance of Count Otto, who turned up almost as though he had sprung out of the ground and looking very crestfallen. He said he had just arrived from London. When it came to questions, however, his replies were so sulky, that the Duke let the matter drop, thinking that there was probably some romantic adventure behind it. With the return of his son and of his mistress, the Duke beamed with joy. And in order to dissipate a slight embarrassment they had felt at their meeting again, His Highness took them out to dinner and got so merry towards the end that he tapped on his plate with his knife and fork by way of accompaniment to the piano in a neighbouring room.

On waking next day, which was Tuesday, Charles d'Este received from the hands of the valet who drew back his curtain, a letter in a black-bordered envelope which had been brought by Christiane's maid. He did not like the sight of the letter, which he thought was probably another appeal for help, at the suggestion of Princess Sophie, for a chapel or some charity. So the Duke put off opening the letter till after four o'clock in the afternoon. About two o'clock, Christiane ordered her carriage. She waited a little while, pacing up and down the room in a sort of dream, while Father Le Charmel and the Princess of Hanau carried on a whispered conversation in the corner. At last Christiane suddenly exclaimed: "Let's go!"

"You still desire, my dear child, to go by way of the Père La Chaise cemetery?" Madame Sophie asked.

She nodded her head affirmatively in reply. Old Louisa came in with some luggage, and Christiane, being the last to go out, stopped on the threshold of the door and cast a long farewell look at the familiar room that was as dear to her heart as a friend. So it was quite true: she was leaving Paris in order to enter a Carmelite nunnery at Poitiers. There she would abjure her faith and later on, take the veil and the solemn, irrevocable vows. . . . A death-like silence reigned all around. The wind softly stirred the heaped-up ashes of the grate, where she had burnt some letters and portraits of Hans Ulrich. The most poignant sufferings of affection filled her breast. . . . Then she went out.

"We've two hours to spare," said the Princess, taking out her watch. Nothing more was said. Huddled up behind the windows, Christiane cast a mournful glance at the tree-bordered avenues, the passing carriages and pedestrians. The sight of them was painful to her eyes. She let down the blind and nestled back in her corner. But already the carriage stopped. They were at the gates of the cemetery.

"Go, my daughter, we will wait for you here," said Father Le Charmel very softly.

The temporary tomb of the Blankenburgs, which the Duke had bought half-built from a rich Brazilian, is situated on a small rising not far from Balzac's tomb. Although surrounded by a great number of monuments, whose marble crosses and slabs stand out on all sides, the Blankenburg tomb is distinguished by its tapering marble spire, rich gildings and open turrets with angels at the sides.

Christiane dismissed Louisa after she had taken the garlands of flowers from the old woman. Unlocking the door, she went down the couple of steps into the narrow chapel. Though the place had been kept shut up, there was no smell. The stucco walls were shining white; a number of old faded wreaths lay on the marble slabs, while others hung from gilt-bronze hooks along the walls. In this clean, bright spot Christiane felt no emotion. Hans Ulrich seemed infinitely remote from her, however near were his mortal remains. She knelt down, and bending over the vault, said:

"Adieu . . . adieu . . . adieu. . . ."

Once again she saw him on his bier, his pale face wrapped in linen bandages. He was down there, stretched out and dead. "And this is a dead person that speaks to you," she said, "for I'm leaving the world and going to a place of rest as dark and hidden as yours." She was silent. A gust of wind shook the trees of the cemetery, and the beaded wreaths on a tomb nearby jangled together with a weird noise. Suddenly a shower of rain pattered down, the whole sky streamed with water. "Ah!" she thought. "How cold they must be!" And at the same moment her eyes filled with tears and she broke into sobs and sighs.

"Oh, my dear, my beloved darling! . . ."

And falling to the ground, she cried out in despair: "Oh, how I love you! I love you! Ulrich, take me, open your arms, put me at your side! Oh, speak to me! . . . I want to hear you. . . . Hear me! Answer me! Alas! . . . I implore you. Open your eyes. . . ."

With dishevelled hair she lay on the marble slabs, her tears flowing abundantly like the rain outside, her sobs mingling with the storm. In her frenzy to die, she was about to smash her head against the wall. . . . Suddenly she shuddered, realising that she was shut up all alone with the two dead bodies nearby. The ground seemed to slip from beneath her feet, her eyes slowly closed and the unhappy creature fainted away. . . .

The rain had ceased. Christiane stood motionless before the tomb. A heavy rumbling, pierced by strange noises, rose from the vast city, that spread out before her eyes. She gave a last look at the eternal resting place of her dear brother, and saying adieu, adieu, once more, she went back to the cemetery gates. Louisa told the coachman to drive to the Gare d'Orleans. . . . The train set off and went out of sight,—and Christiane was never more to be spoken of in this world.

✳

The Duke was just getting out of bed, when he deigned to remember the letter, and thus he learnt the news. . . .

"So much for my daughter's respect and love," he said bitterly. . . . And having rung for the milk, which constituted his sole beverage for the time being, he began to play chess with Giulia, while Otto paced up and down the room. Whether because he was really amused by it or because he thought it was a sign of greatness of mind, the old fool took it into his head that day to play the lover, pressing Giulia with his knee under the table, leaning towards her from time to time and saying something to her in a whisper while he rolled his eyes. Giulia was almost scared to death as she saw Otto grow red and white in turns, his throat swelling and his eyes starting out of his head. Happily, the Duke got up from the table after a while, and leaving the game, suggested they should go for a walk in the garden, as the heat was so great.

"Have a drink, if you feel hot," said Giulia.

"Presently," replied the Duke.

Whereupon they went out. The strange thing that occurred shortly after has never been thoroughly cleared up. There was something mysterious about it, and it might have been invented for a novel, at least in the version given by the Italian, who boasted of having saved His Highness's life. He declared he had felt thirsty while mending one of the wax figures in the room next to the Duke's bedchamber. Being alone in the room, he had taken a drink from the Duke's own cup; but as he raised it to his lips, he had been so struck by the rank smell and the strange colour of the milk that he had been on the point of throwing it away without more ado. If the story was true and an

192

investigation had shown Otto to be at the bottom of the affair, as the Duke suspected, apart from the madness and heinousness of such an attempted crime, the excessive danger of the business made it hard to understand. How was it possible to leave the Duke, prepare the poison (supposing, as was done, that it was made of phosphorus scraped from matches), enter the room and throw the scrapings into the milk without letting Giovan, who was working in the next room, hear the least sound? And was not Giovan such a subtle, cunning and cautious man with never a doubt or hesitation? . . . It must be admitted that the affair surprised him like the bursting of a bomb, and gave both him and Emilia plenty to keep him busy with, so that he had scarcely time to work out his arguments.

Between eight and nine on Wednesday evening, Emilia, who had been very unwell for several days, was suddenly overtaken by the throes of childbirth. According to her own statement, nobody was expecting the event less than herself, since it was due to occur the following month. Giovan, who was at supper, nearly choked with astonishment when Teresina rushed wildly in, crying out that her mistress was going to be brought to bed.

A doctor was sent for, and he arrived immediately. But when it came to calling Count Franz, there was a good deal of questioning among all the servants of the house without any information being gained concerning the whereabouts of the young man, who had not been seen for a whole week. Footmen were despatched to several places; first of all, to the apartment which the Count had recently taken in the Rue Taitbout in order to be free in his comings and goings, according to his own words; then to the Imperial Club, and the club in the Rue du Helder.

At last, about half an hour after midnight, the attendant of a notorious gambling den stated that the Count had gone with M. Romero, about half an hour before, to play at the house of Madame Lyonnette, Rue Francois I.

✳

That evening at the house of the new Countess d'Oels—née Léonide Chafiaroux, her real name, as revealed by the marriage banns,—there was a fairly numerous gathering. Ladies of middling virtue, opera girls, Flora van Bloemen, the singer, a Brazilian lady and her husband, and a dozen or so young men of the world, distinguished for their wit, their prodigalities, or their debauchery. There was the young Duke Lussan-Biron, who died at the age of 29, leaving nothing but immense debts, and eighty-three fancy dresses in his wardrobe; the red-haired Schonen; four or five sons of bankers; the Marquis de Courson, M. de Poix, Feuillade, Lyonnette's lover for the time being; the old Marquis de Vivarens and several others.

About midnight arrived M. de Villalba, a young gentleman from Cuba, very wealthy, a novice, and a great gambler. He was immediately surrounded, and after the initial polite remarks, Lussan-Biron, who had met him several times at the club in the Rue de la Paix, asked him whether he was in luck's way, and whether he was a loser or winner.

"At Enghien?" asked Villalba, who understood French badly and spoke it still worse.

Perceiving that the young men were laughing up their sleeves, he apologised very politely and the Duke repeated his question. "Oh, no!" replied Villalba, "I'm not lucky. I lost 20,000 francs yesterday." At the same time noticing Romero among the men surrounding him, he added jokingly that he had lost to that rascal there, and took him familiarly by the arm.

"But he knows French quite well," the Duke de Lussan whispered to M. de Poix, while Romero replied with a grin:

"Bah! bah! You'll get it all back. . . ."

"So I hope," replied Villalba. And he showed his wallet, which was stuffed with bank-notes, remarking several times that he had brought a hundred thousand francs with him.

"That's very well, but don't let it stop at that," said Romero. "Since you so desire, I'm going to give you your revanche. . . . Franz, go and ask the hostess for a pack of cards."

Count d'Oels came on the scene after a while, looking very shrewd and jocular.—Madame la Comtesse so little expected that anyone would care to play that she had had only three or four whist tables prepared; and he went away to give the necessary orders. Shortly afterwards, two footmen appeared, carrying a dirty old kitchen table, over which Count d'Oels threw a green cover. Then a page-boy entered with several packs of cards. Meanwhile Romero took a piece of billiard chalk and sketched on the green cover a plan of Thirty-Forty, as used in Germany. The two players sat down opposite each other, and Romero placed before him a pile of gold coins and bank-notes to the value of about 20,000 francs.

"Franz, are you my associate?" he asked, as he dealt out the cards.

"Indeed I am," replied the Count.

While most of the company gathered round the table to watch the Spaniard play, Feuillade went up to Schonen and de Lussan at the end of the room and stood before them. A lively, whispered conversation was going on between them concerning Romero. Schonen had met him before at Basel, where he had seen him win more than four hundred thousand francs one evening. Moreover, the fame of this remarkable adventurer was such that in the casinos of Germany he had obtained the unusual favour of playing to a maximum of 25,000 francs instead of 12,000.

They returned towards the gaming table in order not to appear too long confabulating. The game was beginning to get lively and the bystanders were laying wagers on the one or the other of the players.

"How now!" Feuillade asked Franz. "You're punting against the bank, although you're the banker's associate?"

"Oh, yes," replied the Count. "Romero has so little luck this evening that I'm obliged to play against my own money in order to make up for my losses."

To be sure, at that very moment Romero struck the table with his fist, and throwing down his cards, got up with a look of fury, vowing he would play no longer.

Whatever Villalba attempted to say merely increased his anger and his vows that he would not play any more. . . . So that in the end the young man, being keen and anxious to win more, suggested to the company a game of little baccara, which began with stakes of from ten to twenty louis and tempted the ladies to play as well.

From time to time Villalba called out to Romero, who remained standing near the table, and urged him to join in the game once more.

"No! no!" replied Romero. Whereupon the other doubled his stakes.—"Come along! Allow yourself to be tempted. It's your turn now. Come along, you're dying with envy! . . ." After a good deal of entreaty, Romero sat down at last, as though conquered and constrained, while Villalba clapped his hands like a schoolboy.

"I lay 3,000 francs," said Romero. "Do you hold them?"

"By Jove, yes!" said Villalba.

"Eight," said Romero.

"I've lost," said Villalba. "Let's double the stakes."

"I hold one hundred louis," said Count Franz.

"Seven," said Villalba.

"Nine," said Romero.

"Good! Let's double the stakes."

"I give . . . eight," said Romero.

"Lost again!" said Villalba.

"I hold two hundred louis," said Count Franz.

"Eight," said Villalba.

"Nine," said Romero.

Everybody was looking attentively at the players, and this gave the opportunity to Lussan-Biron to turn towards M. de Schonen and draw his attention to Romero. Schonen winked his eye as though to say: "Yes, I'm watching him." A minute later they came together and the Duke whispered to Schonen that Villalba had lost his head, that he was going to get robbed, and that, in a word, nobody knew where the fine fellow with the whiskers sprang from.

"The fact is," said Schonen, leading Lussan further away, "the tricks turn up in a very extraordinary manner."

"And there's Franz with tricks at 500 louis in his hand even now," said the Duke. Just then Feuillade came between Schonen and Lussan and whispered in their ear excitedly:

"What does it all mean? Look at the cards."

Romero held his cards fan-like in front of him, but it looked as though there were some quite new cards among them. The Duke examined the pack. There was a striking contrast between the shining, clean cards held by Romero and the slightly tarnished gilt of those that remained on the table.

"The Countess must be informed, since Count d'Oels has gone to bed," said the Duke de Lussan. "Feuillade, go and beg her to come to the yellow room."

In the meantime, with their monocles stuck in their eyes, they went in that direction, very much upset with indignation, and interrupting one another's words. Lyonnette appeared immediately, together with Feuillade.

"Well, what's the matter," she asked. "What is it he tells me?"

They took her into a window-recess and explained the matter to her. Astonishment and exclamations lasted a fairly long time; then came the great question as to what was to be done. Certainly the game must be stopped, but what a scandal, what a sensation! . . . And besides, they might perhaps have to appear as witnesses at the police-court. Feuillade, having been sent to the gamesters, came back immediately, lifting up his arms. It was necessary to hurry up; the stakes were getting bigger and bigger. Villalba had just lost a bank of 60,000 francs; there had been about 130,000 francs on the table. The height of the sum made them make up their minds. They went back to the little gaming room, fully determined.

An extreme silence had followed the great trick which had just been played. The bystanders stood tiptoe in order to observe Villalba, who, pale and trembling, was taking bank-notes out of his wallet. And all their gaping, perspiring faces revealed something in the nature of cruelty, while their eyes were glued on the piles of money and their mouths stood agape with wonder. In the midst of the profound silence, Feuillade's voice broke out:

"This play is too dear, gentlemen. This is not a gaming house."

"It's my usual play," replied Romero.

At the same moment, the Duke de Lussan-Biron picked up the packet of cards on the table and said to the Spaniard:

"You have added some cards, sir," while M. de Schonen put his hat over the basket into which the tricks were thrown after they were done with.

The tumult that followed baffles description. Romero and Villalba sprang to their feet; but Romero had very prudently pocketed everything that lay before him and he was struggling in the midst of the crowd that surged around him. At last, by dint of striking the table with his walking-stick, Feuillade obtained a measure of silence, and addressing Lyonnette, asked:

"How many packs of cards were there in the house, Madam?"

She had had five packs given to the players. Feuillade counted them. There were cards of seven or eight different packs in the Spaniard's pocket.

"Gentlemen," said Romero above the torrent of abuse to which he was subjected from all sides. "You are gamesters, you will understand me. I had won with these cards of the Imperial Club; I believed they were lucky."

A roar of laughter broke out, and above the tumult, Feuillade called out:

"Come, sir, you must give the money back."

This proposal threw the Spaniard into a sort of frenzy. He began to stamp, protest and gesticulate. Suddenly he stopped, turned pale, and doubled himself up in all sorts of contortions, as though he was a prey to one of those pressing necessities which can hardly be resisted. Laughter burst out irresistibly. The women clapped their hands, while some were so greatly amused that they could scarcely stop laughing. Meanwhile, taking the people aside, Villalba told them he had no desire to be mixed up in the affair; at the same time, Courson and Vivarens tried to persuade Count Franz to use his influence on his friend.

"Romero is not my friend," replied Franz warmly.

And he appeared greatly relieved when the Spaniard at last consented to do what was demanded of him,—not as an act of restitution, he declared, putting on a proud look and casting a defiant eye round the company, but by way of gratuitous kindness and because he was quite willing to yield to the opinion of the gallery. Accordingly, he would give back his winnings at baccara, but they should take into account his losses at Thirty-Forty. . . . Whereupon he took a bundle of bank-notes from his coat and, muttering vague threats between his teeth, threw it on to the table.

"Franz," said the Marquis de Courson. "You must also give back what you won as the associate of the bank."

"I didn't win anything," said Franz warmly. And he drew out his wallet. "I brought 35,000 francs with me, and there's all that I have left, 25,000."

The gentlemen glanced at one another in astonishment. . . . But at the same moment, the Duke de Lussan, who had counted the notes thrown on to the table by Romero, said in a mordant, mocking voice:

"There's fifty thousand francs here. We are waiting for the rest, Monsieur Romero."

"That's all I've got on me," said the Spaniard furiously.

This reply produced a fresh outburst of derision, and there was a loud outcry against him. He was pressed and pushed about. Somebody put his fist under his nose, while Madame Barucci nearly gave him a whacking blow. In the height of the confusion, some unknown person upset one of the lamps; and the Beauvais carpet with its hunting cupids and doves, was badly spoilt. In order to see better, the women had climbed on to the armchairs and stood there grinning, struggling, and shouting: "Search him! Search him! Fetch the police!" Then, all at once, they began clapping their hands again frantically. And for a few moments the house was filled with the noise of a great clapping of hands, while the men formed a circle round Romero, who had grown very pale.

Then Schonen, who had kept his eye on the wretch the whole time, saw a bundle of bank-notes issue from the bottom of his trousers. He rushed to pick them up, while the Spaniard moved hurriedly away.

"Oh! it doesn't matter," said Feuillade. "We now know where the nest is."

"I tell you I feel unwell," cried Romero furiously.

"Oh, let him go!" said the Duke de Lussan in a compassionate tone. "You see that M. Romero has a flux of bank-notes."

The Spaniard left the little room, followed by the crowd. Bank-notes kept appearing as though by magic at every step he took. Lussan picked them up one after the other, and after counting them, called out the total: "Sixty-five thousand . . . seventy thousand . . . eighty thousand. . . ." The chase was extremely amusing and accompanied with a constant fire of jokes and comments, most of them rather rude. Unfortunately the amusement did not last very long. Having arrived at the bottom of the yellow room, Romero sat down in an armchair and refused to budge. With closed eyes and looking pale, the poor man seemed on the point of being taken ill.

"Let's have done with it," said Feuillade, hearing three o'clock strike. "M. Romero must have passed on to an accomplice the rest of his winnings. Gentlemen, you are all willing to submit to a search, I presume?"

"Of course . . . of course . . ." was the reply.

Whereupon, Feuillade and Lussan, after opening their coats and revealing the contents of their pockets, went up to the old Marquis de Vivarens, who submitted graciously to be searched. The rest of the company were no less eager. And while they performed the ceremony of turning out their coats and pockets, the young men cracked jokes about the necessity of obliging the ladies to do likewise, especially Flora, who was fat. Suddenly a furious voice was heard:

"Never! Never! . . ." said Count Franz. He was urged to remain calm, but looking ghastly white and with his eyes bolting from his head, he cried out:

"I will never allow myself to be subjected to such an outrage!"

"Since I've allowed myself to be searched," said old Vivarens in an injured tone, "you can very well put up with it also."

"I showed you my wallet," said Count Franz. "That is all I have, absolutely all."

The Count was surrounded and repeatedly exhorted to allow the search. He looked about him with bewildered eyes and kept repeating: "Never! Never!" At last as the crowd drew back a little, a bundle of bank-notes was suddenly noticed lying at his feet.

"Here are some notes," the Duke said to him, as he picked them up. "They've just dropped out at your feet. Take them; they are yours."

"They are not mine. You may keep them," said Franz, pushing them away. And he completely changed colour.

Once these 20,000 francs were counted, there were only 30,000 lacking to make up the total sum. Very shortly, M. de Poix, who was prowling about the little room, discovered them behind an armchair. Then Courson took a pen and worked out the losses. To Villalba he gave back 80,000 francs over and above the thousand louis he still had, 7,500 francs to de Poix, 150 louis to Constance Meyer, and about 25,000 francs to Romero. Finally the Spaniard tried to get the company to give their word that they would not divulge anything about the affair. But they all turned their backs on him and left.

In the ante-chamber, Count Franz found a footman from the Beaujon house, who had been waiting a very long time, unable to get beyond the doors, which Lyonnette had ordered to be closed, as soon as the affair started. The footman came to tell him of the accouchement. He noticed that Franz looked bewildered and talked to himself as he went out to his carriage. He was seen for a moment or two at his apartment in the Rue Taitbout, where, no doubt, he filled his hands with jewels and money-bags. . . . But the deuce knows where he went to from there, to Belgium probably, but thence forward nobody ever saw him again on the asphalt of the boulevard. It is true that for him to return to Paris would have been equal to putting his head in the noose, for Romero was condemned a fortnight later to five years imprisonment and a fine of one thousand francs, while Count Franz was condemned by default to thirteen months imprisonment as his accomplice.

The Duke was not informed of the event till Friday, June 13, at his awakening. He had had a fever and shudders the previous evening and all night long. When he read the fine story, of which the newspapers were full, he was overtaken by a sort of faintness, which made him fall back on to his pillow. The whole day went by in a state of suspense and uneasiness. Although there had already been a grave suspicion of anthrax on account of the acute pain he felt in his throat, and the inflammation that showed itself there, the doctors merely talked at first of a simple boil. But matters became very bad in the night, and the following day it became necessary to inform Charles d'Este of the danger threatening him.

A poultice was applied and anthrax pustule appeared very soon after. The first incision was then performed. The Duke felt so unwell and muddleheaded that he feared anything might happen. Summoning his lawyer, he dictated to him his last will and testament, by which he revoked all his former wills and designated Count Otto as his one and only heir.

Never before had Giulia Belcredi appeared so beautiful as during those days. However much care she took to disguise her affliction, she went about surrounded by a sort of proud glory that adorned her whole person, yet seemed restrained. Otto was dazzled by her; and the two lovers, emboldened by the Duke's grave illness, kept seeking each other's eyes in order to snatch a delicious draft of love through the windows of the soul. The Duke was too ill to notice anything whatever, and his curtains were more often drawn than open. But Arcangeli was never away from the bedside, and the lovers' anxiousness not to let anything escape before such a tiresome witness, was intense and delicious. This exceedingly strained state of affairs did not last long. The doctors made more and more incisions and deputation set in; so that the feeble hope of avoiding their crime, which Otto and Giulia had had at one moment, vanished as quickly as it had appeared.

The Duke's convalescence demanded no less than several weeks, during which time the great bed was moved all over the apartment. Charles d'Este had become more suspicious of draughts and more anxious about his health than Augusta Linden even. Pistols and daggers, lying always at his side, bore witness to other fears of his regarding the Jesuit priests,—his cruel enemies, he thought, who, not satisfied with converting his daughter, would now very likely try to lay their hands on his fortune and even on his life.

Moreover, his way of passing the time was not of a nature to turn his mind towards idylls and pastorals. A monstrous crime had just been committed by a wretch called Hermann and the horrible discovery with its spectacle of seven victims all murdered by the same man, stirred the whole of France. Such was the gay poem which the Duke had read to him day by day and which he followed with the greatest interest.

"What a merry fellow!" he kept saying all the time; "what a merry fellow!" while he squirted water on the Indian vetiver mats. The evaporation, mingling coolness with the odour of the flowers standing in Chinese vases, increased the pleasant languorousness of the dim, magnificent room, which was more suited to the reveries of an amorous caliph than to the Duke, who did nothing but feed on terrors and nightmares. He was particularly delighted when the newspaper reports, after detailing the murder of the five children and the wife, came to the poisoning of Kinck, the father, by means of prussic acid. In order to prepare the poison, Hermann had thought out a most ingenious method, and the Duke begged Giulia to read the description of it to him carefully.

The murderer had made use of two retorts, one with a large orifice and the other with a long, narrow neck. He had put the one into the other. Then, by means of an ordinary spirit lamp he had distilled in the bigger retort some yellow prussiate of potash, sulphuric acid and water; and the smaller one, having a damp cloth at the bottom, had acted as recipient. The chemist-expert declared that there was no other way of fabricating the acid so that it would keep.

At this point, Giulia's eyes met those of her lover. Then, by way of reply, they both cast a horrible glance at Charles d'Este, who was reclining on his bed of gold and silver embroidery, and playing with big bars of massive gold, which he was then collecting from all over Europe. The poor crowned child, so happy with his bauble, was quite oblivious of the dangerous viper curled up by the hem of his garments.

From that very moment, the poisoning of Charles d'Este was decided on and prepared. At first the idea had seemed to them like a dream, a vain amusement, a piece of fiction which they imagined and which seduced them with the opening prospect of their complete future happiness. And now, a few days later, the two lovers awoke with their minds fixed on and saturated with the possibility of their crime. Giulia and Otto talked it over. Everything was thought out and arranged. The poison they chose kills without leaving the least trace: death would no doubt be attributed to the breaking of a blood vessel or to heart failure. Moreover, Otto was to wire immediately to Prince Wilhelm for permission to inter the Duke in the old cathedral of St. Blaise, which contains the tombs of the Guelphs. Thus the body would be removed from inquisitive doctors, if, by possible chance, there should be any.

Various domestic happenings obliged them to put off their project for a while. Then again, there was the death of Emilia's baby, which was given a sumptuous funeral with lots of flowers and lights. They considered that two funerals so soon after each other from the same house, would draw too much attention. Unfortunately the end of the ceremonies brought them up against the Italian, who, either because he had altogether new eyes or by a mere chance, realised that Otto and Giulia must have pressed very close together, as he saw them come through the door. Certain ways and looks, which he had thought to catch by surprise, had already made him wonder a good deal. More familiarity was betrayed by the two lovers than they suspected. It was as though one smelt it with the nose.

"Oh!" thought the Italian. "Let's beware!"

And from that moment, no dog on the scent could have been more patient and attentive than Giovan.

Although he saw a lot to make him think furiously, he was obliged to use the tricks of cunning in order to get sufficient proof. He sealed the doors of Otto's and Giulia's apartments with a hair; and in the morning, the seals were found to be broken. He sifted very fine dust on the floor of the corridor leading to Giulia's room; and the footmarks plainly showed where the lover had come from. He was all agog with this discovery. But as to telling His Highness about the matter, he was unable to make up his mind, no matter how eager he was to speak it. Charles d'Este's blind affection for his son and for his mistress, and Giovan's own lack of favour with the Duke, made him afraid of having seen what he ought not to see at all,—and as for the proofs of his allegations, how was it possible to get them accepted?

✳

One afternoon, between four and five, Arcangeli happened to be in Emilia's room. She was up for the first time after her accouchement. Arcangeli was not a little surprised to hear footsteps, pretty heavy ones too, overhead. Now, he knew that the attic was empty and nobody dwelt there except the rats. He questioned Emilia, who replied that she had heard the same noise several days running, but had paid no heed to it, thinking it might be a manservant.

"In the afternoon?" asked Giovan.

"In the afternoon," she replied.

Now, Charles d'Este was in the habit, after standing at the top of the terrace and watching the parade of his horses, of going to lie down for an hour or so. During that time the lovers were quite at liberty. "That's who it is. I'll find out," thought Giovan.

Leaving his sister, he went and consulted one of the numerous plans of the house, which were locked up in His Highness's study. The attic with the dormer window over Emilia's apartment bore the number fourteen. Giovan could find out nothing more at the moment, as he had to go and attend to the Duke.

He remained with him till eleven o'clock, and was going up to his room by the narrow servants' staircase when he suddenly took it into his head to pay a visit to the mysterious attic. He climbed a storey higher, passed along two or three corridors with his cellar-lantern in his hand, roamed a while about the dreary waste of joists and plaster, and came at last to the door with the number fourteen painted on it. He had taken with him a large supply of master keys, so that he entered the room without difficulty and locked the door again carefully.

A first glance round by the smoky light of the candle revealed to him little beyond a great bed with wreathed columns and a brocaded canopy. It had been Christiane's at one time, but after the death of Hans Ulrich, she had had it removed from her apartment. There was also a jumble of furniture lying about the place, which was, in fact, merely a lumber room.

He went the round of it cautiously and found nothing suspicious in all the clutter except that he noticed a couple of those wreaths of plaited straw that are used for standing retorts on. And greatly disappointed at not finding the marvels he had expected, he was thinking of going away, when the sound of a footstep came from the end of the long corridor. He stood stock still for a moment, his eyes staring, his heart beating; then he swiftly blew out the candle, crushed the smoking wick with his fingers and slipped noiselessly under the enormous bed, biting his sleeve in order to keep from breathing.

Suddenly the door opened and Giulia entered the room, while Otto followed with a small lighted lamp. She carried with both hands a large china basin full of cooked tangerines. She was wearing a red rose in her ear, having passed the evening with the Duke; and the train of her green velvet robe, embroidered with a mosaic of silver, pearls and gems, rustled and trailed to and fro behind her. She placed the basin on the table. Otto put the lamp at the side. Then, gazing into each other's eyes, they stood for a moment speechless.

"But it's for tomorrow . . . for tomorrow," said Otto in a low voice.

She said yes with a nod, and Otto began to walk up and down the room with short, regular turns. Meanwhile Giulia placed on the table a sort of silver saucepan, taken apparently from among the utensils, which the Duke and Miss Sinclair had once used for their cookery. Giulia made in it a mysterious mixture of water, sugar, and orange blossom. Then she put a lighted spirit lamp underneath it, and the saucepan immediately started to simmer. Otto stood leaning with his fists on the table and watching her attentively. Outside, the night was serene with large twinkling stars.

"Put this carpet over the window," said Giulia, pointing to the dormer-window. "Some servant might notice the light."

She drew from her bosom a slender flask of cut crystal, richly gilt, in the stopper of which was adjusted a hollow silver tube, the smallest ever seen and as thin as a needle. Through this tube flows drop by drop the precious balm of essence of roses, which is said to be the foam that gathers on the rose-water canals winding about the gardens of the King of Persia and of which that

Prince sometimes makes a present to certain courts of Europe. Indeed, the empty flask had come to Giulia from the Grand Duke Vladimir.

"Ah!" said Otto. "Is that where you've put the . . ." And he did not dare pronounce the word "poison." She took from her hair a fairly large diamond pin, with which she made a deep prick in several of the little oranges. Then with the long beak of the flask she introduced a drop of deadly poison into the heart of each orange through the prick, and dipped them in the hot syrup in the silver saucepan, so that when the thick layer cooled and whitened, not even the most experienced, eye could have distinguished the poisoned fruit from the good and wholesome.

"No!" said Giulia after a while, taking an orange from the plate. "This one's too lovely for him." And after taking a bite, she offered it to Otto. The latter, however, no doubt deeply wounded at the sight of such a present from his old lover, remained sullen and frowning and coldly defended himself against Giulia's laughing attempts to put the orange to his lips. She ended by throwing it away peevishly; and throwing herself back in his arms, she gazed up at him steadily. Otto's eyes became more brilliant, his hands wandered over his mistress's open neck; his heart beat faster. She led him towards the great four-poster, under which the Italian lay hidden, more dead than alive.

The little lamp was burning; nothing stirred in the narrow room. Only from time to time, Giulia muttered a few incoherent words, like somebody dreaming aloud. Then she raised her voice a little, and Arcangeli shuddered, hearing Charles d'Este's name.

"I shall want a couple of handkerchiefs," said the young woman, dreaming. . . . "I shall be obliged to touch the body."

Then she added excitedly:

"But, if he were to fall down and split his skull against the furniture!"—for the sight of blood filled her with horror. The young man made no reply, but as he lay with his face in the pillow and his arm stretched above his head, he suddenly began sobbing with a sort of bitter fury. . . .

"Shall we both die?" she said. "Ah! how I would gladly die! . . ."

Filled with a sombre frenzy, he clasped her to him without uttering a word. Little by little his weeping ceased and Giulia pensively stroked his hair. Finally, they left the four-poster and went towards the table.

They said very little to each other. As Giulia looked at the flask in the light of the lamp before hiding it in her bosom, she said out loud that she would pour the remainder, a good third at least, into the Duke's bowl of milk, so that no chance might save him. Otto took the lamp in his hand and Giulia picked up the china basin. Then they both went noiselessly away.

More than a quarter of an hour had to pass without a sound of anything suspicious, before Arcangeli ventured to creep out from his hiding-place, where he had scores of times been on the verge of collapsing or revealing himself. He shook himself, sniffed the air, and took off his shoes. Then, barefoot and lighter than a cat, although his legs and body trembled, he crept back to his room and shot the bolt.

He was filled with a great terror and a swarm of whirling thoughts. He already saw himself dead, a victim at his master's side. One moment he wanted to go and wake him up, run out and expose the plot, and very nearly came to ringing the great bell of the house; the next moment he sank back into his chair, as though aghast. Thus he spent the whole night, neither going to bed nor dreaming of doing so. About six o'clock he fell asleep in his armchair, being duly guarded by a big piece of furniture which he had drawn up against the door. He did not wake up till noon.

He sprang up in a fright. Nevertheless, he felt something like a mean and secret desire to know that the thing had been done while he was sleeping. He stood listening. Not a sound. Grey clouds were scudding over the sky; pigeons were cooing on the roof. Suddenly there came a knock on the door. He gave a start, cast a look of terror in all directions and then went and talked through the key-hole. It was only a message from His Highness, who was waiting for him in the bathroom.

"All right, I'm coming!"

The manservant went away and Arcangeli removed the barricade. As he walked down the dim corridors, he expected any moment to feel the thrust of a dagger in his back.

✳

About that time there appeared in the newspapers a good number of articles and drawings descriptive of the house and the famous bathroom, which was the pride and glory of the unhappy Duke. The room was circular and reached by way of a winding corridor. It was the interior of the Russian cupola dominating the buildings and got its light from a window overlooking the Place de l'Arc de l'Etoile and from four small mosaic domes, painted gold and blue and pierced by openings in the shape of stars and crescents. The walls were covered from floor to ceiling with very fine mirrors, which, on being opened, disclosed gigantic cupboards containing the innumerable flasks, ointments, creams, and pomades which the Duke used. Opposite the door stood an enormous malachite dresser, as big as the high altar of a cathedral, and containing in the vaulted upper portion three silver basins with hot, cold, and tepid water taps. It was full of toilet articles of the richest and most diverse variety, all set out on the various little shelves.

When Arcangeli entered, the Duke was up to his beard in the great malachite bath, which was situated under one of the little blue and gold domes and reached by four white marble steps. Giulia Belcredi had just finished reading aloud, and Otto was walking up and down the room.

Though His Highness always bathed with a dress on, the bath was hidden for decency's sake by a cloth embroidered in red and blue in the Russian style.

"Good Heavens! What's the matter? My poor Giovan, whatever do you look like?"

And as Arcangeli began to mutter something, the Duke, without any further compassion, ordered him to open the morning's post as usual. The Italian's shaky voice was lost in the noise of the water, with which the Duke kept warming up his bath every minute. Besides, the first letters were only requests for help or audiences from former subjects of His Highness, so that the Duke, fed up with the great heap of letters that still remained, ordered them to be thrown into the fire. Whereupon, he asked for his dressing gown.

"*Mon cher seigneur*," said Giulia. "Aren't you thirsty? Won't you have a drink?"

"Indeed I will," replied the Duke. "Let them bring me my milk. . . . And see, I beg you, that my sweet-bowl is filled with sugared oranges."

"I'll see to it, Monseigneur," said Giulia.

Sharp gusts of wind shook the garden trees, while thunder began to rumble on the far borders of the sky and roll up towards Paris. Otto stood by the window tapping nervously on the pane and watching the sky grow darker, till in a short while it was quite black. The burning olive-stone embers, which were keeping warm the irons for the Duke's beard, crackled in the brazier; and the old greyhound, Caesar, came and nestled against his master with a long whine. Clad in a white dressing gown, the Duke sat at the bottom of the room, having his feet brushed in a large bowl of almond water by Arcangeli.

"Beware, don't eat any," Arcangeli hastily whispered in the Duke's ear.

"What d'you say?" said the Duke.

Otto turned round, and there was a long silence, during which nothing was heard save the water dripping monotonously in the bath. A cold sweat stood on the Italian's brow. He was on the verge of fainting with fright. It was almost all he could do to lift a trembling finger to his lips, and again he stammered:

"Don't eat any. They're poisoned. . . ."

The same moment a clap of thunder burst with a terrific din, and a blinding flash, which seemed to set the room on fire, revealed at the end of the corridor Giulia, livid and thunderstruck, carrying His Highness's gold sweet-bowl and a large cup of milk on a tray,—then all was blotted out.

"Ah!" she exclaimed. "It gave me such a fright. I almost dropped the tray."

"One can't see at all," said Charles d'Este. "Giovan, close the shutters and light the chandeliers."

Arcangeli hastened to light the brilliant gas candles, which hung in five circles of rock crystal from the middle of the domes. Then he went to the window. The rain was pouring in torrents from the heavy, dark sky.

In the distance a regiment of soldiers was marching through the downpour on its way to a station, war having been declared against Prussia three days previously. There was a fleeting glimpse of the drooping flag, followed by long, blurred files of men; then Giovan closed the iron shutters, which were padded with raw silk.

"There!" said His Highness. "Now we're all to ourselves. Giovan, come and dress me."

While the storm thundered outside, Charles d'Este sat in a great armchair of crimson velvet with gold fringes and gilt woodwork, like a man waiting to be shaved. The Italian drew towards him one of the busts of coloured wax, which stood on a crimson velvet pedestal and was so well-modelled from life that it was hard to distinguish the copy from the original. Then, sitting in front of the Duke, Arcangeli opened his box of colours and began to paint his master's face. Using colours diluted in gum or pastel crayons, he restored the Duke's obliterated features; but, that day, his hands quaked so dreadfully that only a miracle saved the patient's eyes.

"A little more carmine on the cheek . . . the bend of the eyebrow is hard. . . . But what's the matter with you? Come now, you're going off your head!" the Duke cried out in a rage.

The lights shining on him from all sides made yet more startling his strange pink face, which was reflected many times over
by the surrounding mirrors. The claps of thunder went on without ceasing. The roof of the house rattled under a furious downpour. Neither Giulia nor Otto spoke any more. What thoughts
were passing through their minds in those supreme moments, as
they stood on the brink of the abyss? Otto's look was dark and
forbidding, his face enflamed and crossed by livid spots. From
time to time he screwed up his features as though to chase away
a worrying wasp. Giulia was ghastly white, but remained superb
and unmoved. Perhaps at that terrible moment, their hearts were
touched by some sense of horror and regret. If they had no hesitation whatever, if no remorse came to haunt and horrify them
with their crime after they had received so much kindness and
so many advantages from the Duke, one might be tempted to
believe they were acting under a direct inspiration of the wicked
Angel himself, beyond all human explanation.

"Giulia," said the Duke of a sudden, "will you pass me my
sweet-bowl? . . ." And taking an orange, either by chance or
because he had understood Arcangeli's warning, he called out:

"Come, Caesar! Hop-la. . . . That's for you, Caesar!"

The greyhound caught the orange in its open jaws, but
scarcely had he crunched it, when he fell down dead.

"Oh! oh! What does this mean?" said the Duke, rising to
his full height and aghast with emotion, though his painted
face seemed to show no change. Otto and Giulia rose at the
same time.

"Poor Caesar!" she said in her embarrassment. "What has
happened to him, then?"

"There's something unwholesome in these oranges," said
Charles d'Este in a raucous voice.

"Ah!" replied Giulia Belcredi, "you're always trying to make
things unpleasant for me, Monseigneur. . . . One would think
you were ready to suspect me."

"Don't accuse yourself," exclaimed the Duke.

"Monseigneur," replied Giulia, "I've eaten them myself. I was eating them just now. . . ."

"Poisoner!" Cried Charles d'Este, unable to restrain his feelings any longer. "Poisoner!"

A revolver shot resounded. From the entrance to the corridor, Otto had fired on his father.

"Ah! traitor!" roared the Duke, snatching his revolver from his pocket.

A second ball missed his head by three inches, as he quickly stooped behind his armchair. He fired. Otto staggered, fell to the floor, and remained as though lifeless on the threshold of the door.

"Giovan!" cried the Duke. "Here, take my revolver. Shoot that hussy for me!"

"Oh no!" said Giulia. "I shall be able to die by myself."

Then she added in a strident voice:

"Old fool, old fool, to think even for a moment that I loved you! I loved nobody but Otto, d'you hear? . . . Otto! . . . He execrated you. Everybody execrates you . . . I, your son, your brother, your flunkeys, everybody, everybody, everybody!"

And like a delirious woman, she began to cry out:

"Assassin! assassin! assassin! Seize the assassin!"

"Stop shouting or I'll kill you," said Charles d'Este.

"Be off," she cried. "I know how to die." She sank on to her knees by the side of her lover's body, kissing his lips and pressing him to her bosom; then, noticing that her skirt was slightly drawn up, she rearranged it.—"Farewell, Monseigneur," she said. "I'm thoroughly tired of this world. Eat in peace, when I'm dead. . . ." And leaning with one hand on the floor, she put the deadly flask to her lips and fell back all at once.

A flash of lightning, so dazzling that it pierced the shutters like a long shaft, seemed to bring down the cupola with the terrific clap of thunder that came after. The lightning had struck one of the eight lightning-conductors with which the roofs of the house were fitted.

"We shall leave Paris this evening," said the Duke to Arcangeli, who seemed to appear from nowhere. . . . And seeing the body of Otto, Charles d'Este cried out:

"Parricide! Assassin!"

But his voice seemed to be smothered in his throat and he stammered with a deep sigh:

"My son . . . my son . . . so he did not love me!"

X

TOWARDS the middle of August, 1876, there were given at Bayreuth some magnificent and very remarkable performances of the opera pieces composing the Niebelung Ring. *The Rhine Gold* was played on the 14th; *The Valkyrie* and *Siegfried* on the following days; while August the 17th saw the first performance of the opera which brings that immense drama to a close, namely, *The Twilight of the Gods*.

About four o'clock in the afternoon of that day, Mr. Smithson was walking up and down in front of the theatre in the company of Baron von Cramm, whom he had just met. The latter had left Charles d'Este's household three years previously and was living at Blankenburg. Hence, after the usual greetings, he asked for news of His Highness, Count d'Oels, M. d'Andonville, who was back in Normandy, and even of several former domestics; to which Smithson gave appropriate answers.

"What about Augusta?" said the Baron.

"She died at Rome," replied the American. And he added that the poor lady had ended by falling into such a sad state of paralysis and other evils, after her son's flight, that death had been a happy release for her.

"Ah!" said Baron von Cramm. "And what about Count Franz?"

"He is said to be living in retirement with his wife in some out-of-the-way corner of Bohemia," replied Smithson. "Count Nostitz, I believe, received him as steward of a large estate."

"And Signor Arcangeli?" asked von Cramm, lowering his voice.

"Oh! don't say another word about him!" replied the American. . . .

After a few paces up and down in silence, they both stopped to look at the very animated scene before them. The Bayreuth theatre is built on an isolated, narrow height, which stands above the town and is reached by a gently sloping roadway. The weather was extremely beautiful. A great number of vehicles, cabs, ancient berlines, and carriages with powdered footmen were going up the side at a very slow pace between a couple of hedges of onlookers and peasants from the neighbouring villages. Whenever a prince passed by, the crowd shouted. Joy shone in every face and the name of Wagner was heard in every mouth.

"Ah!" said Mr. Smithson, who was calmly surveying the groups with his lorgnette. "Here comes His Highness."

At the bottom of the height appeared the Duke's magnificent landau, drawn by four high-stepping dapple grey horses with plaited tails. As the traffic of carriages had already begun to grow less, the landau advanced alone in the middle of the road, re-splendent with varnish, satin, polished brass and escutcheons.

"He has changed a good deal," said von Cramm, his eyes glued to his lorgnette.

And as he was exactly the same age as the Duke, he began, no doubt in order to set his mind at ease on his own score, to refer with a look of compassion to the fatigues which so much travel-ling about had brought upon the Duke since his departure from Paris. He counted them one by one on his fingers. First, Naples, which the Duke had been obliged to leave on account of the hor-rible eruptions of Vesuvius; Rome, where he had grown weary of the finest view in the world, the gardens, the suburbs, the Tiber meandering across meadowland and country, the snow-capped peaks of the Apennines on the horizon; then, the Hague, where His Highness in his first enchantment had thought he was going to settle forever. The houses were beautiful, and, as the bricks were frequently painted over, they always looked new. Chains guarded the footpaths, while the roads and highways were so clean that carriages could drive along them without raising a speck of dust.

From behind the shining window-panes women watched the passers-by or watered pots of tulips. But very soon, the Duke suddenly became unwell and he had to quit that land of dykes and marshes. At last he settled in Geneva, where he kept shifting about from one hotel to another, restless, ill and dissatisfied.

"And Otto?" asked the Baron, bending towards Mr. Smithson's ear.

"The same as ever," replied the American. "His madness increases with the attacks and becomes a sort of frenzy. The Fathers of Charity, who have had charge of him for the past year, have given up all hope of his recovery."

"Yes!" said Baron von Cramm. "It would have been better if his wound had been a mortal one."

At that moment, some musicians appeared on a balcony of the theatre and played a fanfare of trumpets on a theme from *The Twilight of the Gods*. It was the signal that the opera was about to begin. The groups of people on the peristyle dwindled away; and Baron von Cramm, not caring to be seen by the Duke, whose landau was just drawing up, took a hurried leave of Mr. Smithson.

The horses stopped before the steps and the few remaining onlookers made way. The Duke was sitting back in the carriage, his head leaning forward and his face looking violet-red. He seemed not to have noticed that the carriage had arrived. Mr. Smithson had to touch his arm. He turned his eyes slowly and then said in a gentle voice:

"Ah! there you are, Smithson. Giovan did not care to accompany me. He says that it bores him."

Whereupon, the poor Duke rose with difficulty on to his feet, and aided by a couple of footmen, alighted with shaking legs from the carriage; and bending over his stick, while he gave his other arm to the American, he began to walk under the peristyle.

A thrill swept through the assembly when Charles d'Este made his appearance. It grew into a sort of muffled clamour when, leaning on Mr. Smithson's arm, he began to mount the steps leading to his armchair. He was now of so inordinate a size that he could scarcely move. Moreover, he was eaten up with gout, his hands swollen and twisted and his feet so puffed that he could no longer put up with any but black velvet footwear. Owing to a strain, his body had burst at the navel, so that it had to be supported with a sort of silver girdle, and a wretched affliction in another part of the body kept him in constant fear of the slightest accident. Nevertheless, he had insisted on wearing full dress and appeared that day in his grand uniform of black and gold with the medals of his orders and a hat with a tuft of plumes.

Seated, with no one in front of him, in an elevated place above the seats, the lower tier being cut away by the bay of a corridor, Charles d'Este found the eyes of the whole assembly directed upon his own, and he remained motionless, gazing with unseeing eyes and looking absorbed in thought. A few gas lamps between the pilasters and half-columns adorning the stucco walls, shed a dim light over the vast hall which was built in the style of an ancient theatre. A clamorous throng filled the red velvet tiers rising from the orchestra to the "Fürstenloge," the Princes' Box, which was draped with crimson velvet and gold fringe and occupied the entire width of the vast hall. All the other places were, without exception, the armchairs of red velvet.

Suddenly a small door facing the stage opened, and the Emperor Wilhelm entered the Imperial box. Everybody immediately stood up and acclamations burst forth, while His Majesty saluted. Behind him came the Prince of Prussia with his Princess at his side. Then followed the King of Bavaria, the Grand Dukes of Mecklenburg, Baden, and Saxe-Weimar; after them, the Duke of Coburg, the Duke of Anhalt, the Duke of Saxe-Altenburg,

Prince George of Prussia, Prince Hohenzollern-Sigmaringen, the Duke of Leuchtenberg, Prince Romanowsk, and Prince Wilhelm of Blankenburg. The tumult, shouts of joy, stamping, and waving of handkerchiefs by many of the women during this ceremonial entry lasted until His Majesty and all accompanying him were in their places. In the midst of so many sightseers and genuine enthusiasts, Charles d'Este alone remained seated, turning his back upon the Princes and Emperor with a display of contemptuous unconcern.

"Old fool!" said His Majesty, shrugging his shoulders;—and he was bending over to the Princess of Prussia in order to draw her attention to that eccentric Charles d'Este, who was being much talked about of late, when the gas suddenly went down till there was very little light in the hall, and the footlights rose in front of the curtain. A profound silence fell upon the gathering. Then all eyes were fixed on what the adepts of the master called "the mystic abyss," which was the spot where the orchestra was completely hidden from view by a sort of wooden jutting between the stage and the auditorium and awaited the signal to strike up.

Hans Richter lowered his wand and the musicians played the prelude. Then the curtain parted, disclosing a gloomy landscape. Lightning rent the darkness on the jagged peaks; and seated on the rocks were the three Nornes, daughters of Erda, white-haired and frightful, weaving the chain of destiny. Venerable sisters, ancient spinsters! The First embraces all the Present in her thought, the Second all the Future, the Third all the Past. Outside and without them, there is nothing. Their eternal vigil makes the life of the universe and all creatures. The pupils of their eyes are the bounds of all that exists. They were singing at their task, and their fateful words spoke of Siegmund and Sieglind, of Siegfried and Brunnhilde. Suddenly the thread snapped between their fingers and, terror-stricken, the Nornes vanished into the bosom of Erda, the earth.

And, as though at the bitter voice of the Norne of the Past, the Duke's thoughts went back to ten years ago; he saw himself again at Blankenburg. Then it was he who was acclaimed whenever he entered the box of a theatre; the swarms of baseness, flattery and adoration crawled at his feet. But those intoxicating days of his reign had only served to prepare the cruelest misfortunes of every kind, even that of casting at last that great and absolute master into an abyss of powerlessness and obscurity. Ah! how dismally fateful was that icy dawn when he had left Wendessen, forsaken his beautiful duchy, which he would never see again! As he got into his carriage, he had asked Wagner the title of the last opera of *The Ring of the Nibelung*:

"*The Twilight of the Gods*, Monseigneur. . . ."

And as though the words had contained some sort of curse, from that day began the slow and sombre twilight of the Duke's life. Little by little he began to fall asleep; for the last few months he had been growing drowsy at all times, waking up with a start when he was spoken to. Of a sudden he fancied he saw Claribel standing before him. She was wrapped in a peaceful light, her eyes staring, her lips pale, and she was holding a skull in her hand. She stood motionless for a fairly long while without utter-ing a word. Then she vanished;—and the Duke woke up with a start, struck cold by the vision and unable to recover his breath for a few moments. Alas! what did she want of him, his Clary, his last born? Death, which had taken her away, had opened the door to many other phantoms; and since that time the domestic Plagues had never been withdrawn from over the Duke's family. First it was Hans Ulrich, who was discovered one morning dying in a pool of blood. And a dark rumour concerning the cause of his death had increased the horror of it, while Christiane's grief and wasting away had only served to develop the dark and ter-rible enigma. Then there were Otto's scandalous follies, Franz's disgusting marriage. . . . Soon after, the Duke had received harder and more intimate blows. He had been deeply grieved by the ungrateful manner in which his only remaining daughter had forsaken him. His honour, dignity and rest had greatly suffered on account of Franz's infamous cheating at cards. It was an ineffaceable blot on his name! the trait of baseness and dishonour! But very shortly after, it had been surpassed by the monstrous crime of Otto. . . . Thus, the proud race that had once held all Germany under its yoke and shone with its great men of all kinds, kings, emperors, saints, ended in an abyss of blood-stained mud, with bastards, thieves and parricides.

And the Duke's heart was broken.—Moreover, what had he been himself? An unnatural son, a crud father, a terrible husband, a detestable master, jealous, capricious, restless. What happiness had he tasted, what grandeur yet remained to him, who wished to have everything at his feet? He was alone, more than unfortunate in his family, his brother, his uncle, his children, torn within by poignant catastrophes, with no one to console him, bearing his de-crowned brow through all the hotels of Europe, left in the hands of two or three menservants, who ruled him despotically, no longer doing anything except through them, having given up to his buffoon his taste, his judgment, his ears, his eyes. Moreover, he was broken down and ridiculous. Night was rising around him; the shadows were thickening. Those hard times had been the twilight of his breed.

The moments of drowsiness in the heavy heat of the theatre suspended his gloomy thoughts for a while; and sometimes the music and show also turned them aside, though he could not long remain attentive. He would put up his lorgnette whenever a riband, a face, or a sparkling medal caught his eye; but while he was surveying the dense throng of spectators, he would sink back into his reflections. Certainly, this remarkable festival, which had been so long prepared and discussed, was like a congress of all Europe, at which all the highest and greatest in rank and art ought to be present. But whom did Charles d'Este see there? Lots of industrialists, grown rich with their foundries and factories; businessmen, law-mongerers, who had pushed themselves forward by the vilest use of the pen, or law-court-spouters; bevies of beautiful adventuresses, now admitted everywhere to exercise their unclean trade; and the rest, men of letters or newspaper reporters; all mixed up, levelled, confused. There was no longer any rule, any hierarchy. An arrogant middle-class mingled at their pleasure with the overlords, even with the very sovereigns, so greatly did the world seem to have been intoxicated with the spirit of revolt and innovation.

Then the Duke, who for three days running had persisted in turning his back to the Princes' Box, stood up with a sort of sprightliness,—the whole assembly was acclaiming the Emperor as he returned at the end of the second interval,—and bowing very low and slowly, saluted His Majesty. He now pardoned him for having annihilated the sovereigns of Germany and crushed the last remnants of that grand and noble feudal order.

Devoid of everything and forming no body in common, what would these princes have been able to do against the turbulence of the people, the violence of the new spirit and unbridled, triumphant licence? Whereas a single chief and guide with his tents, banners and army of devoted soldiers could range himself in battle against so many insurgent forces, crush them and restore everything to submission and duty.

But as he resumed his seat, Charles d'Este noticed not far from him two Jews of well-known name, who carried on the greatest money business in Europe. He turned pale with disgust.

It was to them and not to him that the particular greeting given by the Emperor Wilhelm was addressed; and that act of prostitution, as it were, by a prince, who was so stinting of his favours, showed fairly well the power they had. Yes! the Jews were now risen above the heads of kings. That voracious and enemy tribe, ever busy sucking the life-blood of the peoples by all the cruel means that covetousness can devise, had, century by century, amassed in the lining of its tatters all the treasures and gold of the world; by this means, kings, prelates, emperors, the earth, labour, commerce and even peace and war, were held captive by a few filthy Jews who did with them what they pleased.

Their plunderings, turned into a science and financial strategy, had made them masters of this Golden-Calf-worshipping age; all bowed their heads before them; their daughters entered the bed of princes and mingled the vile mud of the Ghetto with the purest Gentile blood.

The Duke turned away with disgust from the sight of these hook-nosed usurers; but his eyes fell at once on a group of ill-dressed men, who had an impudent look, enormous hands, creased shirt-fronts and the goat's beard of the Yankee. They were Americans, and said to be the wealthiest people in the world: this one possessing petrol wells, that one, immense stores, that other, herds of cattle, while a fourth, short and ruddy, nick-named the Commodore, owned the steamers of the Atlantic. All these "milliardares," obviously sprang from the depths of the people, and Dicky Bennet still wore little earrings. Before getting rich they must have been swine-herds, lumbermen, tramp steamer pilots, railway conductors, pioneers. And only to look at them, as they lolled cynically in their seats, was enough to realise the offensive arrogance and pride of rudeness advertised in their whole bearing, and a stupid, magnificent contempt for the arts and refinements of old Europe.

Then the Duke saw the infinite multitude of people, workers and poor wretches, like an immense abyss, from which furious waves were about to surge up. Independence and indocility were invading the social fabric from too many quarters to be stopped everywhere. If the water was held back on one side, it immediately penetrated by the other; it was even welling up underground. Yes! the fatal time was drawing near. All the signs of destruction were visible over the ancient world like the angels of wrath over a doomed Gomorrah. And what would come after? What dark future awaited mankind? Free and equal, subjects of nobody, not even God, against whom their scientists would create wonders as Pharaoh's wizards did, they would knock the world about with holes and machines in order to pierce mountains and shorten the continents; but puffed up with the pride of Matter, they would, so to say, burst with it. All the flower of Life being withered, the graces fled to heaven for shelter, no head rising above the oppressive level of a monstrous equality, the earth would soon become a trough of filth, in which the herd of mankind would wallow and have its fill.

Amid profound silence a solemn march was played. It was the march of the death of the gods, for Siegfried, the hero, had just been killed and through his death all the gods were dying. The Duke listened appalled to the funereal lamentation, which was so disquieting in its horror and superhuman majesty. It seemed to him to be mourning for all that he had known and loved, mourning for his children, mourning for himself, mourning for the kings, whose death-agony he was somehow witnessing, mourning for the twilight of the gods.

He remained deep in thought till the very last accord of the piece. Wagner appeared on the stage in deference to the calls of the whole assembly. His eagle eyes were shining; his tortured features, which were as though kneaded by the force of genius, were pale with emotion. He made a short speech and disappeared. The Duke hurried out and got into his carriage, which managed very luckily to get him out of the crowd, so that it did not take him a quarter of an hour through the deserted streets of Bayreuth to reach his house.

Charles d'Este found Arcangeli waiting for him in the drawing-room with a collection of cakes, grapes and peaches. He ate a few muscatelle grapes and drank a little sherry, complaining all the while of being very, very tired. But before going to bed, the Duke insisted on writing to his lawyer at Geneva. It has since been conjectured that he wished to send him a few lines for his will, or at least, in order to cancel the one deposited with him. However that may be, when the Italian returned with a writing-pad, the Duke was sitting in an armchair between a couple of footmen who had assisted him to it. He said nothing as he saw Arcangeli approach. Suddenly it was noticed that he was stuttering, and the same instant he fell forward in an apoplectic stroke on Arcangeli, who caught him.

The whole house was astir in a moment. Help was sent for, but the Duke was beyond hope. The first doctor to arrive had him laid on a sofa and bled him; but only very weak signs of life were obtainable. In less than a couple of hours, all was over; during which time Arcangeli was suspected, pretty rightly, of having helped himself in advance to the Duke's valuables; for very little money was found in His Highness's desk. His precaution, moreover, was quite opportune, for neither he, nor Franz, nor Christiane, nor Prince Wilhelm, nor the King of Hanover, nor any member of the family, nor any friend or servant had a single mite from the will. Mr. Smithson was the only exception, being put down for a legacy of one million. The will was published in several newspapers and gave a good picture, even after death, of Charles d'Este's character.

LAST WILL AND TESTAMENT
OF HIS MOST SERENE HIGHNESS
CHARLES D'ESTE,
DUKE OF BLANKENBURG.

In the name of the Father, and of the Son,
and of the Holy Ghost.

Being at this moment in the town of Geneva, at the Hotel Beaurivage where I am living, December 14, 1875, I, Ferdinand Charles d'Este, sovereign Duke of Blankenburg, Luneburg, Wolfenbuttel, etc., by the grace of God, sound of body and mind, have written with my own hand this present will, which contains my last wishes.

I will that after my death my body shall be placed in a coffin of the following description:

It shall be made like the coffin of my father, only larger; it shall be of the best wood, lined with the finest dark red Genoese velvet, fitted with gold braid and fringes.

On either side shall be my full coat-of-arms, with all my decorations embroidered in gold, as they are painted on my white State coach; at both ends, top and bottom, a German K, with the royal crown.

On the top of the coffin shall be a silver gilt crown reposing on a velvet cushion adorned with very rich gold braid and fringes. Underneath, my knight's sword in gold, with its tassel and belt, my stars and decorations, that is to say, the great Ones, which need not be returned to the Grand Masters.

On top of the coffin there shall also be my portrait painted by Funica.

The interior of the coffin shall be fitted up like a bed with all the accessories.

I wish my body to be embalmed, and if better for its preservation, petrified according to the process printed in the accompanying instructions.

My funeral shall be conducted with all the pomp and splendour due to my rank as a sovereign.

I desire my body to be placed in a mausoleum above ground, to be erected at Geneva in a prominent and befitting position.

The monument shall be surmounted by a statue of myself on horseback and surrounded by those of my father and grandfather of glorious memory, according to the design attached to this will, in imitation of that of the Scaligeri at Verona. My executors shall cause the

227

said monument to be constructed, ad libitum *of the millions of my succession, in bronze and marble by the foremost artists.*

I declare that I leave and bequeath my whole fortune, without exception, and particularly that important portion of the same which was forcibly taken from me and retained since 1866, with all the interests, in my duchy of Blankenburg, to the town of Geneva on condition it pays the legacy of one million which I bequeath to Mr. Smithson, my High Treasurer, who has always served me well and faithfully. If this is not easy to read, as I have re-written the sum, it is one million that I give to him.

I make the condition that the executors of my will shall not enter into any transactions whatsoever with my unnatural relations, Prince Wilhelm of Blankenburg, the ex-King of Hanover, the Duke of Cumberland, his son, the Duke of Modena, or with whomsoever of my so-called family.

I wish that after my death has been well certified, my executors, among whom I nominate Mr. Smithson (and the other shall be designated by the town), shall have my body examined by five doctors of medicine and surgeons in order to make sure that I have not been poisoned and to make a detailed report, written and signed by them, on the cause of my death.

The present will and testament, written entirely by me, I have signed with my hand, at the aforesaid place, year, month and day as above.

CHARLES D'ESTE,
DUKE OF BLANKENBURG.

＊

In accordance with the Duke's will, the dissection of the body was made in Geneva, in the presence of Mr. Smithson; and all the organs were so unhealthy and spoiled that the physiologists were astonished that Charles d'Este had lived as long as he had. The brain, when weighed, was heavier than that of the average man, the stomach was of great capacity, the liver and the lungs were engorged. The badly embalmed entrails were placed in an urn, where they fermented, making it burst with an intolerable odor during the funeral ceremony, and causing a great fright among those present.

1877-1882.

www.ingramcontent.com/pod-product-compliance
Lightning Source LLC
Chambersburg PA
CBHW050256110726
47898CB00007B/2432